# THE ECHO OF A LOST DREAM

## MAI L. HERRERO

Content Advisory: This book is intended for mature audiences and contains graphic violence, explicit sexual activity and disturbing imagery.

First edition

ISBN: 978-84-09-34057-6

Editing by Lucy Rose York
Editing by Lucy Christmas
Illustration by Nomad Visuals
Cover design by The author

*For my father, and in loving memory of my mother*

# Contents

Prologue       iii

P A R T   I

Chapter One       11

Chapter Two       23

Chapter Three       35

Chapter Four       43

Chapter Five       60

Chapter Six       70

Chapter Seven       81

Chapter Eight       87

Chapter Nine       99

P A R T   I I

Chapter Ten       115

Chapter Eleven       126

Chapter Twelve       133

Chapter Thirteen       141

Chapter Fourteen       152

Chapter Fifteen       163

Chapter Sixteen       171

Chapter Seventeen       180

Chapter Eighteen                                190

PART III

Chapter Nineteen                                203

Chapter Twenty                                  209

Chapter Twenty-One                              221

Chapter Twenty-Two                              231

Chapter Twenty-Three                            246

Chapter Twenty-Four                             259

Chapter Twenty-Five                             274

Chapter Twenty-Six                              282

Chapter Twenty-Seven                            294

Chapter Twenty-Eight                            308

PART IV

Chapter Twenty-Nine                             319

Chapter Thirty                                  321

Chapter Thirty-One                              330

Chapter Thirty-Two                              335

Chapter Thirty-Three                            337

Acknowledgements                                340

About the Author                                341

# Prologue

Obsessions can be sinister or angelic; that was what my mother used to tell me. But I didn't take her words to heart when she told me of such things as vice and virtue.

In the beginning, I was a boy full of hopes and dreams, a dream much greater than myself, a dream that had a price, and a price that I would pay for heavily.

This is the story of that ignorant boy, of myself, forever ago.

# PART ONE

Scourged,
Torn,
We once were. . .
Smothered,
Plunged,
We become. . .
Death,
Combusted,
Eternally, we'll be. . .

# Chapter One

The first time I felt it inside me—it was like a heart-beat, but not quite. There was more. The drumming sounded as if I had three hearts in my small chest. Each of them pounded to its own rhythm, unsynchronised. Something was calling.

In the quietness of the evening, when the last rays of sunlight touched the windowpane, a loud noise echoed within me.

I thought of when my mother would play chords on her small lute. I pictured myself doing the same. But in my hands, there wasn't a musical instrument, there was clay – fresh, soft, almost feminine clay that my mother had bought me on my tenth birthday.

I strung and glided the clay along my fingers. And a pure, raw yearning coursed underneath the softness of my skin. It circulated, pressing upon the tip of my fingers like strings that vibrated from someone else's touch. It was like I could almost talk to it or even hold on to it. Then, I began to form this yearning sensation into something tangible. I thought about the shape of my mother's hand when she played the lute, and I started to mould it.

I was halfway through making the model, blindly following the urge from within, when I heard a twig snap just outside the door of the hut. I knew that it was my mother because I recognised the sound of her footsteps.

'Mother,' I called out. I wanted to show her what I was making out of the clay she gave me. But when she came through the door, I could see from her face that she wasn't having the best day. There were shadows under her blue eyes that I hadn't noticed before.

'My dear Jacobo, I got you some dinner.' She placed a cloth-wrapped bundle on the table and picked up a basket. 'I'm going to get some blooming moonflower. Eat your dinner, all right? I won't be long.'

I watched her move swiftly from the table to the cupboard, then from the cupboard to a small bench next to the door. She picked up a candle before she was out again.

I was tempted to continue working on my unfinished sculpture, but I didn't want to upset my mother. Besides, the smell of fresh cheese was hard to ignore. I moved to the table where a cloth-wrapped bundle laid on top. Unwrapping it, and there it was, a fresh cheese as well as a small loaf of bread. I sat down and started my dinner.

When I had the last bite, the wooden door opened again. My mother entered with a sigh. She removed a shawl from her head, and I could see her long red braided hair hanging down her back, almost touching her waist.

She walked to the cupboard and put the white flowers in a jar before she came over to me. I watched her curiously while chewing the last piece of bread.

'Oh, my dear boy,' said my mother as she placed her hand on my right cheek. 'I know you have something to tell me. I am quite exhausted today. I think I should rest.'

As I looked into my mother's eyes, I could really tell that she was tired and maybe a little downhearted. But at least, she was smiling at me.

'Why don't you come to bed with me after you wash your face and hands?' she said. 'Make sure to get all those clay out of your nails, all right?'

'Yes, mother,' I said, smiling back at her.

My mother kissed my forehead, and I watched her disappear through the tiny bedroom that belonged to the two of us.

Oh, my mother . . . the first beautiful woman I ever learned to love. She sacrificed everything for me, for this brown-haired boy who knew nothing about life or death and nothing about eternity. I was young, naive and foolish. I didn't come to understand the love and care that my mother had for me until later in life.

My mother was my friend and my caretaker and the only company I kept, for I had no other friends of any sort. I suppose the richer boys thought I was too poor to mingle with, and the poorer boys thought I was too boring to play with. But that didn't bother me. I thought my time would be wasted spent with them, running about here and there, playing with swords. I was filled with curiosity for the world inside me.

I went to the bucket of clean water and washed my face and hands, making sure to get every bit of dirt out of my nails. Then, I followed my mother and climbed in next to her underneath the blanket.

'Mother, can I come with you to the market next time?' I asked.

'Of course, my love, I'm surprised you asked,' she mumbled. Mother put her arm around me, and soon her breathing slowed.

I curled up close to her, breathing in her unique scent from her clothes and her skin; it was sweet and aromatic. Whenever she wore that scent, I knew that my sleep would be ever so peaceful.

I snuggled up closer to her, and soon all the troubles in my head seemed to cease for a while.

Our next days were spent collecting herbs from the woods that mother mixed and ground until they formed a particular shape and had a particular smell.

When I wasn't moulding clay, I helped her collect some more strange-looking plants and flowers. Sometimes we quietly worked next to each other; my mother with her herbs and I with my clay. Time passed quickly when we were busy.

When the weekend arrived, my mother prepared to set off to sell the herbs in the market again. This time, I joined her.

We walked a long way through the woods, past rows and rows of asymmetrical tree trunks until we arrived at a narrow path made of rows of rocks placed one after another. There were no more trees standing tall beside me; instead, there were tall stacks of stones that mother told me were houses. The first time I saw them, I was fascinated by those stone buildings. They were a shade lighter than the clay I possessed and a shade darker than the cider my mother used for cooking. But their size! I stared up in wonder at them as we walked along a small alley.

'Mother, why haven't you told me about any of this before?'

'Probably because I'm always more interested in listening to your stories,' she said.

'Well, what else have you seen that I haven't?'

'Oh, let's not talk about that. Better that you see the world for yourself.'

Sometimes I wondered if it was because of what she had seen that we ended up living where we did.

Castellfollit de la Roca was a small town. The only way in and out was over a stone bridge. The hanging town, it was called, for it was on top of a flat mountain, with the balconies of the houses overhanging the edge. This town was cut off from the cities and therefore from life. And then, our hut was beyond the woods, even more remote than that little town in the middle of nowhere. So when I first saw those tall, big buildings, it was the first time I was awestruck by something other than my clay-moulding.

We came out of the narrow alley into the market square, which was full of people buzzing around. There were also children around my age running here and there while their mothers were yelling at them.

We headed to a small empty wooden table, and mother started to pull jars of herbs from her bag and line them up neatly. I recognised the colourful herbs she had ground to make paints for me. They ranged from light to dark: orange like autumn leaves and the dusk sky; olive green, pine tree deep green, the light green of fresh leaves; brown like a tree's bark. And red! Oh! The deep red of pig's blood. They each had a unique smell of their own.

When we were done setting up, more people started to show

up. I suppose all the fascinating colours and smells either attracted or scared the passers-by away. Some of them were curious
enough to ask what these things were, then they would whisper
in each other's ears and quickly stride off. I noticed a woman
holding a young boy's hand. When she saw us, she looked down
and walked past without a second glance. But not all of them
acted that way. Some men came to our table and asked for potions of herbs for pain relief, or even to cheer their mood, and
women came for scented potions. My mother would hand them
different coloured herbs in exchange for small coins.

The boys in this small town started to take notice of me,
another boy their own age. Some quietly approached me when
I was wandering around observing the stone buildings. I wasn't
aware of their proximity until I heard a noise behind me and
turned to see three of them staring at me, their eyes wide. I suppose they were scared of me, but when I did nothing to show
them that I could do them any harm they started to come closer,
then closer, until I could see a freckle on one of the boys' faces.

'I don't think you are as scary as my mother told me you
would be,' said the freckled boy.

'And I don't think you can harm me in any way,' said a shorter one, who stood a bit further behind.

I was curious about the way they had addressed me, for I
never thought that I could seem harmful. I was thin and pale,
and without my dark hair, I might have looked colourless.

'My mother told me that your mother is a witch,' said a golden-haired boy, who stood on my right side.

'But my father said she is too pleasant-looking to be a real
witch,' the shorter boy said.

'That is because a witch can transform herself from an old hag to a beautiful woman,' said the freckled boy. His hair was red, like my mother's.

'What is a witch? And what is a father?' I asked them.

All of them chuckled.

'How can the son of a witch not know what a witch is?' the golden-haired boy said. 'A witch is a woman who has evil powers, who would steal children if they wandered into the woods and eat them alive! And your mother seems to be selling dark magic!'

I was surprised by this and angry. 'That's a lie! My mother would never do any harm. She takes good care of me and makes me delicious food – and she got me a birthday present!'

'Well, that sounds just like my mother,' said the freckled boy. 'She does all those things you just said for me. Well? What is your name, then?'

'Jacobo,' I said.

And that was the end of their fear.

When I look back on it now, I realise those boys had lies and hatred put into their little heads. Like blank paper, they had absorbed all the lies as their truth. But since those boys were still innocent, and the lies that their parents told them hadn't been fully embedded into their core, they chose to put fun before fear. And they welcomed me into their little sword game as they said they were lacking one of the characters.

We performed a story of The Cid. One of the boys used a wooden stick as a sword and poked me with the pointy end. I asked him why he would do that, and he told me that I was a villain that The Cid had come to slay.

It was interesting at first, those tales they told, and I urged them to tell me more. But they only knew that The Cid was a hero who had slain his enemy, and because he won, nothing else mattered. I soon lost interest, for their arguments and childish conversation bored me. I got lost in my own thoughts about the clay figure I would be going home to create.

'Jacobo! You were supposed to kneel after I said kneel! You didn't even listen to me,' said the freckled boy.

I told them that I would comply, but after the third time that I failed to follow their instructions, they gave up on me.

'Let's go, lads. I guess we just have to wait for Isaac to get better and join us again,' the golden-haired boy told his friends. Then he said to me, 'You can go back to your witch mother now.'

My brows furrowed. I was irritated – not because of how they had discarded me, but because they kept filling themselves with those lies. They hadn't learned what I'd told them earlier. And I hated the way they accused my mother of being a witch when they knew that it meant something bad.

Walking out from the small alley between the stone buildings, feeling the hard stone under my feet, I sought out my mother. I found her right away, for her fiery red hair stood out amongst everyone else.

'Jacobo! Where have you been? We must get back before it gets dark,' my mother said when she spotted me.

'Are there more things you have not been telling me?' I asked.

'What is it? What have you seen this time?' she said. 'There are many more things I haven't told you, my boy. But since you have started to be curious about something else other than your

18

clay, we will start the lesson soon! Now, off we go, help me carry these back.'

'What lesson?'

'Books. I am going to teach you how to read and write.'

'Why do they say that you are a witch? And who is father?'

My mother looked at me with her blue eyes that became sad all of a sudden.

'I am not a witch. Who told you that?'

'Just the boys I met. But I don't really like them.'

'Of course, I am not. And your father is far, far beyond these woods. He is not coming back, and I'd rather not talk about it, not now. But aren't we happy, just the two of us? Are you happy with me?'

'Oh, yes, mother.'

I never knew who my father was, for my mother had never mentioned him to me. When I was old enough to know how babies are made, she explained that a man must impregnate a woman, and that the man who did that to her was my father. But that was it, and my curiosity about my father faded away from my head. It was good in a way because it made my mother's lines on her brows relax when I didn't ask any further questions. But after that day at the market, there were some that didn't fade away. The words that those boys had said, the way they had accused my mother. I loved my mother, and I didn't want anyone to hurt her. The accusation made my body uncomfortable; it filled my inner self with turmoil.

When I wanted to forget about that discomfort, I turned to clay moulding. And once I realised that I could make a building from clay, I imitated it. The next day, I formed clay in many square shapes, waited for them to dry and stacked them all up until it became a small place that my mother and I could fit in. But that was it.

Something in me was still yearning, unfulfilled. It would only be left at ease if I started to embed those sensations into something solid. I took out the incomplete sculpture of my mother's hand from the damp box I kept my clay works in to prevent them from drying out. I wetted the sculpture and built up from the base that I had left unfinished. Each layer upon layer, I let my own self diffuse from the softness of my fingertips through the softness of clay. After it was done, even though the piece looked complete and I was satisfied, I still couldn't grasp the reason for its being. And so, I put it away inside a cabinet.

A week later, my mother started to teach me a lesson as she had promised. After realising that I had been missing out, I sacrificed some of my time in learning how to read rather than spending it all on clay moulding.

For months on end, I paid attention to the alphabet and words that my mother taught me. Within a year, I learned how to read and write. And read I would – all of the books that my mother got for me. My new ability to read allowed my mind to travel far beyond those woods and mountains without having to leave my home.

Those books also developed a sense of something else inside me, for I felt like the range of my emotions expanded. Each book gave me new feelings that I had never experienced before. Everything seemed to be intensified, especially the yearning inside of me. I started to ask my mother more questions about why the people in a book behaved the way they did. I also asked her about all the discomfort that I didn't understand, until she had no more answers for me.

I would try to mould different kinds of figures while listening to the echoing sound inside of me, until I realised that I couldn't because I didn't understand these intense, new emotions. Most of the figures would be left incomplete, and I couldn't stop myself from smashing some of them on the floor.

One day, just out of boredom, I went through the row of finished clay figures that I kept inside the cabinet. Within it were many small sculptures that I made years ago in the shapes of small animals I found in the wood – little birds, squirrels, mice, animals that I had often seen. When I lifted those small figures and ran my fingers over them, there was a tingling sensation in my chest. It transported me back to the moment when I created each figure, even if it was just for a short second. I felt the small glimmer of joy and happiness of that time, things I had not felt in a while.

Then, it was like a light shone upon me, for I realised that a part of myself, my emotions, my own soul, was embedded within those figures. The yearning and calling from the depth of my being were forever captured and locked inside the figures I made. It was like déjà vu, when smelling a scent unlocks a memory, evoking the fragments of a past experience. But when I held one of my sculptures it was much more than that. It didn't just transport me to a vague memory of a specific moment; it brought me back to the distinct emotion once again, exactly like the first time I had felt it. And the figure seemed to be alive, like

I had created another life in between my hands. I felt so fulfilled, knowing that part of my soul was forever embedded within it.

My eyes shifted to the far right of the cabinet, where the sculpture of my mother's hand stood. The end of each finger was formed into the head of a mystic creature sprung from my imagination. I made each of them to symbolise each uncomfortable feeling that I didn't understand. They seemed to be arguing with each other. But now, once, I lifted it up and clung onto it, I understood it perfectly – the discomfort or feeling that I didn't comprehend before was struggle. And it was this feeling of struggle that I had embedded inside it. But now, as I held the sculpture in my hand, I didn't even need it to remind me of that emotion because it had already come to haunt me again. I was struggling. I was feeling the forceful restraint of being unable to understand my own emotions, and it erupted into a newfound frustration.

I knew that I wasn't good enough, and I craved for more.

# Chapter Two

The morning I left the hanging town, I was seventeen; not yet a man but no longer a boy. My journey began when I walked across the stone bridge, down the mountain and out to the wide-open path that was surrounded by tall mountains and woods on both sides.

That morning, I didn't bring anything much with me except my rabbit-skin bag filled with bread and cured ham. I had managed to tuck a knife in the front pocket and some coins that my mother could spare. But the most important thing was that I had my clay moulding skill with me, and that was all I needed. I was ready to go on an adventure of my own, to search for a master of sculpture.

On the first day, I spent all of my time on the road, walking with a goal but without a destination. I let my instinct guide me, hoping to reach a big city where the master would reside. As dawn turned into day and then into dusk, I had assuaged my hunger with almost all the food in my bag. And as night fell, I sat next to a tree and laid my head against its trunk, hoping to get some rest.

I woke to the sight of soft rays of sunlight on the horizon and with a numbing pain in my body but the wonder and excitement were still intact within my heart and mind, and so I continued on with my journey.

On the second day, after a long walk, my legs were sore, my feet swollen, and my stomach cried with hunger. I stopped beside the road in search of food that nature provided.

It was getting dark, and I didn't know how long I had been walking, for my head was always ahead of me. Even as I was walking among rows of trees, my imagination was elsewhere, beyond those mountains, far away in some grand city, or even in that little home of mine where my finished sculptures were lined up along the shelf. I also thought about the unfinished sculptures I had left scattered under my bed and the possibility of a life I could have given them if I was good enough. But the pain that seeped out of every muscle brought me back to where I was, to the reality that I was still in the middle of nowhere.

The last ray of light was already beyond the horizon, and the shadow of the night was creeping closer. I had never been scared of the dark, for darkness brought me calm, and calmness brought me a sense of focus. And when I was in such a state, I could think more clearly, like I had become a wiser version of myself. And as I had lived all of my life in the hut deep in the wood, I had learned how to survive in the dark.

I took advantage of the last drop of light to seek out something that would cure the twisting pain in my stomach. It didn't take me long to locate a meal. I would have recognised the smell of ripe apples anywhere. That alluring scent brought me to rows of apple trees at the edge of the wood. I plucked a red ripe fruit off the branches and crunched it between my teeth. Freshness and sweetness exploded in my mouth, bringing me unspeakable pleasure. Slowly, the happiness oozed inside my chest like those juices that coated my tongue. Just that sweet bite of apple made my heart bloom with joy.

I don't know if it was luck or fate, but as I was munching on the apples, I heard the sound of slow gallops and wheels breaking through the pebbles on the road. I hurriedly collected as many apples as I could and tried to follow the sound. I must have been too greedy, for the moment I ran from the tree, apples spilled out of my bag, dropping onto the ground. I went back and picked some of them up, but I could see that they were bruised now.

When I was finally out on the open road, a horse with a cart came into my line of sight, closing in on me now. An old man sat behind a medium-sized black horse, the reins in his hands and a candle lamp glowing beside him.

'Oy!' the old man shouted as he spotted me. The horse came to a halt. 'Who is there?' he said with a tone of alarm, but when he saw my face, it changed to a milder one. 'What are you doing alone in the middle of nowhere, boy? And in the dark!'

'I came from the hanging town in search of a master of clay. I was sitting by the tree when I heard the sound of your horse and your cart,' I told him.

The flickering light showed lines on the man's face. He was older than I expected, but his head was covered with a hat, so I could not tell if old age had reached his hair yet. His hands were rough and dirty from some kind of hard labour.

'Well, I don't think you will find anyone in the dark, except wild boar,' he said.

'Where are you headed, Señor?'

'To my house, of course. It's dark.'

As I stood beside the cart, the horse moved towards me, sniffing at my bag. Its dark eyes looked straight into mine, and I knew that it wanted the apples.

'Oy, Blanco must like you, eh?' the old man said. 'Normally, he does not approach strangers at all.'

'I'm not sure if he likes me, but he must like this.' I rummaged through my bag and pulled out an apple, showing it to the old man.

'Can I feed him?' I asked.

'Of course, you see that he wants it, don't you? What is your name, boy?'

'I'm Jacobo, Señor . . . ?'

'Martín,' the old man replied.

'Señor Martín, may I ask if the nearest city with a big market is near to where we are right now?'

'Not for another full day's walk. I say, why don't you come with me? Me and Blanco here don't have much, but at least I could provide a roof over your head and food in your belly. At my age, I do not wish to see a young man with a future like you die in the middle of nowhere!'

'Oh! Señor. Are you sure? I really don't mind finding shelter under this tree, for I have slept outdoors many times.'

'That is quite unusual! You said you are from the hanging town?'

'Yes, Señor Martín, but I live further in the woods.'

The old man paused and seemed to think for a while. After a few seconds, the wrinkled skin between his brows relaxed. 'Hop on now, boy, before I change my mind.'

I could not believe what I had just heard. I must have stood my ground because the old man said, 'So, are you coming or not?'

'Oh! Thank you, Señor! I am in your debt, then,' I said as I collected myself and hopped up onto the wooden seat while Martín scooted over to the other side.

Blanco and the cart moved off slowly along the dirt road and then turned to the left through the woods, where the mark of cart and hooves on the dirt ran like a permanent scar, showing that he must have travelled this path every day for I don't know how long. The cart swayed its way further along the path, passing rows and rows of trees.

I took this quiet moment to ask Martín where had he been before I heard his cart coming my way.

'I was at Don Vicenç's house,' he said.

'Where is it?'

'Not far from here.'

'Who is Don Vicenç?' I asked.

'My employer.'

'May I ask, what do you do?'

'You are a curious boy, aren't you?' said Martín, raising one eyebrow. 'Haven't you heard that curiosity kills a man?'

'But I'm just a boy,' I told him.

'Well, every boy becomes a man—and one day you will be a man, and that is when curiosity could kill you— Here we are, boy! Hop down and help me open the barn, will ya?'

'Yes, Señor,' I said.

As I hopped off the cart, I stole a quick glance at the house between the lines of trees. A window showed a flicker of light from within. Even in the dark, I could still see the rural house was single storey and made of stones. It wasn't big, but it wasn't small, either. I went straight to open the door of the wooden barn. I didn't want to show too much of my curiosity, as Martín seemed to mind his privacy, and I didn't want him to change his mind and send me back to the road. At first, I thought that Martín was living alone, but then I must be wrong, for I heard the sound of a little child crying inside.

Martín brought the horse and the cart into the barn after me. I helped him untie Blanco and poured some food into the wooden trough for him while Martín unloaded his stuff from the cart. I peeked in and saw brown jars securely closed on top of the cart. Martín only lifted off a white sack that sounded like it contained something made of metal, for it clinked and clanked when he slung it over his shoulder.

'Come, boy. It's time for dinner,' he said, and I followed.

'You have a son or daughter? I heard a crying sound when we first arrived.'

He didn't answer, just raised his eyebrows at me. And I kept my mouth shut. I thought I would soon find out anyway.

When we got inside the house, Martín took off his hat, and I could see that his hair had already turned grey. A second later, a woman, who I supposed was a bit younger than Martín, for her hair had started to turn grey, and her face was lined with age, came forward to greet him. Alongside her, stood a little girl, whose eyes were red in evidence that she had been crying earlier. When the woman's eyes came to rest upon me, her expression of joy shifted to confusion.

'Martha, this is Jacobo,' Martín said. 'I found him on the road on my way home. He is looking for a master of clay.'

Martha's confusion was still apparent. She didn't react to Martín's comment.

'Oh, my dear Rosalia, what is the matter?' Martín shifted his attention to the little girl, who clearly wasn't used to seeing strangers. She moved back and hid behind Martha's skirt.

'Martín?' Martha said, her expression unclear. It was a mixture of recognition and doubt, but behind it, I could feel a certain warmth.

'I have decided to give Jacobo some shelter. I will bring him to Don Vicenç's place tomorrow,' said Martín.

'Oh, dear Lord,' said Martha, her expression was still unreadable. A silent exchange seemed to pass between the couple.

It was Martín who broke the silence. 'I have decided,' he said.

'Right,' she answered. 'Then, please come in,' Martha addressed me, 'I have prepared enough food for all of us.' The warmth in her face was still there, but the doubtful expression was replaced with sympathy. I didn't really understand the situation, but all I could do was to accept their generosity without asking any questions.

Martín quickly kissed Rosalia's cheek, then Martha's, before he carefully placed the white sack on the bench near the door. He reached out his hand for the little girl to take. Martha urged the girl to take Martín's hand before she walked away to prepare for tonight's meal.

'Who is he?' Rosalia spoke up, her voice was soft and unsure.

'Dear Rosalia, this is Jacobo,' said Martín.

The little brown-haired girl in a white dress looked up at me with her green eyes. She didn't remind me of anyone in particular, but those innocent eyes of hers did remind me of myself when I first asked my mother if I could accompany her to the market.

'Hello, Rosalia,' I said, but the little girl said nothing back, only kept her round green eyes on me.

'Rosalia, do not be rude. Why don't you say hi to Jacobo? He is going to be my new apprentice,' said Martín

I averted my eyes from Rosalia's face and looked at Martín in surprise, and with curious eyes and mind, he must have read my expression, for he told me, 'I think it's your lucky day, boy. You might have found a ceramic maker, not a master, but I believe I can teach you a thing or two.'

'Oh! Señor, you know how to make sculptures?'

'I would say so. That is one of many jobs I do for Don Vicenç, and I am in need of an apprentice, for there is too much work for me to do alone. So, tomorrow, you will come with me to Don Vicenç's place, and I'll speak to him about you.'

'I—I thank you, Señor! I am in debt to you again. But this time, I cannot think of a possible way to repay it.'

'Just learn from me and do what I suggest, then your debt is paid, boy. Now come, let us eat, shall we? Martha and Rosalia must be starving already. Today, I was overloaded with work as Don Vicenç needs everything done before his ship leaves the port.'

I didn't exactly know what I felt at that moment, shocked perhaps, by the game of fate or some sort of luck that was handed to me, unnoticeably. My thoughts went straight to my mother. I should write to her to tell her what I had just heard from Martín's lips, but I put the idea away, for it had to come into reality first. I would have to get on working with clay and having Martín teaching me. If I wrote to tell her before all this had happened, I would just be writing my dreams away.

Martín signalled me to follow him to the table that was laid in the middle of the house. I followed him mindlessly as my head was spinning with what I had just heard and the possibilities of what was to come.

Martín pulled a chair next to him out from under the table. I sat down beside him. As my senses of reality began to slowly fill into its spot, my eyes started to wander around the house. All the walls were made of stacks of stones, but the colour was different from the buildings in the hanging town.

The quality of Martín's house was far better than my hut in the wood. It was blessed by space and equipped with necessary furnitures. A stove and a table for cooking were placed up against the wall. The table where we were seated was big enough for all of us, and it would allow two more adults before it felt crowded. There were also three more doors that led to other parts of the house, which must allow Martín's family to live in a luxury of space. Whereas the hut that I stayed with my mother had one common space, one tiny bedroom that belonged to my mother and another tiny room which now belonged to me. Not so long ago, that tiny room used to serve as a storage room where my mother kept her herbs, but as I grew older, we had to move the cupboard and every jar of herbs into the common area where we cooked, worked, ate, and experienced new things in that same space because it only fitted me and my growing limbs.

I didn't learn the sense of rich and poor until I saw the difference between the house in the hanging town and my hut in the wood. And I grew to develop more of this sense of inequalities through books when I read about castles of kings and queens. I realised that my mother and I were poor, but at that moment in time, it didn't matter much to me because all of my attention was thoroughly focused on clay moulding.

Martha placed a ceramic plate with meat stew and mushrooms in front of us. I felt so blessed at the moment, not only because of the smell of the stew but also the bowl in which the stew was served. It was shiny, its colour so bright and well preserved. I ran my hand over the rim of the bowl, and the feeling that I got was very different from the ceramic I made back at home. There was a pattern of leaves flowing at the rim, but most of the drawing was obscured by the stew. I don't remember the taste of the stew that well. It must have been great, but I could not wait to see what was beneath, so I quickly ate up everything inside the bowl, scooping all of the contents into my mouth until the picture became clear. It showed a jar of red roses.

'Señor Martín, how can the colour look so bright here on the bowl? and it feels like there is a layer of something shiny on top of it—How did you do it, Señor?' I asked, disturbing the conversation that was happening, which I wasn't paying attention to.

Martha looked at my face, her brows lifted. 'Well, well, I thought you were starving, Jacobo. And I thought you loved the food I made.' Martha chuckled before she added, 'Oh! Martín,

I think you have found your apprentice.' Then she directed her gaze at me again. 'Martín here will teach you how to make it, Jacobo. Can you believe that he was complaining to me that he needed assistance because his work was so busy!'

I smiled at Martha, feeling a little shy from the comment she made about the food. 'Of course, I love your food, and I am very thankful, but I was just curious about this magnificent technique.'

'Boy, I love your enthusiasm,' said Martín. 'I would love to teach you a technique or two, but first, we have to see if Don Vicenç allows you to be under his employment. I will bring you to his place tomorrow,' said Martín.

'Can I go to visit Don Vicenç, too?' A little voice from Rosalia rang up.

'No, no dear, it's not a place for a little girl of your age,' replied Martín.

'But he can?' said Rosalia, pointing her small finger at me.

And that was the first time I noticed that the girl must be around the age of five at most. I wondered how Martín and his wife managed to have a kid at this stage in their lives. I knew that over time, a woman's ability to have a baby decreases. I wasn't careful with my words when I asked, 'Is she your daughter or granddaughter?'

Martín turned to look at me with lurking brows. He signed and said, 'I think that your curiosity will be a problem. There is one thing I want to tell you before you meet Don Vicenç.' He looked into my eyes, and I can see the seriousness in them. 'If you get to work for Don Vicenç, try to stay out of his business. And as a curious boy as you are, try harder! Double your efforts to stay out of his business! We are his employees. We do not interfere with what he does. We do not judge anything he chooses to do. Show me your worth, make me see the passionate boy I believe I see in you.'

And, surely, I promised Martín I would.

# Chapter Three

In the morning, Martín woke me up before dawn. It was still dark. Looking outside through the window, I could see that none of the light had yet escaped from the sky. The only light that allowed me to see the looming silhouette of Martín's face was from the flickering candlelight on top of the table, where we had dined together the evening before.

Last night after the meal, it was past bedtime for Rosalia, so Martha had taken her to bed right after she had finished putting away the ceramic bowls. After Martín prepared a place for me to sleep, we said good night, and I fell asleep the second after I heard the door of Martín's room shut.

I awoke on top of a long wooden bench near the stove, and to which I was grateful. Even if my long legs stuck out beyond the length of the bench, it was far better than sleeping against the tree trunk.

Martín told me that if Don Vicenç agreed to let me work, I would have to stay at Don Vicenç's place in case he needed my help for other physical tasks in the household. And another reason was because there were no more spare rooms in his house for another soul to sleep. To all of this, I had agreed. 'Anything would suit me.' I remembered saying this to Martín. 'Anything at all, just so I have a chance to learn from you.'

'Boy, time to get up,' I heard Martín's voice and saw his silhouette standing beside me. 'There is a lot of work to be done. We will leave in fifteen minutes. You can wash at the bucket over there.' Martín pointed to a wooden bucket that appeared next to the stove. 'Ah! And let us hope that Don Vicenç is in his best mood today,' said Martín before he disappeared behind the entrance door.

We did leave the house exactly after fifteen minutes. I didn't have a chance to thank Martha or even say goodbye to Rosalia as we left quite early. I helped Martín getting the horse and the cart ready while he put the white sack of what I supposed was a metal tool from at the back of the cart along with those brown jars.

'What are in those jars?' I asked spontaneously out of curiosity.

'Clay and stuff, that is, boy,' Martín said without looking at me while he was leading Blanco out of the barn. My eyes followed the objects covered by white fabric on the cart as it slowly exited the door. I thought about the clay that lay inside, and I was full of enthusiasm to get going with my day. When the last inch of the cart passed the radius of the door, I impatiently closed and secured the lock back at its place and hurriedly hopped up to the seat next to him, feeling more impatient to reach Don Vicenç's place and get started with the clay.

I could see the orange light already peeking out from the horizon once we exited along the same scarred dirt that we passed yesterday. But as I looked up, the sky above me was still dark. The only light that guided us down the road right now was from a glowing flame inside a small lamp that was swinging on the side of our seat as Blanco pulled us forward. I looked to the ground where my shadow had formed a weird, inhuman-like shape. How the light could play out such illusions. It had stretched out my limbs and fingers; my body became a shape I could not recognise. It didn't scare me, but I turned away. I noticed the cart creaked in the same rhythm along the whole path, and my uncanny shadow swayed and twirled to the sound like it was dancing. Along the way, neither of us said a word.

Martín eventually spoke up first. 'No questions today, boy?'

Upon hearing Martín's voice, my head snapped away from my uncanny dancing shadow and focused on the old man next to me.

'I do have many in my head, Señor,' I said, 'but I am trying to suppress them as you said I should not put my nose in any of Don Vicenç's business.'

Martín's eyebrows quirked up. 'You do learn quite fast, don't you, boy? Then, why don't you tell me more about yourself?'

'Of course, Señor,' I said enthusiastically. 'But, truthfully, there is nothing much for me to tell you. Back in the hanging town, I lived with my mother in a small hut. But I left because I wanted to learn from a master, Señor. I felt like I was not good enough, and all those books could not provide me with what I wanted to know. Then, I met you. And you sheltered me, and now you are leading me to what I have come to find.'

'You know how to read?' asked Martín curiously.

'Yes, Señor.'

'How peculiar. Your mother taught you?'

'Yes, she also taught me how to write,' I said with a wide smile, feeling proud of my mother.

'Well, she must come from a well-to-do family?'

'Oh, not that I am aware of, Señor,' I said. 'My mother only told me a bit about my grandfather. He was a physician in some big city. I have never met him, but as far as I know, she told me that my grandmother died when my mother was young, and after my grandfather passed away, she didn't want to live in a big city, so she moved to a small town.'

'I see, I see,' Martín nodded up and down in the same rhythm as the cart swayed left and right. 'And you said that you are from the hanging town,' he said, his brows knitted as if he was trying to process his thoughts. Eventually, he continued, 'Yes. I think I have heard of it. Oh, did you say that you only lived alone with your mother?'

'Yes, my mother told me that my father passed away when I was very young,' I told Martín. I recalled my mother's face when she told me that my father was dead. The relief in her eyes seemed to be saying that she'd preferred the state of the man being dead than alive.

'I see, boy, you must have been through a hard time, living with only your mother. How do the two of you get on, then?'

'Oh, we have a good time, just the two of us. We are happy. She earned some money from selling herbs and some of my sculptures. But the money just keeps us day to day. Sometimes we can't afford to buy necessary tools for our work. But we never lack food, Señor. There is always food to eat in the woods if we look carefully.'

Martín nodded as he stared in front. He seemed to be lost in the process of his thoughts again. I shifted my gaze to look in the same direction. All I could see was the dark path ahead of us. The sound of the cart and Blanco's hooves still played in the same rhythm along the way. Suddenly, Martín's head snapped my way. 'Do you believe in God? Jacobo,' he said.

'God? Which one? I have read about a lot of them,' I answered, unsure of where Martín was diverting the conversation.

'Of course, a smart boy like you must know which God I am talking about.' Martín rolled his eyes. 'But, from what you have said, you can just tell me what you believe in. I won't judge you. I won't tell another soul, either.'

'I'm sorry, Señor, I would have to tell you the truth. I do not believe in God or any other gods.'

Martín turned and held my gaze. With just the dim light from a lamp, I could see in his eyes that he was being serious. 'But you should have faith, boy, you should. Because I think God has sent you to me. I am going to tell you why I took you in and why I didn't question you . . . much.'

'Why do you think God has sent me to you, Señor?' I asked as I held his dark blue gaze.

'Because, as Martha said, the day before, I was telling her about asking Don Vicenç to hire some help as I am overloaded with different kinds of work. You see, Don Vicenç is a perfectionist. Each and every piece of work has to be perfect in order to be accepted. And as you can see, I am old now, and I struggle with my eyesight. So, I might not have perfected my work like before. And then you, boy, you came out of nowhere and told me, with that enthusiasm of yours, that you are looking for a master! If God hasn't sent you to me, then I do not know who did.'

'I'm not quite sure about that, Señor. But I believe that it's a lucky day for both of us,' I said with a big smile.

'Let us hope so, boy,' Martín replied. 'As I said, Don Vicenç is very particular with who he hires as well as with the details of work, and as my age does not seem to be slowing down, I, too, do not like it when my work is not perfect, do you understand me? We only make the best ceramics.'

'Of course, of course, Señor! I will learn from you and work hard because right now, I do not like it when I do not know how to make my work perfect.'

'Good! We will be able to solve both problems, boy. And second to all of that, I do like you after all,' Señor Martín smiled. Even though the light was dim, I could see that his smile was genuine.

Blanco dragged us on.

'May I also ask what kind of ceramics you make, Señor?' I said. 'Only plates and bowls?'

'Oh, no, we also make jars, cups, saucers, vases, and sometimes figures.'

'Figures . . .' I heard the whispering words upon my tongue, and I smiled a silly and innocent smile at Martín.

As I still could not see any silhouette of the house looming out of nowhere, I assumed we were still making our way towards my destiny.

'How did you get to know Don Vicenç, Señor? You talked a great deal of him. Is he even older than you?' I said.

I must not have been careful with what I said again, and my words must have slipped out not quite right because Martín was eyeing me speculatively. 'Even older?' he said, but eventually, he laughed. 'Well, boy, I am old, I know, I know that well. But Don

Vicenç is still young, not as young as you, of course. But I'd say that he's the most charming man I have ever known. When you get to meet Don Vicenç, you will see that he is a man of . . . wonder. How should I put it . . . hmm . . . let's see. Yes, my master is a man of wonder indeed! He has bad days and good days. We all just wish every day could be a good day for him.'

'How long have you been working for him?' I said.

Martín looked at me with contempt. 'I was a man of bad fortune before I came to know his family,' he said. 'I was under the employment of his grandfather, Don Luís Velasco, a very good man, indeed. But he passed away years and years ago now. Don Luís helped me when I was around your age. I was a rat on the street, stealing food in the alleys of Barcelona. I was caught and was going to be punished, but Don Luís helped me. He said I reminded him of a boy he met when he was young, a friend of his. And after he found out that I was an orphan, he took me in and gave me housework to do; however, later on, he saw that I was more useful with other handiwork, so he sent me to work as an apprentice for his ceramic and porcelain business. You see, boy, I used to have the steadiest hand.' Martín looked at his now, old and calloused hands. 'However, a couple months later, Don Luís passed away from old age, but his son, Don Alfons, who was Don Vicenç's father, treated me kindly just like his father before him. I have what I have today because of Don Vicenç's family. Do you know that I met Martha at his place? She was one of the maids. We fell in love. Don Alfons didn't forbid our marriage, instead he gave us his blessing! The house you saw yesterday belongs to his family, but he let me and Martha stay there in exchange for the work I have done for him. This debt could have never been paid in full, do you see it?

'So, I swore that I would be good use to him until the day I die. But when Don Alfons passed away from an accident, his son, Don Vicenç, was about nineteen, and he took on his father's estates and his business. I thought Martha and I might have to move away because we weren't so sure about . . . Let's say Don Vicenç is not his father. But, in the end, he let us keep the same life only to keep my promise that I gave his father. And yes, I swore to Don Vicenç the same promise,' said Martín.

I watched the yellow flickered candlelight reflected in his eyes. Martín was almost in tears.

'I would never be able to repay that kind of debt, either,' I said. 'Just like I will never be able to repay you this debt. The opportunity you have given me, Señor.'

'I'm giving you a chance to prove yourself, boy, to help me with ceramic work, and if what you said is true, that you have the knowledge and experience of making ceramics, then I will teach you everything I know.'

'Thank you, Señor! I am sure. I will be of use.'

'We'll soon see, won't we?'

# Chapter Four

The outline of the building looming over the trees wasn't at all a house in my point of view, for I used to live in a hut made of wood, and I would call Martín's place a house, but what I could see in front of me was surely a castle, and a strange-looking one too.

What made this castle unique was that it was built in a particularly peculiar style. It exuded a sense of mystery, but at the same time, it showcased its charm which lured me to explore what secret could be lying within.

The castle was tall, but if I counted the windows, it only had three storeys, though each floor must have had a very tall ceiling.

I looked up at the top. It didn't consist of one even roof, but it was distributed into a different height. In the middle part of the building, the roof extended taller than the right side, and on the right side, the roof stood taller than on the left. If I hadn't looked carefully, I would have thought that three houses were built on top of the castle. Each with a roof of its own.

Once the cart came nearer to the castle, the first ray of light hit the front part, reflecting on the sandstone, which heightened the orange glow of sunlight into an intense reddish-yellow gleam. The colour burst in my eyes as if the castle was bathing in an angry flame. The glow lasted only a few seconds before it was overshadowed by the clouds above. But then, I was able to see the castle the way it really was. The whole place was made out of sandstone, except for the window frames that were made of dark maroon bricks, jutting out of the sandstone surface. The building itself wasn't built in a plain square shape like the ones in the hanging town, but there were corners and a sharpness all around.

On the second level, there was a large overhanging enclosed balcony that was formed on the side of the castle, and I supposed the weight of the balcony was held by the eerily crafted gargoyles underneath; their tails coiled down until the wall of the first storey, their faces were angry and fierce, and it seemed like they were staring right down at me.

One particular thing that caught my eye as I observed that overhanging enclosed balcony were the objects that framed the upper triangular part of the window. My eyes shone like the texture of those shiny creatures. I knew that it must be made of ceramics because it had the same effect as the bowl in Martín's house. Those creatures were some kind of reptile, similar to a snake, but their bodies were made up of reddish scales, and each of them possessed more than one head.

'Señor!' I blurted out with enthusiasm, 'Are those ceramics? Did you make them?'

Martín flinched. 'Why don't you shout louder and wake the whole place up? Which ones are you talking about?' He spoke in a loud whisper.

I looked at Martín with wide eyes and pointed to those mystic creatures.

'Oh, those, yes, I did, but I made it according to Don Vicenç's needs. I told you he is a man of wonder. Since he was a boy, he always loved reading different myths and tales. But if you ask me who put it there, I'd tell you it wasn't me.'

'Oh, no, I don't care who put it there, Señor. What attracted me was its texture and colour.'

'Then, that is glazing techniques and the same technique I used on bowls and other items. You will learn it from me soon enough.'

I gave him another silly smile, feeling excited and overwhelmed.

'Oh, and what is that tree?' I asked once I saw a strange-looking tree at the side of the castle. It wasn't so tall, but its leaves were extremely long, hanging low until it almost reached the ground. Looking at it, it reminded me of a hairy creature with crooked and twisted dark bone, and its eyes and face were hidden behind that thick green fur.

'That is a weeping willow tree,' said Martín. 'Don Vicenç is also a great traveller. He brought it back from one of the strange places he visited.'

'I see,' I said to myself as I kept on glancing at every corner of this place, feeling afraid that I might have missed any of the detail. I thought to myself, Don Vicenç is truly a man of wonder.

As we moved past the front door, my attention came to a halt at a great double wooden door. It was decorated with wrought iron. Carefully, I observed, the iron had been shaped into large eight-pointed stars formed by long tails of gargoyles on the door knocker. Their snarling faces could easily scare away any unwanted guests.

The cart moved slowly past the castle and came to a halt at the rear of the castle where the stable was located. To my surprise, the stable was built in a normal manner. I was about to jump off the cart and go to the door, but someone else had already done that for me.

'Good morning,' said a young man who was approaching Blanco.

'Good morning, Andrea. This is Jacobo. He is going to be my new apprentice,' said Martín.

Andrea didn't wait for me to introduce myself. When he looked at my face, he just snorted before ignoring me altogether and led the horse away. I didn't quite get a good look at Andrea, but all I know was that he possessed a crooked nose and curly brown hair that covered half of his face.

I hopped down and looked at where Andrea was taking Blanco. The barn was full of horses, their heads stuck out from the wooden fence, and there were so many of them on both sides of the barn, all in different sizes and colours.

Martín pulled the cart to the right, next to several others. He pulled it to a halt on one of the empty spots. And as usual, when the cart came to stop, Martín removed the white sack and slung it over his shoulder. He motioned me to take one of the jars to the right, which I did. And when he headed out of the barn, I did the same.

Before I exited, I turned to look at Andrea once again, but he was nowhere to be seen. Somehow, I was disappointed, not because I expected him to be my friend, but I just didn't want to start off on the wrong foot or to have any bitter feelings towards anyone. However, when I knew that I was about to enter the castle, my excitement overcame the idea of Andrea's unfriendly behaviour. I looked up at the tall castle from behind. I could see that it wasn't lavish like the facade, for its windows were installed in a plain manner, a hole with glass between the sandstone. And I supposed the interior must be quite gloomy as the windows were much smaller, and they would only allow a small amount of light to penetrate. I wondered if my room was going to be the one with or without a window. Would I be sharing a room with Andrea or someone else? I was sure that this castle must have had more than twenty servants.

I was still imagining all the possibilities when Martín called out my name. 'This way, boy,' he said. 'As servants, we do not use the front door.'

'Are there many people living in the castle, Señor?' I asked.

'Did you even hear what I said before?'

'Yes! Do not use the front door.'

Martín gave a curt nod of the head before heading towards a small wooden door, which led us directly to the kitchen. No one was here yet. I thought it must be because it was still early in the morning, but the fire in the oven and the hearth were already lit. A dim fire was the only source of light in this vast space as windows were scarce in this part of the castle. I looked around the dim kitchen, the size of it alone must be the same as Martín's house.

The ceiling was lined with sandstone, and large wooden pillars were laid on top to hold the weight of the castle. The same kind of sandstone formed the four sides of the room evenly, but the floors were uneven and could trip up anyone who wasn't looking carefully where they were going.

At the right corner of the kitchen, two large brick-lined fire-places, darkened by age and fire, stood alongside each other, one bigger and one smaller. The big hearth consisted of an oven with a dome shape on top. Beside it laid piles of ceramic kitch-enware that hadn't been glazed or fired.

There was also a large wooden table in the middle of the room, where worn wooden kitchenwares that must have been through a lot of soups and gravies, lay scattered on top.

At the furthest wall in front of me stood a large wooden door, and to the side, a much smaller one. I guessed that the door on the left-hand side must be the one that I should go through, according to Martín's instruction; I made my way there. But before I reached the corner, a large wooden door in front of me swung open, and an older woman came through. Her eyes shone with surprise before they regarded me with scepti-cism a second later. The woman was plump with sagging skin on her chin. Even though she was round, she possessed angular bone features and a sharp nose. I thought if this woman was thin, her face would look exactly like the thin skin on top of a skull. Her eyes were bulging and hooded at the same time, and maybe that was the reason her face looked as if she was scepti-cal about everything. Her two front teeth were large, extending further than the rest. Her hair that escaped from a plain white closed cap was greyish. I had never seen anyone so hideous.

'Agnes,' Martín spoke up. 'I was coming to find you. The boy's name is Jacobo. I'm going to ask for Don Vicenç's permis-sion for the boy to help me out.' Martín told the plump woman named Agnes before my mouth was going to betray my thought and send me out that small door I just came in.

'Hmm,' Agnes growled, and I thought about the squeaking noise that wild rats like to make when they find food. 'He has got a face that would melt our young maids' hearts.' She eyed me sneakily and continued talking to Martín, but not once did she divert her gaze away from me. 'Don't tell me he is another one of . . . you know, a lost child.'

'Oh, no, just my apprentice to-be,' Martín replied.

'Well, has Don Vicenç agreed to have him?' The woman finally looked away from me and walked towards Martín.

'Not yet. That is why I want you to tell me when he is awake. So I can talk to him about it. Please, call on me if he is awake, would you? I've got to get on with my work. There is a lot to be done.'

'All right, I can do that,' Agnes said.

Martín turned to me, 'Jacobo, go up first and when you enter, do not wander around. Just go up the stairs through a small door, and at the end of the corridor, you will find stairs, then go straight to the highest floor. That is where we will work, understood? I am going to get some bread.'

'Yes, Señor, and nice to meet you, too, Señora Agnes,' I told her and hurried away. When I tried to reach for the door handle, it squeaked and the door burst open. Luckily, I veered back quickly, or I might have ended up with a bleeding nose and dropped the jar in my hand. Two young maids, who were carrying a pile of white sheets in their hands, stopped in front of me, two pairs of eyes lit up and the corners of their lips started to curl up in amusement.

'Oh, Lord, help us!' Agnes groaned. 'Now, if you girls want to keep your job, continue with what you are doing. Be on your way! Do not just stand there and give this boy your sweet smiles!'

Both of the women giggled as they continued eyeing me when they scooped past me. They must be around my age or a year older.

'And you,' said Agnes, pointing my way, 'do as Martín said. Go upstairs now!'

'Oh, yes, Señora. Right away.'

I entered through the small door, and once it was shut behind me, I signed with relief that I had got away from Agnes.

A long dark corridor was in front of me; the only source of light was coming from a faint glow of a single candle that stood on a wrought iron candle holder on the wall. There were rows of doors along the left side of the wall. Slowly, I trod the stone floor, imagining what lurked behind those doors. I looked behind me, and I could hear a faint conversation between Martín and Agnes. Knowing that Martín wasn't going to come in right at that moment, I could not help myself from checking out what those rooms were. The door clicked open easily. Peeking in, I saw the silhouette of kitchen objects, finished ceramics similar to the bowls I had seen in Martín's house. A feeling of excitement and contentment consumed me as I could not wait to begin learning about the glossy technique that preserved and enhanced the colours on the clay's surface. I was so overwhelmed that I hardly noticed the heavy jar that I was carrying.

I closed the door and kept on walking until I reached the end of the corridor, and there, the stairs that Martín had instructed me to use were hidden behind the corner of the stone wall. I went straight up, treading carefully upon the sandstone so that I would not trip and break the jar and have Agnes coming for me.

Upon reaching the second floor, I peeked out to see what lay in this part of the castle, and again, I was met with the same structure of corridor that showcased the same rows of small wooden doors. But on this level, instead of a plain wall on the right side of the corridor, there were big double doors just like the one in the kitchen. The women's voices that penetrated through the doors made me realise that this must be the maid's quarter.

I climbed up further until the stairs led me to the third level. My heart thumped faster from the effort of climbing up the tall staircase. I peeked in and found out that this part of the corridor was completely dark. A light breeze flowing across my face; it carried a certain smell, a mixture of scents that seemed familiar but yet unfamiliar, and I could not put my finger on it.

I stood there, trying to make sense of a memory that was stuck inside my mind, but the sound of footsteps and conversations between women from a level below interrupted my thoughts. I didn't want to be caught wandering around, so I hurriedly climbed further up.

The staircase was smaller and much steeper now, and the steps were no longer made of stones but of a dark shade of wood that seemed to have aged with time. It was quite a challenge for me to go up the steps with one less hand to balance myself.

Once I reached the top, I knew that this level would be a place where I would spend most of my time. There were no corridors here, just plain wooden walls with a small wooden door in the middle. The ceilings of this part of the castle sloped down from the top. It must be the attic that I had seen earlier, the one that looked like it was segregated into small houses at the top.

I walked to the door impatiently, looking forward to getting the weight off my arms. But as the old wooden door gave in to a hard push, a horrid stench came rushing into my nostrils. I could not decipher what it was as the scent was not embedded anywhere in my memory. Out of the dimness, I couldn't tell exactly what it was that caused this horrid smell. I cast my eyes that had now adjusted to the dark around the room. There were pieces of broken ceramics scattered on the floor. I thought the smell must be from a different source of clay that Martín had gotten from a different kind of place, a mixture of dirt and unknown substances that came with it.

I placed the jar next to the table in the middle of the room, as there was no space available on the surface. And once my hands were free, I skipped over the scattered pieces of ceramics and went straight to the only window that was fixed between a sloping wooden panel on the left side of the room and opened them in the hope of a fresh breeze of air to get rid of the smell. The small window gave in easily. When the wind blew inside, I felt better and less like I was trapped inside a damp tomb.

Turning back to face the dim room, I could see that it was small compared to the size of the castle. And it looked even smaller with the sloping ceiling above my head that covered half of it. All the space on the vertical wall had been taken up by tall shelves, except for the small door that was trapped between them. The wall, where the narrow door stood, must have been newly installed as it was plastered with red maroon bricks, which was different from the usual sandstone wall, and the bricks didn't seem to have aged like the sandstone.

I looked further around. On a messy table, there were half-drawn earthenware, tools and colours stored in a glass container. I walked over to the table and observed all of the objects on top of it. The colour in the glass looked so luminous compared to the colour that my mother had made for me from natural substances. And the plate was so neatly drawn with shapes of vines and foliage. I would have to pay close attention as the lines were so thin and delicate.

I now understood the loss of sight that had happened to Martín. If I were to work in this dim room, I might lose my eyesight by the end of the week. The first thing I wanted was to light a candle.

Back at my hut in the hanging town, even though the place was small and the table I shared with my mother was tiny, our hut was bright with all sorts of natural light coming in through the windows from every direction. I wondered why Martín had to work in such a dim place, while the castle must have more than twenty or so rooms.

I found a candle on the corner of the table and tried to light it, but the only way was to go down and light it with another one that was already lit. Before my decision had been made, the door opened, and Martín entered with a candle in his hand.

'Oh, Señor, I was about to go down and light this candle,' I said.

He signed. 'It's good that I am here. I just told you a minute ago not to wander, and you just told me that you were going to go back downstairs.'

'Oh, right,' I said without looking at Martín's face.

'Here is some bread, boy. Eat it up. I am going to light all the candles.' Martín handed me a piece of big bread wrapped in a thin white cloth.

'Thank you, Señor. How about you? Have you eaten?'

'Yes and no. I do not have much appetite in the morning. But you are young, you must eat up before lunchtime.'

Martín lit up the candle on the table, which it instantly brightened up the room. He walked across the room and lit more candles that I hadn't noticed were there before.

'Better?' said Martín.

I raised my eyebrows, still chewing the bread in my mouth.

'The light, of course.'

'Yhe . . .'

'Do not talk while you chew,' he said.

I could not help smiling and kept talking with my mouth full of bread. 'You sound like my mother,' I told him.

He rolled his eyes and said, 'Lucky that I am not your mother, then.'

I gave a little chuckle to his comment and swallowed the last piece of bread before I walked over to Martín's side when he brought out one of the tools from his white sack. Looking over it, I saw an old leather tool roll and eroded hammer, chisels, and fettling knife. Martín didn't waste his time after he rolled out the leather roll; he started to explain all the details of how to use each tool. I listened to him attentively as many of these tools I had never laid eyes upon before.

All of the tools inside the leather roll were new, for the ones outside the roll were eroded with rust and seemed like they were antique from their appearance.

'Do you always carry,' I held up a wooden handle of the rusted hammer in my hand, 'This?' I held up another rusted knife. 'And this, as well?'

'Just leave them where they are. They are more valuable to me than they look and more than you think, boy. They were a personal gift to me from Don Alfons. And they have the best grip of all the others, you'll see. Now, put them down, and come over here.' Martín walked over to the sloping window, where a low chair was laid on the floor; in front of it was a spinning wheel with a flat surfaced stone placed inside a large ceramic bowl, and next to it a bucket of murky water.

'Do you know how to use a spinning wheel?' he asked.

'Oh, no, Señor, but I know what it is,' I said

'Are you a fraud?' He said with a deep frown between his brow. 'Do you really know how to make ceramics?'

'Of course, yes. I mean, no, I am not a fraud, but yes, I do know how to make ceramics. I really make them back at home. I wish I could just show them to you.' I told Martín, frowning as I felt a little put out by his comment. 'I did make plates and cups for my mother. I know some of the firing techniques, but it's never perfect like what I have seen from your house. And I formed them with hands and not with a wheel.'

'I see, I see, I am sorry. I do not mean to call you a fraud. Now, I will tell you how to use this wheel. It's quite easy if you really know the technique.' Martín said as he sat down on the low chair, dipping his hand into that murky water. 'Oh, and remind me to change this water, would you?'

'Oh, sure, Señor,' I told him.

'Now, the clay. There are many kinds of clay, but the one I

am using right now is earthenware clay. It must be the same one as you use because it's easy to find around here.'

'Yes. And the white one in the jar I was carrying earlier?'

'You opened it?' Martín said with fright, his eyes widened. 'If the clay is hardened in any way, you will be back on the road in a second!'

'Señor, I only looked at it for a second, but it's well covered now, and I am sure it is still just as it was.'

'That clay is rare, boy. Don Vicenç got it from France. We are attempting to make porcelain, like this one,' Martín said as he walked over to the covered shelf. He carefully moved the white cover a little to the side, just enough to pick out a small bowl. I wondered whatever was behind these covered shelves must be of value or importance to Martín. He walked back and showed me a milky white, almost translucent bowl; upon it, there were unique blue drawings.

'This is Chinese porcelain,' he said. 'It requires a different firing temperature, and it's more fragile. Don Vicenç got it from the Far East. I could say that I am a good pottery maker and a great pottery painter, but I could not mix those clays, and I don't even know what kind of minerals they contain. That stuff is outside of my abilities.'

'Oh, and by the way,' Martín said with a grim look as he caught me looking at the shelves. 'Don't get too curious about those shelves or what is behind that door. I know you are going to try to find out, but I'm going to tell you now they are very valuable things to Don Vicenç. So, stay away. You do not want to break anything. Do you understand me?'

'Yes, alright, Señor,' I told him firmly as well as assuring myself.

'Good! Now let me show you how to use the wheel. The techniques are in the shape of your hand, boy. Look at it. The curve of our hands is so perfect. And with a little movement of the hands, you can form different styles, wide neck, narrow neck, high neck, low neck, you name it. If you want to create a curvy shape, just bend the part of your knucklebones, cup your hand like . . .' Martín curled his hand in a shape of a letter C. His hands were coarse and wrinkled, but they were a strong pair of hands that had gone through the course of history. 'There, like this, like you are holding a bowl with both of your hands, yes. And, you must already know to always keep your hands wet, or else the clay won't glide well. Now, come, sit here and try it.' He got off the little stool and made a space for me to pass. I stepped over and sat down. With a wheel that was constantly spinning, I began the process exactly how he had shown me, feeling the wet and soft clay underneath my palms.

Martín squatted down to look closely at the process. 'Form the clay with steady hands, and the right pressure exerting from your fingers . . . yes, like that! You see it there? And if you press your hand a little stronger, the clay glides up and that part becomes narrower. Oh! Perfect, boy. You have such a natural talent.'

I could not help smiling and feeling proud of myself.

'You have such a gift, those steady hands and perfect pressure of yours. Back at home, if you did not make pottery, then what did you make?'

I looked up and pulled my hands away from the clay. 'I mostly make figures.'

'What kind?'

'It wholly depends on whatever I'm feeling at the moment. When I feel something so . . . intensely, and I want to capture it, I tend to make them according to my feelings. So, it's mostly in the shape of an animal, or a human, or an abstract object or even creatures from my imagination. But recently, I felt like I could never get it right. There was something missing. I could not feel or rather, I could not understand, and I do not know what to make of it. I believed that I was not good enough, so that was why I wanted to learn, Señor, to become better; so that I don't feel frustrated, and that I can feel the sense of fulfilment again.'

'Hmm! Very interesting. What do you feel right now?' He asked

'I suppose, I feel . . . excitement? As I am eager to learn,' I said and smiled at him.

'Then, you must make one exciting figure for me.'

I nodded and let the idea sink in. 'Of course, I will, Señor.'

'But first,' said Martín as he walked back to the shelf, placed the Chinese porcelain back and retrieved one specific jar with handles on the outside. 'Can you try to copy this shape? I need you to learn how to make this jar here. Add the handle on the side too.'

And so, the next hours were spent forming a jar with a round bottom, curvy neck, and finishing up with a wide mouth. Two curvy handles were added on both sides. Martín came and went in order to observe my work. He didn't say anything about it. I could see that he nodded contentedly before he went back to his seat at the table in the middle of the room, then quietly, he resumed his half-painted jar.

The room flickered with candlelight and natural light that finally shone through the small window above my head. The quietness was calming, but I could hear the household had already awakened. Then, there was the sound of footsteps slowly coming up on the wooden stairs, and after a few minutes, Agnes burst in.

'Don Vicenç has taken his breakfast, and now he is in the study room. He seems to be in a good mood today,' Agnes announced.

'Oh, right, Agnes,' Martín told Agnes before he hopped down from his stool. 'I will go down and talk to him right away.' Then, turning to me, he said, 'Stay put here, boy, finish up. Let's see if I come back with good news for you.'

Agnes walked to where I was sitting, looking over with interest. 'Well, well, you will be of use for Don Vicenç. I wouldn't be able to tell which one is made by you or by Martín.'

'Oh, Señora Agnes, thanks for your kind words,' I said with enthusiasm.

Agnes didn't respond, but she wriggled her nose, looking quite uncomfortable. I wasn't sure whether it was because she hadn't regularly received gratitude in her life or because of the foul smell.

Agnes walked towards the door and told Martín, who was cleaning up his hand on his dirty aprons. 'Just be quick, Martín, before his mood changes.'

# Chapter Five

Before Martín left the room with Agnes, he told me not to touch or break anything as he wasn't very convinced about leaving me alone with my curiosity, and he added that if he were to come back and find out that I'd ignored what he'd said, I would find myself back on the road, sleeping with wild boar once again. It wasn't a possibility I wished to happen, and not only that, I believed my luck would not extend so far.

Thinking back about how I had come to meet Martín, I still could not, in a way, believe that on the second night of my journey, when it was getting dark and when the pain of imagining myself sleeping against a tree was becoming so upsetting, I met a man who claimed to be a master sculptor, who also offered me a place to sleep.

Martín had asked me whether I believed in God, and I had told him the truth. At that moment, I wasn't sure which gods he was talking about, as I have read about so many of them. Though I supposed he must have been talking about the God that everybody in the hanging town had put their faith in, the same God I had read about in a book called the bible.

I had told Martín the truth that I was an atheist. But I did believe in fate, and I thought that it must be the beginning of what I was destined to find.

My mother didn't believe in fate. She also didn't believe in God, or rather she had given up on him, for among the trunk full of my mother's past life, right at the bottom, I found a beautifully bound volume of the bible, the kind that village people could never own. The book seemed to have been untouched for years, but still, she had it in her possession. My mother had never talked to me about the reason why she had lost her faith in God.

Like my mother, when I first read the bible, everything seemed reasonable, but as I read on, I could not bring myself to believe everything in it. I thought the words of God, and his stories and even the practice of the catholic church were just some kind of encouragement that allowed people who were lost to believe that they weren't lost and for them to build up strength and have a pillar in their life, or even to make them feel better about themselves. But I wasn't one of those people, for I knew that I wasn't lost. I knew exactly what I wanted, and I was strong enough to be my own pillar.

I didn't wish to ask God for guidance or his forgiveness. I didn't want to bother him as much as I didn't want him to bother me.

My mother didn't disregard everything. I knew she still had a strong judgement between righteousness and wickedness, of such things as goodness and evil. She believed in her own principle, that living a life under the conduct of righteousness would lead to a more courteous one, whereas if choosing to lead life immorally, that person will end up losing the principle of humanity and will be left in the state of total depravity.

My mother saw the world as white and black, but I could see

it in many different shades and tones because I believed there was so much more than just right and wrong. There were more elements that could be added up before I could define it in colour, into what was considered right and what was considered wrong. I also believe that it depended on each person's value of life. If the cause of your action was done with good intention, but your action was considered unethical, I would not categorise that action as immoral. And whatever the person chose to do – as long as it enhanced the harmony of everyone as a whole – then I would consider whatever that person did as ethical.

I never argued with my mother, even though I didn't believe in her principles. I didn't want her to feel bad, to the extent that I would have lied if that made her feel good. I didn't know the limits of where my values stood, and I supposed that I would have to wait and see.

When the clay glided smoothly underneath my hands, I fell into a deep concentration. Every pressure I exerted was right, as the jar formed in a perfect shape just like the example Martín had shown me. And upon floating in that moment when time seemed to cease, I felt something flutter. I could not tell where it had started, but it shuddered me like I was shaken awake from my soundless dream. My attention shifted from the clay as I glanced around the room, hoping to catch sight of that certain stimuli. But everything was still and quiet, except for the flickering light from the candles and the sound of the pottery wheel that was still spinning endlessly underneath my hands.

Was it just my imagination?

I shifted my focus back to the clay, but again, I could feel it, though this time I realised that it wasn't a movement that came from outside. It was rather an urge, or an undiscovered feeling that vibrated from within my core, like I was listening to a low snarl of a wolf that left an echo in my hollow chest. It growled within me, knocking upon my flesh, yearning to be released. These feelings were beckoning to me. It made my heart beat faster and my skin prickled. I was trying to search for something that must have been hidden somewhere. It kept calling and calling . . .

The next minute when I awoke from an unknown sensation, I found myself standing in front of the small wooden door in between the shelves. Slowly but still blindly consumed by some unknown rapture, I reached out, placing my right hand on top of the black metal handle and upon turning it, the door clicked, but it didn't budge.

But that instant, another door behind me was thrown open. 'Jacobo!'

I flinched to the excruciating noise and quickly turned to find Agnes at the entrance.

'What are you doing? Did you not hear what Martín said?' She raised her voice with the utmost annoyance.

I looked at Agnes' bulging eyes, then back at the door. I was still confused about how I ended up where I was standing.

The call of the unknown, the humming and rattling in my chest was all gone now as if I had imagined it, as if everything that had happened was just a daydream. After a blink, I was brought right back to reality. My heart started to slow down its rhythm, and within my reality, I was faced with Agnes and her angry stare.

Looking back at my hands that were still on the handle, they were all dirty with the clay. I quickly withdrew my hands and wiped them on the brown cotton breeches, and regretted it right away. Everything was all worn out and dirty.

'Damn it,' I cursed softly.

'What did you just say?' Agnes said.

'Oh, did I say something?' I said.

Agnes signed and frowned, her hands placed upon her large hips. 'Martín told me to find you because he didn't trust that you would listen to what he'd said, and guess what? He was absolutely right!'

I remained quiet but kept my eyes on Agnes.

'Oh, now you have nothing to say?' Agnes stared at me challengingly.

I ignored her accusing eyes and said, 'Um, do you happen to have some spare clothes? Especially breeches? Señora Agnes.'

Agnes rolled her bulging eyes, snorted and said, 'No, you are not going to meet anyone except Martín and only sometimes, me, and we could not care less about how you look. Anything else you want to say?'

'Um, then, maybe could you not tell Señor Martín about what you saw?'

'Absolutely out of the question! I am going to tell him everything.' She smiled her rat-like yellowish teeth at me. 'Now, follow me!' Agnes squeaked. She mumbled something ahead of me, and the words I caught was something like 'nosy little devil.'

I had no choice but to follow Agnes. I looked back into the room, as some sensation still lingered, but everything was just as it was, the candles were flickering, and the wheel was still spinning, and all the fluttering and growling was gone.

Upon closing the wooden door, I noticed that wet clay was still clinging to my hands. And because Agnes had called me 'little nosy devil,' I followed her and placed my dirty hands on her upper back, leaving a stain of clay on her white-coloured shirt. She turned and looked at me ferociously, though she failed to notice what I had done. It appeared as if I was losing balance and was going to trip, so I used her to regain my balance.

I smiled at her without uttering a word. Agnes rolled her eyes and turned back. With hands placed on the handrail, she started to continue shifting her feet down the wooden stairs. Her pace was so slow, and her plump body was blocking the whole staircase. She took forever to take each step down the steep stairway, and I was standing on the same step for more than ten seconds before I could put another foot down on the next one.

'Remind me to tell Martín how much he owes me for making me go up and down these horrendous stairs!' she groaned.

'Yes, Señora Agnes,' I told her, but I wasn't really going to remind Martín about it.

As we reached the ground of the third floor, the perfume scent was strong against my nostrils again, so contrasting to the smell up in the attic.

'Did you notice the smell in the attic?' I said, wondering.

'No, I didn't,' said Agnes quickly, without turning to face me.

'And what is this smell? It seems nice, and it is . . . quite familiar, but I don't know what it is exactly,' I said

'It must have come through that door, from the master's quarter, of course,' said Agnes. 'The smell is not for people like us. It's one of Don Vicenç's creations, you see? He made those scents and turned them into marvellous perfume.' Agnes talked

65

as if this was something grand, some invention that Don Vicenç had discovered. I thought about how my mother had done it all those years, long before I even started to get obsessed with clay moulding. She had created these fragrant scents from scratch, out of all the herbs and flowers, mixing and storing them with water and oil. If I was obsessed with clay moulding, I would say that my mother was obsessed with herbs and medicine.

I followed Agnes as she walked through the third floor corridor, the pitch dark one that I previously saw when I first came upstairs, but now, one of the candles on the wall was lit. Even so, it didn't really help brighten the place up at all.

'Where are we heading to?' I said, looking through the dimness and trying to make out what lay in this part of the castle.

'To where you are going to sleep! You have permission to stay and help Martín,' Agnes told me without looking back.

'Oh!' I could not help smiling foolishly to myself in that dim corridor. But all of a sudden, Agnes turned around, hands on her hips. The flickering candlelight above her head gave a dark shadow to her face, making her sunken cheeks look all the more hollow.

'I must tell you this,' she said, looking up at me straight into my eyes. 'There are rules in this place. Rules that need to be obeyed. If you fail to comply, you will be out, or even worse, you will be punished. Do you understand? And I do not want Don Vicenç to waste his opportunity and time just because you could not keep your prying eyes to yourself.'

I nodded, eyes wide, half listening to Agnes and half wishing her to turn away because of how uncanny her face looked from the effect of the light. Agnes pointed towards a large double door that stood to my right. 'And this door,' she said, 'as it's connected to the master's quarter, you are not allowed to enter, ever!' Then pointing at me, she said, 'You are not to wander around the woman's quarter on the second floor. And do not enter the master's quarter from any door, ever! Do not show your face to Don Vicenç. Stay deft and blind to our master's business.' Her brows furrowed as she seemed to be thinking of more 'don'ts'. But instead, she turned back and started to walk further into the shadow where the candles didn't reach. 'That will be all, for now.'

I followed Agnes further along the corridor until we reached the end. Once my eyes started to adjust to the dark, I saw another row of wooden doors on the left side of the wall.

Agnes pulled out a bunch of keys chained together in a large circular metal shape from her pocket and fumbled with it until she found the right one. The keyhole clicked; Agnes pushed it open. It budged, then stuck. She exerted some more force, bumping her plump body against the door until it finally yielded and groaned open.

'No one really comes to this part of the house,' she said. 'That is why it's stuck, but you can apply some oil to the hinge later.'

I nodded and followed her inside. The room was small, with a small window in between a stone wall like the one in the attic. But thankfully, this room didn't smell, all of the walls were straight, and the ceilings were tall. I didn't feel like I was trapped inside a small tomb.

Even though there were three beds cramped next to each other, I felt that the room was empty. There were no personal belongings that gave any history or charm to the space, no jar of flowers, no drawings, not even dirty clothes on the floor. All the beds laid empty. The hay-stuffed bag mattresses were missing. Apart from the other small cupboard that stood against the wall on the right side of the room and a chamber pot beside it, everything else was empty and bare. It was true what Agnes had said, no one had really been to this part of the castle because every surface in the room was covered in dust.

I didn't expect to be sleeping alone in a private room in a big castle that was surely full of servants. And when I realised, I felt a feeling of luxury to have a room of my own. But then I also longed to have some company, not because I was scared, but I just didn't want to feel empty, or was it loneliness that I wanted to avoid?

Agnes told me this part of the castle used to be the quarter for the male servants, but since there were none, the rooms were untouched. I found it weird when Agnes told me that there were no menservants. I thought about the labour work that I had always done to help my mother. I didn't ask Agnes about it, though I did ask her about Andrea, the stableman, where does he live? And she told me that the stableman lived in a stable.

I looked at Agnes, who was standing near the door, observing me.

'If you have the privilege to stay here under this roof, you also have the privilege to clean it yourself. Oh! And, of course, empty your own chamber pot. Even with a face like yours, no young maiden, who is not your wife, would be willing to empty it for you.'

I swallowed when the picture of a woman, who wasn't my

mother, entered my head. My skin crawled at the thought of it. A woman who was to be first, my lover, then my wife . . . It was a picture I wasn't capable of forming in my head. I let that image drop and focused on the chamber pot beside the cupboard.

'Yes, Señora,' I said.

'Stop calling me Señora, I am no Señora here. Just because you are young, you think I am old to you?'

'I would have to say yes, Señora Agnes.'

Agnes rolled her eyes and walked towards the door. 'You can go down and get a bag of haystack from Andrea later. Now that you know where to find your room, you can go back to work. And when you are not working for Martín, I will expect you to do some physical jobs. But you only take orders from me and not from the girls. Do you understand? Here, you must make yourself useful. Don Vicenç hates lazy people, especially lazy boys.'

'Yes. I suppose when Señor Martín does not require my help, I can help you. Just tell me what to do, and I'll do it.' I shrugged.

'You are hired to help Martín, so your main job is that. But we just need a little help here and there.' Agnes grinned.

'All right, shall we head back upstairs? I still have an unfinished jar to work on. And I don't want Señor Martín to find that it's dried up before I am done with it,' I said.

'I am not going up those stairs again. I am done for today. I have to go back to work. You can go back to Martín now. He must be waiting for you with your lunch,' Agnes said before she left, her heavy footsteps echoing down the corridor.

# Chapter Six

When I went back to the workroom in the attic, I found Martín hunched over a stool at the table in the middle of the room, focusing on his work. A breeze carried the air through a small window, and what was supposed to feel refreshing got mixed up with the smell of food, clay and that horrid smell which had completely thrown my sense of smell upside down. I ignored the effect and that unpleasantness when I approached Martín. With a silly smile and sparkling eyes, I told him, 'I can't believe what Agnes just told me. Thanks to you and Don Vicenç!' My happiness and excitement were so overwhelming that I had to restrain myself from hugging him.

'Boy, I just did what I thought was right!' he said as he looked over at the pottery wheel. 'And I can really see that you have talent. You are almost done with the third vase. I am very impressed! Come now, don't just stand over there and let the clay dry up. We must finish everything before the ship sails.'

I walked over to a stool under the sloping ceiling and sat down.

'Drip some water on the clay,' Martín told me without turning away from his work. 'Oh, and after you are done with that piece, you can eat, and I will teach you the glazing and firing technique.'

'Sure,' I said.

I got into the rhythm, and the clay moved according to my desires. I got lost for a second, dwelling within my reverie.

It was less than ten minutes when I got off the stool and stood hovering over Martín's head. As he noticed my presence in his peripheral view, he looked up at me, his face full of surprise.

'What? Are you done?' He said, glancing over his shoulder at the pottery wheel, where my perfect vase stood waiting to be dried. And when he turned back, his eyebrows furrowed, his face was a mixture of astonishment and bewilderment. He shrugged his shoulders and handed the plate with food to me.

I quickly unwrapped the thin white fabrics and found a bread stuffed with cured ham, but it was enough for only one person. 'Have you eaten?' I asked Martín.

'Yes, with the others, but as you are working for me, you don't go mingling with Don Vicenç's servants,' said Martín.

I could almost recite his exact words when he told me to stay away from the maids now.

'Our master won't like you being around his servants,' Martín continued, 'but at least he allows you to stay under this roof. It's very generous of him. Oh, and you will get paid at the end of the month. Even though if it's not much, I think you might be able to get a new pair of . . .' his eyes lowered down at my dirty breeches, 'Um, breeches.'

'What? I will also get some coins?' I said, surprised, all of the annoyance forgotten. Truly, I didn't really expect to get a roof, food, a teacher and, after all, a coin, all at the same time. 'Now I know why you talk highly about Don Vicenç. I would be telling others the same thing.'

Martín gave me a smile, and it showed that he was happy for me.

I thought of my mother. If she had known about my current situation, I was sure that she would have been happier than I was feeling happy for myself. I made a note in my head to write to my mother about my new-found situation. My eyes shifted to the bread next to Martín, and my stomach started to cry out in gratitude.

I devoured the precious cured ham in less than two minutes, and before I was about to swallow the last bite, I said impatiently, 'I'm ready, Señor. You can tell me about the glazing and firing technique.'

It was the second time I saw Martín roll his eyes at me, and I remembered not to talk to him with my mouth stuffed with food. He didn't say anything to scold me in particular, but he led me out of the room with a painted vase in his hand, down the stairs, and back to the kitchen to where the big ovens were, all without saying a word.

A group of people I didn't get to meet earlier were standing in a different corner of the kitchen. And a buzz of cooking utensils rattling against the other objects rang throughout the whole room. I saw Agnes chopping a tomato on the big table, but she hadn't noticed mine and Martín's presence yet.

The woman who was cleaning the dishes near the door I had just entered turned towards the commotion. When she caught sight of me, her eyes gleamed. I remembered her from the morning. She was the one who almost opened the door in my face.

'I suppose you got the job, then, if you are still here,' she said with a bell-like voice as she wiped her hands dry upon the apron. 'What is your name then?'

'Flor,' Martín said, interrupting me. 'He is my apprentice. Leave him alone. And you too, Jacobo, remember what I told you before. Keep your distance from Don Vicenç's servants.'

Flor's smile faltered a little from Martín's comment, but she managed to give me a quick wink before saying, 'Nice to see you, Jacobo. I'm Flor.' Her whisper was low enough, so Martín didn't turn around and give her another round of warning. I smiled back at Flor and walked after Martín.

From his loud footsteps, other servants, including Agnes, turned in our direction. I heard a gasp and a whisper that followed.

'Oh! Who is it, Señor?'

'I hope my future husband looks at least half like him.'

'He must be around our age.'

'Oh look, look, Alba, look at his face!'

'Enough!' Agnes shouted, and instantly all of the whispers and clinking of kitchen utensils ceased. Everything went quiet for a second. Then came a booming command, 'Back to work!' Agnes shouted, and the kitchen utensils started to clink once again.

'You girls, if I see any of you talking to him, you will be out of this place tomorrow morning,' Agnes said while waving the knife in her hand around. When she turned, the pointy end was directed at me, and her face gleamed with slyness, 'And you, I am watching you.'

I restrained myself from saying anything and forced myself to smile against the distasteful thoughts that had started to flare up in my head.

'Agnes, I need to use the oven,' said Martín, interrupting her.

'Fine, fine,' the plump woman answered, looking annoyed. She turned to the maids, 'Isabel, Flor, I think the bedsheets you washed in the morning must be dry by now. Go and fetch them, won't ya? And Alba, take the girls with you and see if the master needs anything else.'

'But we just came back from his room,' said one of the girls, who must be Alba.

'Then go clean the other rooms and make yourselves useful. Out of the kitchen now!' Agnes said with her two extended front teeth-rattling upon the lower ones.

Flor and Isabel left whatever they were doing and walked out through the back door, the same time as Alba and the other girls left through the big wooden door.

One thing that I noticed about the maids here was that they were all beautiful. They possessed round eyes and sharp noses and jaws. Their hair was worn down, spreading across their backs. Each of them had a different hair colour, ranging from blonde to strawberry blonde and chestnut to dark drown. But Flor had a unique fiery red colour that was similar to my mother. She also possessed such white skin, so contrasting with her intense blue eyes.

Martín and Agnes sighed at the same time before Agnes went back to more chopping and ignoring us altogether.

Martín called me towards the big oven.

When I looked through the small opening in front, I could

see that the stack of plates I had seen earlier was now laid layer by layer, segregated by a flat stone. Martín threw more wood inside the oven and lit the fire.

The oven was made of stones, stacked together in the shape of a dome. It must have been through a lot of fire as the stones were darker than everywhere else.

'Look, this is how you place the object in the oven,' said Martín. 'You must elevate the stone up from the floor around it. I would say three inches. And you don't want to stack everything up together in one go because that would restrict the airflow. I separate each level by putting the brick on the side as a post, and I lay a flat stone on top. Make sure that the stone is laid properly on top of the post. Uneven weight distribution could crack your work. Do you understand?'

I nodded and followed what he said enthusiastically.

'You see, these ones are already painted, fired and glazed,' he continued, mentioning the plates, 'We have to put them through a second fire and keep it going for about eight hours. After that, we wait around twelve hours to let everything cool down. The room will get quite hot. Everyone complains whenever I have to use the oven in the summer, but what can I do? The oven outside has a crack and needs some repair, but I have no time to do it. So, I suppose everyone just has to endure a bit of heat.' Martín shrugged as he looked over his shoulder and raised his voice, 'Agnes! I have lit the fire, so—'

'I can see that. I won't let that thing quench the water out of me. I'm leaving now,' Agnes shouted back before Martín had finished what he was saying, then she threw the knife down, wiped her hands and left through the master's door without looking back at either of us.

Martín shrugged again and turned his attention back at me. 'Right, while we wait, I am going to tell you a bit about what we are working on.

'So, there are many types of pottery and many styles. They're made up of different kinds of clay, which require different processes and techniques. The same kind of clay, if painted with a certain kind of technique, can be sold at a different price. I work on several types, for example, lustreware, tin-glazed pottery, or sometimes ceramic figures. But, you see, over here,' he pointed to a stack of already painted plates near the stove, 'most of them are lustreware, but they are very unique because of the way they are painted. You must have seen that normally lustreware is painted in foliage and similar repetitive patterns, but for me, I prefer to have them painted like the painting on the canvas. And that is why people prefer to pay more for my work.'

'Like the roses I saw on the plate at your house?' I asked.

'Yes, boy. And imagine beautiful scenery during your favourite season or a religious scene, they are what I like to paint as well. These things are very valuable, you see. But I have those plates at home because Don Vicenç allows me to keep some of my work.

'And you must be curious about the glazing technique. I'm going to explain it to you.' Martín reached for a bucket. 'So, glazing is a substance made with fine glass powder and various metal oxides. I also like to add some oil to the water. Oh, as well as gold and honey. It's my little trick. And once you mix them all up, you will have this,' he showed me what was inside the bucket. My eyes lit up as I saw a thick liquid with a glimpse of gold colour. Martín then reached for the vase that he had just painted and applied the substance onto the surface with a brush.

'Be sure that the object is completely dry before you apply this,' he said.

'So the purpose of glazing is to preserve and brighten the colour?' I asked.

'Oh, not only that, it also prevents liquid from evaporating or seeping into the open pores of the objects,' Martín said as he placed the glazed vase down. He got up and took one of the plates from the stack near the stove, and came right back to where I was.

'Now, this is the finished Lustreware.' He handed me the plate. I observed it carefully.

As Martín detected the gleam of excitement in my eyes, he said, 'You see, after the firing, the glazing that I mixed and applied would cover and fuse into the clay, so that is why the plate is shining and shimmering like gold with a touch of opalescent sheen. The colours also brighten up, and they will forever be preserved underneath.'

'And the effect would work the same with ceramic figures?' I said.

'Exactly. You can preserve your work through time.'

Martín's words rang through my ears. Not only could I embed my feelings within the sculpture, but I could preserve the figure that I had made for its longevity.

The ceramics were such fragile objects compared to their value to me. I wondered what the outcome would be if I broke one of those finished sculptures that I had embedded my feelings in. I was scared that the feeling would evaporate into thin air, and I would never be able to feel it again, so I never thought of trying it.

Since I had stepped inside this castle, my frustrations were slowly disappearing until I could no longer feel the storm in my chest. It was like I was beginning to breathe again; I was beginning to feel, like when I used to discover a new story in a book that brought a new emotion out of me.

Martín had long since gone, but I still found myself in the attic, working on what I obsessed over. I managed to finish seven vases before Martín told me that I was done for the day. I could not wait for him to allow me to make whatever I wanted, so I spent time alone after Martín had left, forming and sculpting my emotions alive.

The obsession with clay moulding became more and more ferocious in me after Martín had taught me the right technique of glazing and firing. Now that I was back creating figures, and I was able to embed my feelings within them once again, all emotions began to surge through my blood and course through my veins. Upon my hands, I kept moulding and moulding, sending everything I felt into the sculpture. Layer after layer, each and every curve of the figure, I beat on, hoping that my feelings would be embedded inside and that someday it would remind me of all the feelings that I had felt in my life.

Hours passed, and there it was on the table in front of me, the new emotions I had experienced, created tangibly in the shape of a skittish horse—its left hind leg kicking up in the air and its head swayed to the side, tossing its untamed mane to the wind. My excitement had been embedded within this horse, and the horse itself became alive.

After I was done with the piece, I hid my creation away in fear that Martín would find out that I had been doing my own thing instead of what I was paid to do. I would have to find time to fire and glaze it later.

That night, in my quiet and lonely room, I dreamt of a black stallion. I was on its back when it started to gain speed through a valley underneath a starry night sky. The wind whipped across my face and blew through my hair. I could hear the horse's powerful breath and feel every inch of its strong muscle. As the horse sped up, the thousand dotted stars I had seen earlier appeared before me now like a long glowing indefinite line. My heart thumped so fast that it matched the rhythm of the horse's gallops each and every time its hooves beat against the hard ground. Adrenaline rose up through my veins like I had never experienced. I was flushed with energy and emotion.

I exited into a world that wasn't my own. Everything around me seemed like a dream within a dream, like I was floating within a new universe. The horse kept on running and running with a speed that never seemed to cease.

In front of me, I could see a vast and dark bottomless hole, but I didn't want to stop. The horse was connected to me as if we were one. We beat on until we reached the edge, and upon that moment, it jumped off, and I let go of its mane. We were flying in a gravity-less state. I wasn't scared of death at all, and all I could think of was wonder.

It was only for a second that I floated in-between space and time, and when gravity was doing its job, I was dragged down, plunging into the dark bottomless hole. A butterfly feeling in my stomach began to overwhelm me, but I jolted awake from a bang at the entrance.

I was sweating, and the drumming of my heart was still reverberating in my chest.

'Get up!' Shouted a dark silhouette that stood at my door. 'Go cut the wood before Martín arrives!' It was Agnes.

After all, wasn't it only ten minutes since I had fallen asleep?

# Chapter Seven

I expected to meet Don Vicenç and make my existence known to him as well as express my gratitude for having me under his employment with meals waiting to fill my belly and a bed to lay my body. But I never caught a glimpse of my master since the day I arrived, or a week after, or even a month after. Don Vicenç still remained a mystery to me.

Since the day I arrived, I never proved myself unworthy of the gratitude that Martín had given me. I hadn't been mingling with other servants. All of my time was spent in the attic, working long hours for Don Vicenç, even when the light from the candle was my only companion.

Martín and I together, we made a shipload of kitchenware. I didn't know when the work would end. He told me that the first ship had sailed, and all of the luxurious kitchenware that we had fired would already be travelling out of Spain, so we needed to start a new set, to fill a new ship where they would be distributed among the elite in Spain. We had another load of work to do. Some days, I would find Martín with me, working late at night, pressuring me to speed up my work.

'Señor Martín. May I ask,' I said, breaking the silence in the dimmed room. 'Before I was here, did you have to work on these by yourself?'

Martín was sitting on a stool, drawing on a jar on the table in the middle of the room. I saw his back expand as he inhaled then he gave a long sigh. It took a while before Martín answered, 'Of course, what do you think?'

'And you always stayed until this late at night?' I kept asking.

'Now, just get into the point. What is it that you want to say?' Martín said.

'Don't you miss Martha and Rosalia when you stay this late?'

'Of course. But this is how I feed them. I work and I earn the money. And working hard is the way I repay my master, too.' Martín finally dropped the paintbrush and turned towards me. 'You see, boy, trading is one of the things that brings Don Vicenç's wealth. And my work is also one of the things he trades, so, now you see that I am helping him and he is helping me.'

I had got Martín to where I wanted the conversation to go. I was constantly inquisitive about the master, for I had been there for more than one month, but I had never seen even his shadow or heard any whisper of his voice through the walls.

'So, now I'm also helping him by helping you,' I told Martín. 'But when will I be able to meet Don Vicenç? I have only heard about him, but I have never seen him.'

'You work for him, that's right, but your work doesn't require you to talk to him, so there is no reason for you to meet him in person,' Martín said.

'But my master cannot remain a mystery to me forever. We are living under the same roof, and even if I wasn't allowed to enter the master's quarter, some days we would cross paths.'

Martín rolled his eyes and turned away. He picked up the paintbrush he had put down earlier and continued working. 'So, that was what you wanted to ask me about? Our master. Didn't I tell you that curiosity kills a man?' He said with his back turned towards me. 'Don Vicenç is a man of status and social standing. So, a man like him is always busy. He is usually socialising with the people of his society somewhere outside of his castle.' He took a pause. 'But well, sometimes, like very soon, a company of his friends, the lords and the ladies, would come to grace their presence at his estate, to spend their leisure time, and to buy his art pieces. Maybe very soon you'll see him.'

I nodded and stored this new information of my master in the drawers of my head.

The routine of my life for the next few weeks was the same. I spent time working in the attic until I could no longer force myself to focus. Then, I went back to my room, feeling completely exhausted. The comfort of my bed swallowed me up into the dreamless night.

I woke up again before the dawn broke out in the sky, cutting wood for Agnes and doing other tasks that I guessed Agnes had invented just for me. And the day went on like this until the sunlight hid behind the horizon.

Even though I was holding ceramic in my hands and doing what I loved, I found it redundant. Each and every day, I was making the same shape of pots, plates, cups and vases, none of which were the figure that I loved. Those pots and plates had no life. They lacked story, and I could not embed my emotions within them as I did with the sculptures I'd left back at the hanging town or the horse figure hidden under my bed.

I was unfulfilled.

I was unsatisfied.

I didn't know what was happening to me. I missed having defined feelings, and I wanted to feel again. I was like a burnt-out fire that needed more fuel.

My mind came to a pause one night after a long day of focus. Martín was already long gone. I got off the stool feeling quite tired, and I went straight back to my room.

That night lying on my bed, I felt restless. It was odd because night after night, after a long day working, I would find myself exhausted and the sleep would consume me without me noticing it. But on that particular night, I could not sleep even though I was feeling fatigued.

I didn't know what I was feeling inside, and I could not explain it. But it was there, tightening in my chest, in my heart and in my mind. After twisting and turning in my bed for a while, and when sleep didn't come, I finally sat up in bed and walked towards the window. The moon was bright in the sky, but its glow wasn't the same yellowish gleam like it should be, but rather reddish. It reminded me of the colour of my mother's hair.

My mother . . .

The tightening in my chest grew, but in my head, I was resolving the feelings that I didn't understand before. I came to realise that it was longing. I missed my mother, and my subconscious was blaming me for not writing to her. I was so busy and obsessed with my work that I had forgotten to think or to feel.

I trailed my eyes back to my hands that were resting on the window sill. They were still smudged with dry clay, and as for my nails, every one of them had clay stuck under it. I looked at my clothes, they were also dusty and smeared with clay. My mother would never allow me to pass through my bedroom door looking like a mess. She would tell me to go clean myself up and change into clean clothes.

I remembered her voice in my head, so clearly that it was like she was in the room with me. But when I turned away from the window, my vision had already adjusted to the dark: all that I could see was this small room of mine, three empty beds laid next to each other. Trailing my eyes further to the cupboard, one of the doors was ajar, and even in the dark, I could even see that they were empty. The whole room was empty, just like myself.

I was lonely with my new life in this strangely shaped castle. Even though I was working alongside Martín, I didn't have idle talk with him. I could not tell him that I was unfulfilled. He was my master, and I did whatever he needed me to do. More than that, I didn't even have anything to talk to him about, because I hadn't been feeling. I was just a body being controlled by a task. I had tried to let my mind sweep through the possible journey of what would have been or through different tales that I had read back in the hanging town. But even when I was feeling something emerging inside of me, I still had to keep it hidden and keep my mouth shut. I would be clinging on to a hope that tomorrow Martín would tell me it was time for me to create any figure I wanted, and that my routine tasks were done. I was longing for my hands to be able to shift from a different angle and finally let them be free.

I also longed to tell my mother. Back at home in the hanging town, after hours and hours of living in my imagination and after being in my head for a long period of time, I would form all sorts of stories in my head, and by the end of the day, I would tell everything to my mother.

I felt bad about myself that I had forgotten about her. I wondered how she must be doing. Did she go to the market on the weekend? She must be worried about me, mustn't she? When I told her that I would like to go search for a master and to explore the world, she didn't object. Instead, she looked at me with understanding and told me that she had anticipated that the day would come.

As I grew up, I knew that my mother was a person who usually keeps her feelings to herself. She didn't like to express it. The day I left, she didn't cry. She didn't say anything much. Although I parted with her blessing, I told her that it would not be long until I would be back to tell her stories at our tiny table in the middle of our cosy little home.

Time went by fast, and three months had already passed. Three months of me completely forgetting to write to her.

I came back to lay on the hay-stuffed bed, staring at the ceilings, and I let my eyes close and thought to myself that tomorrow I would not forget to ask for paper and ink.

# Chapter Eight

I woke up abruptly to the sound of horse hooves and conversation. I thought it was already late in the morning, and I had overslept. But when my eyes adjusted to the dim light, it was still very early. The sun must have had passed the horizon only a few minutes ago. The household must have awoken earlier than usual today.

I got out of bed, grabbing the clay-smeared shirt from the headboard of the bed next to me and put it on. Looking out the window, I expected to see movements of Martín and Blanco or the maids from below, but I could not see anything or anyone. The noise had already died down, leaving only a distant conversation coming from the other side of the castle.

Even the horizon was cast with a light; clouds gathered and completely blocked out the sunlight. It was gloomy, like the sky before the rain.

I would need an extra candle to be able to work in such dreary surroundings.

After washing my face and rinsing my mouth, I went straight to the workroom, expecting to find Martín there, but he wasn't in his usual spot on the same chair behind the same table. How peculiar. I ignored his absence and lit all the candles in the room. Then, I went to my usual spot behind that same stone wheel.

Seeing the clay in front of me, I felt excited and thought about working on my own thing, but when I looked up at the shelves in front of me, the top part was empty, which meant that I would still have to fill it up with nine or ten more vases. And if Martín was to arrive later and see me working on something else, he would not be pleased. I already knew that he didn't trust me with my curious nature, but I could not have him lose his trust in my work.

I inhaled sharply to exhale the frustrations out of my veins, but my nostrils caught that weird smell again. I thought I must have been used to that smell, but there it was, embedded within the stone wall of this room. This time, it was something sour like the smell of cider, but I could not place the exact smell of it yet. I decided to get off the chair and open the small windows for the breeze to come in. From the outside, I could hear a rustling movement coming from below. Tiptoeing and peeking through the window, I saw Andrea leading Blanco and Martín's cart inside the barn. I wondered where Martín had gone. Even if it was still early in the morning, it would be considered late for Martín as he usually arrived at the attic before sunrise.

I could see Andrea coming out of the barn again. I watched his movements and how he always walked with his face looking down at the ground. Andrea rounded the corner and disappeared, but a second later, he led black horses and a wondrous golden carriage with him. I had never seen anything so magnificent, the intricate carving on the upper part of the carriage and its shiny gold colour. I was lost in the beauty until the carriage completely disappeared inside the barn. I didn't know who the carriage could belong to, then I thought about what Martín had told me about elite people that often come visit Don Vicenç.

Their arrival would not change my situation, as I was confined to work within the attic, and I was never allowed to mingle with anyone anyway.

I came back to my spot and sat down. Without Martín, the room was completely quiet, except for an echo of voices carried in by the wind from an open window. I concentrated on finishing my task and filling up all the shelves.

When my mind became so focused, the quietness became louder in my head. I could feel that flutter again, just like I had felt before, a vibrating in my chest, a sudden intensifying feeling that was responding to something that was calling me. My head snapped up, but when I looked around the room, everything was so still. I tried to ignore that particular yearning and focus on the vases.

My hands plunged into soft clay once again. But the further my state of focus, the quieter the room became. And that was when the fluttering sound started again. There was something else, too, a little soft, wailing noise. But where did it come from? Perhaps Don Vicenç was receiving a guest with a child? That yearning inside me was still calling me, but I didn't let it consume me this time. Once my mind became its own master, all of the summons were gone.

By the time the fifth vase was done, my stomach was wailing with hunger. It must have been late now, but still, Martín was absent, and his absence meant that my breakfast and lunch were three levels below me. It must have been around noon, and I was left with two dilemmas, to stay here and starve or to ignore Martín's and Agnes' commands: never to wander around by myself, especially when there were guests. I recited their words in my head, and I could even see their faces speaking these sentences. But they left me no choice, for I wasn't determined to be so obedient that I was going to starve.

Quietly, I slipped out the room, tiptoeing downstairs with eyes and ears alert. Passing the third floor was easy, as it was always quiet and often dark. No one had really come to this part, and even Agnes didn't seem to care to change the burnt-out candle on the wall. The door that led to the master's quarter seemed to be forever untouched, and the only sign of my master so far was the scent that escaped through the wooden door.

When I reached the second floor, I peeked through the corridor. There were no movements there either, but voices could be heard, echoing along the wall, the voices of men and women's laughter. And in between the sound of laughter, rang a sobbing sound. It was unmistakable, and I hadn't imagined it. A woman was sobbing, and it came right from the room next to the stairs. It must belong to one of the maids who was certainly upset about something. I was curious, but I didn't want to enter the women's quarter and cross the invisible line drawn by Agnes, so I slowly walked away down the staircase, leaving the distressed maid behind.

As my feet touched the stone of the ground floor, the booming noises of kitchen utensils and Agnes' command rang loud and clear.

'I want to see those ingredients chopped when I'm back.' I heard Agnes shouted while her footsteps approached nearer and nearer to the door where I was. And in no time, the wooden door in front of me burst open, and I was staring straight into her probing eyes.

The crease between her brows tripled as she saw me, 'You! Where do you think you are going? Huh?' Her squeaky voice pierced through my ears.

'I—' I didn't get to finish my sentence when she walked towards me and grabbed my arm.

'Where is Martín? Who told you to wander around! Go back upstairs right now!'

I was surprised at her force. This woman's grip was much more powerful than I expected.

'Señor Martín hasn't been at the workroom all morning,' I said quickly. 'And I was very hungry, that is why I came down to see if I could get something to eat.'

I could see her face pondering Martín's whereabouts.

'Why don't you go back to your room and take a day off. No, you better go out and come back again in the evening. I do not want to leave you alone in the attic if Martín is not going to be there with you.'

'If you suggest so, Señora Agnes,' I said dryly, but in my mind, something popped, and happiness burst all over.

'Oh, and your food,' said Agnes as she grinned. I knew that Agnes thought she had this authority over other servants in the castle. Maybe she was debating under that grin whether or not she was going to give me what I asked for. But as it was her job to provide me food and she was very obedient to her master, she could not extend her authority over her obligation. She had no other choice but to get me what I needed.

'Wait here, then,' she finally spoke up after a full minute. 'I will get something for you. I hate to climb up that high, and in fact, I am very busy right now. You must see that today the master is receiving guests, and it's not for the like of you to nosy in on any of the master's business.'

'Yes, Señora Agnes,' I said. 'And may I ask if you would be so extremely kind to let me borrow a paper and ink?' I told her, smiling my innocent smile.

Agnes snorted with scornful face. 'What? What do you need them for? It's only for the master, and I don't care about you acting like a smart person. Now, if you want your food, stay where you are and don't move.'

I was disappointed. If Agnes could not give a pen and a paper to me, I could get them myself one way or another, tonight. And it would not be my fault as I had asked nicely.

Agnes walked back through the small door and left me in the dim corridor. She came back a second later with a loaf of bread wrapped in white cloth.

'Thank you, Señora Agnes,' I said.

Agnes stood there, waiting for me to pass through the door to the kitchen and get out of the castle. But if it was going to be my day off, then I had a plan of my own.

'Um, if it's going to be my day off, then I wish to go to the stream to wash my clothes,' I said. 'But I have to go up and get the clothes first.'

'Fine,' she said as if she could not care less. 'None of the maids would be able to wash your clothes anyway. After you get what you want, go straight through the back kitchen and mind your own business, all right?'

'Yes, and thank you for the food,' I told her.

I started to walk away, but Agnes was following me. I turned back to her, and she rolled her eyes, telling me to mind my own business. I quickly ascended the stairs, and when I reached the third floor, I could hear her loud voice from the second floor corridor.

'Flor! Come out of your room now and go back to work. We need all hands on deck to make the master's guests comfortable! Did you even change the bedsheets in the red room?'

I could not hear the muffled voice that came after. I supposed the sobbing sound I heard earlier was Flor. I wondered what had upset her, but I thought maybe that was the way of women, as my mother cried when she was upset about something, and when I asked her, she would say that she was upset because her dress had a hole in it, or that she had stomach pain.

When I reached my room, I could not help biting into the loaf of bread stuffed with cured ham even though I had planned to have my meal by the stream. I was starving. But I had to resist the urge to swallow everything down all at once. Grabbing the pile of dirty clothes from the corner of my room and tucking them under my arm, I quickly left the room. At that moment, I was excited to finally have a chance to go to the stream near the castle and swim a little because I didn't get to spend that much time outdoors being as busy as I was, and lately, Martín was always with me, watching my every move.

When I descended to the lower floor, Agnes and Flor were already gone. I passed the kitchen quickly, and most of the maids were all too busy to notice my presence, except for one of the maids, whose name I remembered as Alba. She turned and gave me a wink before going back to her own task.

Slipping through the back door, I headed towards the stream.

It was already early autumn, and the weather wasn't very suitable for swimming, but I could not miss out on this chance. My mother would definitely forbid me to swim at this time of the year. But she wasn't here; she could not have known.

When I reached the stable, what seemed to be an argument caught my attention. The nearer I reached the spot, an idea formed in my head that one of the voices belonged to Flor and the other was of a man, which if it came from the stable, must have been Andrea.

Flor was still sobbing while trying to form her words. 'No, Andrea, you don't understand . . . It isn't that easy, don't you see?'

'I told you time and time again to be careful! Flor.' Andrea's voice rang out of the barn, following with a sign.

'I—I could not think of it! But now, I do not know what to do, and he doesn't love me anymore! He never comes and sees me, Andrea, and have you seen her? Look at her, and look at me!'

The wailing became worse.

'Flor, Flor, what are we going to do? We have no other choice. We would never be able to leave. Look at what happened after he found out last time.'

Everything went quiet for a while before Flor let out a moan of lament, 'I am sorry, I truly am.'

'Have you told anyone? Have you even told him?'

'No, of course not! How could I? Oh, Andrea. I want to be with him, but he—he doesn't seem to care about me anymore. And the other day, I saw Alba and—'

Flor stopped talking the moment Andrea grabbed her arm.

Andrea had spotted me. Flor turned in surprise, her face blotchy and red from crying. 'Jacobo?' she said.

'What are you doing here?' Andrea said, anger rose from his tone. Even when half of his face was hidden by his hair, it still didn't hide the resentful look on his face or his crooked nose.

'Sorry, I was just passing by. I didn't mean to eavesdrop,' I said.

'Then be on your way,' said Andrea.

'But where are you going, Jacobo?' Flor spoke before I could turn around and leave.

'Um . . . to the stream,' I answered.

'Don't you have work to do? Martín's precious boy,' Andrea said with a scornful tone, but Flor squeezed his hand.

As I had a clear look at both of them, I could tell that they must be siblings. Andrea had beautiful blue eyes, just like Flor. But no one would have noticed how good looking he was because they would first see his crooked nose then his hair that was always covering half of his face.

'Señor Martín isn't here today,' I said, 'And Agnes told me to stay away from the master's business.'

'Good for you. Now you can stay away from our business, too,' Andrea said, grabbing Flor's hand, a sign that they were about to leave. But before they could, I quickly told Andrea, 'What is it that makes you so bitter towards me?'

'It's your face,' said Andrea with a cold look before he led Flor away. 'Come, Flor, we don't want any more trouble.'

Both of them walked past me, but Andrea made sure to bump his shoulder against mine. They both walked away without giving me a second glance.

I didn't know that people could be so hostile.

On the way to the stream, I thought to myself that with Martín's absence, I was starting to get into trouble.

I walked through a narrow forest path. Eventually, the path got wider and wider. And there, in front of me, laid a flowing stream on an open grassland. I quickly ate my lunch and jumped into the water.

I spent a peaceful time alone, easing away all the fatigue in my body. I let the cold water melt away the bitterness in my chest. I lay floating on my back in the water, letting the bright sunlight roam over my face; I closed my eyes.

Shards of light pierced through my eyes and travelled across my face. It burnt, but the contrasting heat from the stinging sun and the coolness of water cleared my head. A group of clouds passed over, blocking direct sunlight for a second before they moved away. I don't know how long I was there, counting the passing clouds from the shadows that covered my face. But at a time like this, when my mind wasn't occupied with work, I missed my mother more than any other day.

I thought about what my mother must be doing. Normally at this time of the day, she would be in the woods, collecting specific herbs before the winter. There was a time when I would help her spot the herbs, but she would tell me that she would prefer me to build a trap so that we could have some meat for dinner.

I did miss my life in the woods with my mother, but I also wouldn't go back to the hanging town. That part of my life was an old chapter.

A large group of clouds must have been passing by as it

overshadowed my face for a long time. I wondered if the wind had brought a rain cloud with it, but it was sunny and bright just a minute ago. My eyes blinked open to check, but instead of seeing the sky, I saw a man's face.

I was alarmed by his presence; how long had he been there, looking down at me. He came out of nowhere as I hadn't heard his footsteps approaching at all. If this was in the woods, and if the man was a predator, I would have been dead.

I stood up, as the stream wasn't too deep.

'I have never seen you around before,' said the man. He was skinny, and it made his face look bony. He must be a middle-aged man. Even though he was slim, I could see from his naked torso that he was a lean man. He had a cold expression that made me realise how the water's temperature was chilling into my bone.

'What do you want?' I said, trying to keep myself calm.

As I said those words, the bony faced man tilted his head. His cold expression remained unchanged. I had no idea what he was feeling or thinking.

'That depends,' said the man, his brows lurked up a little. He squatted down and stared directly at me in the eyes. 'What are you doing here?' he asked.

'I work at the castle nearby,' I told him, thinking that if he was a thief or had any intention of harming me, someone would know that I was missing. But when he heard that I was working at the castle, his brows arched a little higher. 'Ah, then you are my fellow colleague. I also work at the castle,' he said, 'Well, not really, I would have to say I work for the master of the castle because I don't work there, inside the castle. You see what I mean?' the man shrugged and continued, 'Oh, well, I do work inside the castle sometimes. But let just say we are working for the same master, shall we?' He finished his last sentence with a smile that showcased his fine teeth.

When I didn't answer, he chuckled. 'Oh, I won't be running to tell the master that you are slacking off. It's gonna be our secret.' He kept on smiling, but the smile didn't quite reach his eyes. 'I guess I'll be seeing you around then,' the bony man said as he walked off.

The man exuded oddity and lunacy.

I still could not forget his cold stares and several large scars that ran red and angry across his back.

# Chapter Nine

That night alone in my room, with my own shadow from the glow of the candle as my only company, I waited for the noise within the castle to die down, for I had a little plan of my own. I was going to steal some ink and paper for my own sake and for the love of my mother. I didn't know the treacherous reason behind me being forbidden to ever step inside the master's quarter as if it was a crime. But by any means, I could not let myself get caught, for I could lose my job, and then I would be back on the road, searching for another fortune once more.

During those quiet hours in my room, I left the door open, so I could better hear the movements within the castle. Around after midnight, when all the laughter had finally subsided, the servant's part of the castle was left eerily quiet; I could even hear the fire burning away the taper of the candles. Finally, I tiptoed out of my room, making sure that my shoes would not make a sound against the surface of the stone floor. I blew out all the candles in my room and the one on the corridor, where I managed to put it the other day. In the dull light, I was convinced that no one could spot me. The only light guiding me was a faint light from the moon, penetrating its way in through the window, softly glowing in the corridor like a cloud of transparent smoke.

Slowly, I reached the double doors that lead to the master's quarter. I tried my luck on the handle, but as usual, it was chained from the inside. Feeling partly nervous and partly annoyed, I crept further along the corridor with eyesight that had already adjusted to the dark and imprinted memories of those familiar steps. Nevertheless, I had to tread down the staircase carefully, as this part of the castle was completely hidden from every sort of light, and stumbling down the stairs wasn't a situation I would like myself to be found in.

Once I reached the corridor of the second floor, it was partially lit so I could use my sense of sight to guide me along. At the landing of the staircase, I stopped and listened for any kind of noise. There was a faint snoring sound that came from the room far inside the corridor. I didn't have to guess which of these rooms belonged to Agnes.

Finally, I stepped across the invisible line to the women's quarter. Swiftly and quietly, I went straight for the door that would lead me to the master's quarter. The door's handle clicked and turned easily with the force I exerted. With a grin on my face, I slipped inside and made sure that the door closed behind me as quietly as possible, without stirring any unwanted noise or unwanted company.

What waited for me on the other side was another corridor that was also dimly lit. I could see that the passage of the master's quarter was much wider and more delicately built than the servant's quarter. The floor was made of the same type of sandstone, but there were no uneven steps that could be felt underneath the soles of my shoes. The walls on both sides were built with a delicate transparent-like white stone where I could see a brownish-black line of veins running on its surface. I remembered this type of stone was called marble.

I thought I would have to try my luck in order to locate a paper and a pen, knowing that they must be located in the master's workroom or in the library.

I went past a door less corridor until I turned to the right. There, I was met with high ceilings and a wide corridor, where two large doors lay on each side. These wooden doors were decorated with a black wrought iron similar to the entrance of the castle, a gargoyle with a long tail that curled into the shape of an eight-pointed star. And there was also a strong scent similar to the one my nostrils caught on the third level of the servant's quarter. My master must be a delicate man who loved fragrances.

I walked on, and once I spotted that the door on the left was chained from the outside, I chose to go in the right one, expecting to see a room where the objects I deemed to possess lay. I was about to push the door open when my eyes came to rest on the gargoyles' angry faces. In between, their fangs laid a circular iron which served as a door knocker. They snarled at me, but I thought if I had that heavy iron forever placed in my mouth, I would do more than just snarling at the passers-by.

I pushed, and the door groaned and opened inward, and what followed was a foul smell. In the dimness of the night, I could see a vast room. It was something beyond my imagination; a silhouette of different types and sizes of animals stood motionless throughout the room. I thought it was a lifelike sculpture at first, but with a foul animal smell, I realised that they were real, once alive, once free somewhere beyond these four walls. But now, they were just taxidermy, frozen in time, alive but lifeless, always watching but not knowing what they saw.

I felt amazed and disturbed by seeing these animals.

I was amazed because of how they were preserved with only a dull smell and no unbearable smell of death. And how their skin and eyes seemed as if they were alive. In the hanging town, when I came across a decaying animal, the smell would be unbearable, and the corpse would change its form within a day. Although, I never stayed around that long to find out what was going to happen to it after a day because some other predator always got there first.

I was disturbed because even if I was obsessed with preserving my work and my feelings, it was all in a different manner. I didn't want to take life away, but I wanted to give my creations a feeling so that they could come alive. But what I was seeing was a whole new level.

I roamed wildly across the room, stunned by what I was looking at. A long-necked animal stood taller amongst the rest. A swirled horn deer appeared gigantic next to longhorn ibex deer. There were more animals with fascinating horns in the room. It vexed me to see that nature had punished them by giving them these enchanting horns, to which, in return, those horns had attracted humans to claim them as some prize possession.

On the other corner of the room, I saw a striped-skin tiger that I had never set eyes on before. It stood snarling on top of some kind of wooden base as if it was a prize for victory. Next to it, different types of tigers stood motionless; leopards, black tigers and spotted skin cheetahs. Looking closely at the cheetahs, their amber eyes were staring lifelessly at me, and down upon the eyes ran black fur lines, like they were crying an endless black tear.

Don Vicenç, a man of wonder, Martín said once or twice. I didn't doubt it.

I floundered out of the room. I had seen enough. Part of me understood why I was forbidden to enter the master's quarter. It could be possible that Martín was afraid I would find out what was hidden within this peculiar place. I wonder what else laid behind all those closed doors. But, I had to remind myself that I came here with a plan and needed to achieve it and get back to my room without anyone noticing.

Shutting the heavy door after me, the smell of the perfume erased all the foul smell inside the animal room. I thought the scent must be specifically used for that matter.

I continued down a wide corridor until I reached the end, and the connecting passageway forced me to turn to the right. Once I took that turn, I was stunned again by an open space right in front of me. This time it was much bigger and so much more magnificent. I found myself standing on the first-floor foyer, where the open space allowed me to see the stone floor of the ground floor and the high vaulted ceiling, reaching tall to the highest floor above my head.

I wasn't sure where I was, whether this was a fragment of a dream or a reality until I came to a sense that this was a castle of Don Vicenç, a rich merchant, or that he might even be associated with the king of Spain himself.

None of the descriptions in the book I'd read had given justice to what I saw now. Such a place would only exist in my dream. But as I was looking at it right in front of me with my own eyes, the place existed in my reality, but a reality that was far beyond my reach. I realised that the place still had to be considered as a dream, a dream of a place that I dreamt of living in.

The feeling I got was similar to how awestruck I had had felt when I first saw the golden carriage or the room with taxidermy, but the amazement ran deeper as it mixed with something else.

For a moment there, I thought to myself—how could a person possibly live in such a grand place. Surely not a person like me, for I was no one; I was a boy who came from nowhere. Seeing this? I pitied myself and my mother for how fate had thrashed its cruelty in our face. The hut where we lived was the size of that cupboard that laid against the wall on the ground floor. I thought of the place in the attic where Martín and I worked. It was a shit hole compared to this magnificent scene. We were stuffed inside a small room, burning the hours of our life away while the master of this place squandered his pennies on luxuries.

Upon a tall pillar that surrounded the open space, a torch was burning a smokeless fire, illuminating the space with an orange glow. But because the space was vast, the light from the torches didn't reach every hidden corner where darkness flared.

I was staring at the bright orange light of a burning torch, and inside me was burning hot with envious and hatred of unfairness, of why my mother and I, or even Martín, would have to be in the situation we were in, while some people had the means to rub their good fortune in other people's faces. I could not understand why God, as Martín mentioned, would have chosen to bless some people and not others. And why would a person have to be determined by the fate they were born with?

I was lost in my thoughts for quite some time until I realised that I was standing at the edge of the foyer with my hands squeezing so tightly onto the metal rail that my knuckles had turned white. It shocked me, the person I had become momentarily. My hidden dark thoughts were exposed to me like I was exposing myself to every possibility of getting caught. I tried to get my senses back together as I quickly moved behind the nearest pillar, hiding in the corner like an amateur thief. I have to get back into the darkest corner, I thought as I slipped along the dark corridor on the right to where the light could not reach me.

Through the passageway, there was a series of wooden doors decorated with wrought iron in a shape of an eight-pointed star, only that there was no gargoyle watching over. I had no idea which door would lead me to my fate, but I imagined that in one of these rooms, I would find what I had come for. So there I was, ear pressed against the first door I came upon, hand on the handle, quietly hoping that this was the right place.

I listened hard for any possible sounds behind the thick wooden door, but it was all but silent. And there was no evidence of light peeking through the gap between the floor and the door either.

Quietly but nervously, I pushed the door open. All I could see within was darkness, complete darkness. I pushed the door a bit wider, hoping that the burning torches from the foyer would lend me some light. The room appeared to be a big bedroom with a big four-post bed in the middle. A big cupboard, as well as a big table with a mirror, stood in each corner of the room. I could see a curtain was drawn, omitting all the light from the moon to grace upon its beauty. There was a sign of someone sleeping in the bed as the bedsheets were crumpled, and the blanket was half thrown off. I felt somewhat lucky that the person who should be sleeping there was nowhere to be seen, and I knew that I could not find what I came to look for here, so I tried to move to the next door and made sure that the door was securely closed.

I walked deeper towards the corridor. When I tried to listen to any escaping sound from the second door, there was some faint noise. The sound was faintly stirring from the next room. As the castle was deadly quiet, I could hear the noise clearer now like a morning bell. I realised that I wasn't alone in this part of the castle anymore, so I quietly tiptoed away, expecting to be out of this occupied area as soon as I could.

But the sound!

It attracted me. It erupted something inside of me. The sound was, at first, a faint moaning, but it became louder and louder until the shouting became more apparent. It was the voice of a woman. Had she been hurt in that room?

I was tempted to be the hero of the moment and burst through the door. But I wasn't; I was still scared of my presence being detected. But I knew I would feel guilty if I had just left the spot and found out later in the morning that someone had been murdered. Right then, I had decided against my good conscience. Carefully, I peeked behind that door without letting whoever was on the other side notice my intruding presence. I meant no harm, I told myself; I just wished that if the lady was in pain and if she needed any help, maybe I could be of use.

But the thing that I was seeing in front of me wasn't at all the scene of a crime, but rather a scene of aggressive passion. I could see a man on top of a woman, thrashing himself over her. She was shouting as if in pain, but her face showed otherwise. Her body was easing to the man's every move, and her hands were roaming over his body as if she was clinging onto him and would not let him go. The man's body straightened up, and still, she was clinging onto him. She was still shouting as if he had hurt her. Her head tipped back, revealing the white skin of her neck and her long dark hair that trailed against her ghostly white skin. My eyes trailed over her collar bone down until the swell of her blossom breasts.

I gasped at what I had just witnessed. And I let the door shut with a sound in front of me without carefully closing it. My heart was beating loudly in my chest, and I was exposed, unaccustomed to this new sensation that crept up in my core, my skin, and my pores. And I was left ashamed. I knew what I had just seen. I had read about it many times from the books, but this was different.

I cursed myself for being nosy this time, and I didn't have to wait for Martín to scold me. I cursed again for what I had just witnessed and once more for the fact that I still hadn't found what I wanted.

I walked as fast as I could, out of those corridors and through the foyer. My feet shuffled quickly towards nowhere. I was panicking that I was going to get caught, but at the same time, my mind was occupied by the previous passionate scene. The woman's white skin and her intoxicating grin were still floating in my head.

The echo of my own footsteps reminded me of how careless I was, as I found myself pacing around the open space on the ground floor. I really could not remember the path I had just taken. Did I just walk down the main stairs? And how did I end up standing in a dark corner of another corridor? I didn't know how long I had been standing there either. My breath became ragged, and my mind spun, all of which came from the pictures that I was unable to erase from my head. Were they guests of Don Vicenç? Who was she, the woman? And the man?

When my heartbeat slowed down and the adrenaline rush that made my ears ring subsided, my senses began to come back to me. Within the dark and quiet corridor on the ground floor, I could hear another moaning, but this time it was as if the person was in pain. It was a howling of grief, a wailing of pain. It was just a faint noise, but it was there, though I could not comprehend its whereabouts.

As I tried to follow the howling, the noise was replaced by high-pitched laughter that came from somewhere near. The laughter and the wailing mixed up in an unsettling tune, procreating in a miserable air that reminded me of chanting music from the church near my mother's stall in the hanging town. When I turned left, the high-pitched laughter pierced through the air. I tried to back away from it, but the more I scooted away, the wailing noise became louder until it was unbearable, shrouding all senses of merriment within me.

I was confused, and I thought that my mind had been playing tricks on me. I was lost in the darkness under a sensation that I could not grasp. I knew that I needed to go back to my room. The intention of getting paper and ink was now my second priority.

Hurriedly, I walked away from the dark corridor, but I wasn't aware when footsteps approached. It was coming from the turning corner. Someone was coming. Someone must have heard me. But the corridor was completely consumed by the dark. They would not be able to spot me if I could just hide in this dark corner.

Quickly, I moved back and hid, leaning flat against the wall. A flickering light upon a candle emerged from the corner. It revealed the figure of a woman. As she walked closer, the glow illuminated her face, and I caught my breath. It was the same woman I had just witnessed in that passionate scene.

I wished that the woman would have just walked away, but alas, she stopped a few steps in front of me.

'Who is there?' Her voice rang like a bell.

I held my breath.

'Bernado? I thought you were asleep! You have had too many drinks.'

I kept my mouth shut.

'Are you awake? You see, I could not sleep, so I was just getting some air,' she said. 'What are you doing in the dark?'

The soft glow of the light slowly floated towards me. I could not let myself get caught. I quickly darted away from her, out from the dark corner, expecting to slip away, but the woman walked after me.

'Bernado! You are acting weird!'

Upon exiting the corridor toward the open, where light from torches exposed my identity, the woman gasped.

I attempted to quickly slip off.

'Stop! Or I will scream and wake up the whole household!'

My feet halted from her threat. I did not want to cause further trouble. I thought I was already in too much trouble.

I slowly turned to face her.

'Who are you?' The woman asked.

From seeing the woman's face closely, I was dumbfounded by her beauty and the colourful shiny stones on her throat and the ones dangling from her ears. Even in the dark, I could see the stones flickered from the candlelight in her hand, illuminating her face and her round-shaped eyes.

'Step into the light. So I can see you better,' she said.

I slowly took my step, unsure, towards the square of cobblestone where the light shone from above hit the particular spot. The lady also took a step further towards me.

Seeing her in front of me now, a soft orange light surrounded her face. She looked beautiful with a perfectly symmetrical face and a straight nose. She possessed high cheekbones and deep-set eyes. I wondered what colour would shine out of them in the sunlight. The lady looked at me in the same wonderment, her eyes glimmered, and I felt exposed as her eyes trailed over my face and my body.

'Who are you? I have never seen you around before,' her voice rang again, soft and sweet.

'I have arrived not long ago,' I said, enchanted like I had been hypnotised.

'Ah! And may I ask what do you do for Don Vicenç?'

'I work on the ceramics,' I told her.

'With the old man? Well, well, I suppose that you are the one who sculpted the horse? The old man is not capable.'

'The horse?' I repeated her word, unsure if she was talking

about the sculpture hidden away in my room.

'Yes, the one that Count Alfonso is interested in buying. And such a price he is willing to pay. Now, tell me. What is your name?' The woman's round eyes flickered up at me. Her lashes fluttered softly. She looked fragile and sweet, unlike the version of her I had seen before. When I didn't answer her question, she took another step closer.

Surprised by her closeness, I finally gave her my name, 'Jacobo,' I said, my eyes still lingered on her face.

'Jacobo . . .' My name on her lips. Her voice completely hypnotised me.

'And you?' I didn't know the courage I possessed. I knew in my heart that a servant could not address the master's guest like that. But she had rid all good sense in me just by her presence.

Her soft laughter rang out from her slender, diamond wrapped throat.

'I'm Delilah. Well, Jacobo . . .' she took a pause upon saying my name, cherishing every syllable of it. 'I don't know what you are doing around the master's quarter, but I believe it must be something important?'

I didn't answer her question, but my eyes shifted from her eyes to her lips when she said my name. When she caught me looking, her lips parted a little before she sucked in a sharp breath, and it made my skin burned.

She stepped in closer; her presence was so near. I could breathe in her scent now, a sweet smell mixed with my master's fragrance. Her face tilted up to look at my face, and I was unable to shift my gaze away. I looked back into her eyes once again, they were observing me. And unexpectedly, she lifted her hand

and placed it upon my left cheek. I leaned slightly towards her touch. Her hand was cold, but it made my skin burn.

'Isn't it such a pity that a person like you must hide from the world?' Her sentence was like a whisper in my distant dreams.

The heat in my body was growing irresistibly. I longed to touch her, too.

I lifted my hand and reached out slowly, but when my skin was almost upon her face, she withdrew her hand and stepped away, grinning a triumphant smile.

'Well, Jacobo,' said Delilah, as she tilted her head, her eyes narrowed, hiding whatever wicked thoughts behind. 'I won't tell Don Vicenç about your mischief tonight,' Delilah's voice seeped into my ears. She stepped away further and further until I could no longer see the sparkles in her eyes. The candlelight carried her beautiful frame and my fantasy further away from me.

'Why don't you go before someone else sees you?' She said before turning in the opposite direction, her footsteps echoing along the silent corridor. I was drawn into her spell, my legs remained rooted to the ground as I watched the candlelight slowly taking her presence away. Her long hair swayed slightly on her back to the rhythm of her hips, and before she disappeared completely behind the door, she whispered to me, 'We'll see each other again soon.'

# PART TWO

When darkness erupts,
It corrupts my core
Oh, please, mother,
Show me your love
Oh, please, mother,
Lend me your light.

# Chapter Ten

Aloud bang awoke me from my blissful dream.

At the door, Agnes stood with hands on her hips. 'What do you think Don Vicenç is paying you for? You are late! Get up and get to work! I told you not to make me come up those stairs again, and look where I am now . . . I can't believe it. Stop staring at me and get to work. Now!'

I didn't get a chance to answer before the door slammed shut, and I was left alone, trying to understand what had just happened. A minute ago, I was dreaming of Delilah's face, and a second later, I was looking at Agnes' face, which reminded me of the taxidermy in the master's quarter. The contrary was so much for me to bear.

Oh, Delilah . . . she appeared in my dream. Her long hair spread on my face as she lowered herself to me. Blissful were her words, softly eluded into my ears. We were by the stream, under a tall tree that shaded us from the sun. Delilah . . . her face glowed with the sun and her eyes shone so blue and clear like the colour of those aqua blue ponds from the water of the mountain dews back in my home town. She looked at me with the same yearning sensation. Slowly, she drew in closer, her warm breath nuzzled my face, 'Jacobo . . .' My name was so gentle upon her lips, 'I know what you saw last night, and I know what you wish for.'

But now Agnes' loud noise shook all the good sense out of my brain, and my sweet dreams from last night turned into bitterness on my tongue. I wanted to tell her to shut her mouth. And now, I wasn't surprised why Agnes had never gotten married.

Looking out of the small window, I realised that the sun had already been up. 'Ugh!' I groaned loudly from the disappointment that I had overslept and that the memories of Delilah with me by the stream were non-existent.

I quickly washed up with the water from the bucket and went straight up to the attic. Entering the familiar space, I was met with a familiar stench and a familiar old man, sitting in his usual place.

'Good morning, boy,' said Martín.

'Good morning, Señor. I am sorry I overslept. It won't happen again,' I told him.

'It does not matter, boy. It's not that late yet. I would have let you sleep a little more if Agnes had not come in and found out that you were not here.'

'I am sorry, Señor. Oh, you weren't here yesterday, but I saw Blanco and your cart.' I recalled that my voice sounded a little low.

Martín quickly glanced at me before he looked away, 'I know, boy. I was working on something else for the master. He didn't give me prior notice about the arrival of his guests. Actually, he didn't give anyone of us prior notice, so that was why the castle was in chaos yesterday.'

I could see that Martín's face was a little pale and weary, to which I supposed that it must be from the sleep he didn't get last night. Martín glanced at me again and said, 'Did you notice that Don Vicenç was receiving his guests yesterday?'

'Yes,' I said, my voice plain.

'Did any of them see you?'

Yes. I thought. 'No, Señor,' I said otherwise.

'Agnes told me that she gave you a holiday. That was a good idea, isn't it? You have been working without a break since you arrived.'

'I suppose so, Señor.'

'So, where did you go?' Martín kept asking. I was a little surprised that he was in the mood for idle talk today.

'Just by the stream. I didn't meet any of Don Vicenç's guests, but I met a man with brown hair that reaches his shoulders and bright blue eyes. He found me by the stream,' I said as I remembered the man's noiseless footsteps creeping up on me like a shadow. 'He told me that he works for Don Vicenç.'

Martín's face was blank with an expression I could not read. 'That must be Itzal. Yes, he works for Don Vicenç, but he doesn't live here. His type of work doesn't let him stay in one place. I suppose you didn't get into any trouble, did you?'

'No, Señor.'

'Then, there is nothing to be afraid of. But I reckon that you should just stay out of his way like you stay out of the master's way.'

'I will,' I told Martín, recalling, again, the coldness in the man's eyes and the scars that I didn't want to know the cause of.

'Oh, boy, what is wrong with you today? You don't seem like yourself,' said Martín.

I looked at the old man, my brows raised, surprised by his words.

I was unable to notice why would he think that there was something changed in me. Was it that obvious that I was feeling a little off, a little not myself?

'No, there is nothing wrong, Señor. Maybe I am just tired,' I told him, but the truth wasn't because of that by any means, but actually, it was because of Delilah, who had invaded my mind. And of the scene from yesterday, the lavishness of luxuries I could not fathom. What was it that was actually happening to me? I wasn't so sure of what I was feeling, for I could not say what it was that I felt. Was it because I could see something that I wanted but knew that I could not get? Like when I saw those tall houses made of bricks in the hanging town and I didn't have one like them? Or like when I saw those kids in the hanging town carrying beautiful new books and knew that I would have to wait for I knew not of how long until my mother could get me a new one. I would tell my mother so—why did those children have new things and I could not, and why did we have to stay in a wooden hut in the wood and not somewhere with a tall building, too? Then, my mother would tell me that I had to learn to feel satisfied with whatever that I had and not be envious of others.

That was the first time in my life that I learnt about the world of envy. My mother had taught me against it, and of course, I tried to listen to her, but I could not understand the unfairness; on the other hand, I didn't want her to be upset, so I would tell her that I understood what she meant. And now, the world of envy had come to haunt me again. And even if I knew it, I still let it consume me.

Another thing emerged from the back of my mind; I still didn't have a paper and a pen to write to my mother!

'Damn it,' I cursed under my breath.

'What?' Señor Martín looked up from his work.

'Uh . . . Nothing, Señor. It's just that I forgot about something.'

I did totally forget about my mother. Had I not thought only about Delilah, I would have those things that I needed by now.

'I think I just heard you swear?' Martín said with raised eyebrows.

'Uh . . . no. Uh . . . actually, yes. Sorry about that, Señor.'

'Are you sure you are quite well? I wasn't here only for a day, and I can see you are acting weird.'

'I'm perfectly well, Señor,' I told him, expecting him to persist in asking me about the state of my being.

'Hmm . . . if you say so. Well, then let me tell you some good news, boy! But first, I have to tell you that . . . um, that—,' Martín played with his words and could not look me directly in the eyes, 'that the other day, I was looking for you and one of the maids was cleaning your room, and she found that horse sculpture of yours. It was something that I could not ignore. If I had known that you could create that kind of masterpiece, I would have let you do it long ago. I really had no idea how good you are, boy!'

I understood what Delilah had mentioned earlier. She told me that someone wanted to buy the sculpture, but I was curious about why would Martín lie that someone was cleaning my room when he himself must know that as he had forbidden me to mingle with any of the maids, having them cleaning my room was out of the question. And since I had been here, my room had never been cleaned by anyone else except me. For him to have found the sculpture, he must have gone through my room himself. But I didn't say anything, I just nodded to Martín's words.

'Well, Don Vicenç's guest, Count Alfonso Fernández has just bought it!' said Martín

'Bought it?' I said, somewhat irritated by the fact that it had been sold without my permission. I wasn't sure if I wanted to part with it. But wasn't that what I wanted all along? For my work and talent to be known.

'And with the highest price Don Vicenç has ever sold any of his artwork!' Martín continued enthusiastically, with pride shining out from his tired eyes.

'I suppose it's great news?' I said, still unconvinced.

'Of course, of course. I am so proud of you, boy! And more than that, Don Vicenç wants you to make more sculptures for him! If he likes you, which he must by now, you could make sure that he would never desert you. You will have a place to stay. And if you are loyal to him, he will give you what you deserve.'

But what do I deserve? What could he possibly give me? I wasn't sure if the words that came out of Martín's mouth were true. It was true that Martín's life was stable right now, in a way, but the conditions that Don Vicenç was letting his loyal old man work in right now could not be compared to where he himself lived. We were working in an attic with a small window, borrowing light from the candles and enduring this devious smell day by day. We had been selling our souls for his benefit so he could spend it lavishly on his precious castle and his precious taxidermy.

Couldn't Martín see that Don Vicenç was buying his loyalty? And with what? A house? A job? Some security? But I could not possibly say that to Martín's face.

'You don't look so excited. I thought you wanted to make whatever you wanted. I know that you don't enjoy this mundane activity of making these same shaped vases and kitchenware. I can see it in your face. I don't, either, somehow. But that was what the master required, so we all needed to oblige. But now that he wants you to make more sculptures, I suppose, you could use the best of your talent!'

'Yes, Señor Martín,' I said, though I was thinking about the money that Don Vicenç would receive, and the money that would never be mine.

'Well, why do you still look like you just ate something bad?'

Did Martín even know our master's living conditions? He must do.

'Jacobo?' Martín said as he extended his hand and placed it on my arm. He must have noticed the dissatisfaction on my face.

'It's— it's just that I don't understand how the world can be so unfair!' I blurted out, unable to keep it to myself. 'Yesterday I went inside the master's quarter and saw the interior of the castle. Look at where we are now, Señor. You said that you have been working for Don Vicenç since he was young. You have been making money for him, so how can he let you work here? It's so dark and small. I think you deserve better, don't you think?

'And I do not understand why is it that I am not permitted to go anywhere near anyone or even to have a conversation with whoever I want? I have been here for months, and I have heard so many things about the master, but I have never laid eyes upon him!' The words came out of me unexpectedly. But I needed to say it as it had been on my mind for weeks.

Martín signed and placed down the brush and the jar on the table. He looked into my eyes and said, 'So, you said you went inside the castle without permission? Did the master see you?'

That was it? The only thing that Martín cared about? Of everything that I told him. He just worried that someone would see me walking in the master's quarter. I looked at him boldly and undauntedly. I wanted the old man to come to his senses, and he must have sensed it. 'Boy, calm yourself,' he told me.

I breathed in, hoping that it would calm me. 'No, he didn't see me,' I said.

'Now, tell me, in the castle, did you see anything or hear anything?' he asked.

'No, Señor. I just saw the vastness of the castle, and I was scared of getting lost so I gave up and went back to my room,' I lied, trying to remain undisturbed by the images that, once again, penetrated into my mind without permission. Delilah's passionate expression zoomed in and out. Her moaning echoed through the vast chamber of my head. Then, I was dragged back into the room of animals when Delilah's moaning changed into a grotesque beast's groan.

I looked back at Martín's face again. His once serene face had shifted into a stern and solemn one, and none of the warmth in eyes remained. I could see the muscle on his left eye ticked.

Martín seemed convinced with what I had just said. He must have known then that I had sensed that something was wrong, so he told me, 'Trust me, boy, when I tell you to listen to me, you should listen to me. You will know that all of the things I tell you not to do is to protect you.'

I wanted to ask him what he wanted to protect me from, but I kept my mouth shut.

Eventually, Martín continued, 'And why did you sneak in the master's quarter? And when?'

'Last night, I just wanted to find paper and ink. I asked Agnes, but she refused to give them to me,' I said with a hushed and low voice.

'Of course, she must have thought that you were joking. None of the servants really know how to read or write. If you really want them that much, I can get them for you.' Martín appeared to be calm as he inhaled deeply. 'And now, you have to listen to me carefully. I know you think that God or the world is unfair, but you must know this. God has a plan for each of us. Even if it comes with a cost or a sacrifice, it's his will.'

'Do you? Do you understand his plan for you?' I couldn't resist throwing his words back at him.

'Listen to me, boy. I know you think that life is unfair. Don't you think I also thought the same way when I was your age? I used to ask myself the same question a million times. But one day, God answered! He sent me my saviour, who pulled me out of a rat hole and poverty. I was given work and a place to stay. Don Vicenç's grandfather, Don Luís, and his family saved me, and I believed that God had finally answered my prayer.

'God has given a task to prove my loyalty to my master. And I have! I am forever grateful and loyal to my master. I know that to achieve whatever it is that God has set a task for you, there will be some sacrifice. I have proven my loyalty time and time again. I know that I could never be anything close to my master's image. But in the end, I am satisfied . . .' Martín kept talking, and I kept on looking into his deep blue eyes, trying to understand his words.

'Well, I could not say that I am overly satisfied with what God has planned for me. But, as I have already reached this age, I have everything that I have ever wanted. To be able to achieve it, it might take some sacrifice. But eventually, I am . . . satisfied with what I have. You are young; you have a whole path ahead of you. You will learn of his plan for you soon enough.

'And don't you think that you owe it to Don Vicenç that you have a job and a place to eat and sleep? Imagine if I had not found you. Where would you be? What do you think would have happened to you? You need to learn how to be loyal and grateful, boy!' Martín said with resolution.

I was still unconvinced, 'Why are you so devoted and loyal to him. Is it because he has given you a house? and—'

'You do not know what you are talking about, boy!' Martín interrupted me. The old man seemed angry and intense. 'Don Vicenç has given me much more than that! He has given me something I could never repay! He gave me a chance, and he gave me his—,' Martín stopped in the middle of the sentence, his eyes became blank for a few seconds, and I could see moisture in his eyes like he was about to cry. I had no idea what else Don Vicenç had bought off the old man in exchange for his devotion.

When Martín regained his composure, his voice trailed low and somewhat unconfident, 'He—he has given me what I could never have.' Martín finished his sentence with an apparent emotion that beseeched his eyes.

The room became quiet.

'Alright, Señor. I am sorry if I said anything that might have offended you,' I said just to break out the silence that crept out in this room.

'It's alright to say what you think some of the time. But I felt like you're not quite yourself today. I hope that you do understand what I am trying to tell you. And you are sure that there is nothing wrong with you?

'I do understand, Señor. And there is nothing wrong,' I said.

But of course, I didn't understand, and of course, there was something wrong . . . with both of us.

# Chapter Eleven

That night, after Martín got me my writing material, I wrote a letter to my mother about my well-being, leaving out all the details of my dissatisfaction. I folded the letter and put it in the pocket of my breeches. Then, all I had to do was wait for travelling merchants to pass by, so I could ask them for a favour to deliver the letter. Somehow, I felt like part of the task that I was obliged to do had been lifted out of my chest, but still, as the time passed, I could not even think about sleeping because I knew it would never come, so I spent my night alone after Martín left, with dancing candle flames as my only friend.

There was so much, too much going on in my head, a storm of wasps buzzing noisily inside my mind, preventing me from peace and quiet. They roamed over my head, and one by one, they stung me, burying their stings inside my brain. Slowly, their venom seeped through my veins and through my good conscience. They had poisoned my thoughts and burned me with confusion, anger and hate.

I sat there, in my corner, and I felt relieved that the feeling of satisfaction of having clay in my hands hadn't yet been lost. So I went on, hands plunging into the softness of the clay, forming shapes beneath my hands.

Within a minute of deep focus, I could hear the fluttering of movements, but now, it was like that fluttering was twitching in my chest, in my body and in my core, calling out to me to dwell on it, upon which, this time, I fully surrendered.

There, a little inside my core, I could grasp a glimpse of it, a black dot growing, taking its root inside my soul. Softly, it murmured. It was humming a strange tune. Its voice was soft and ringing like Delilah's . . .

I could hear her voice nearer, a little louder as I allowed myself to float under my subconscious.

Going deeper, I could take a closer look at her. But no! it wasn't Delilah that I saw.

She was someone else.

A shadow was obscuring the lower part of her face. Her body was bare except for the thin fabric that covered her nakedness. I could still see the curve of her body and her long dark hair.

The woman noticed my presence, and abruptly, she stopped humming. She turned to look at me, her eyes shone with curiosity, mirroring my own.

Slowly but surely, she approached, her movements flickering like those flames on the candle, causing the thin fabric to cling to her skin, exposing her shape and her full bosom. From her appearance, she looked like an innocent woman who had sprung out of her womanhood, not knowing what kind of sin her body could cause to men. She was as innocent as she was poisonous, skipping her little devil dances my way. When her face was fully exposed to my sight, she was the most beautiful woman I have ever set eyes upon. My words alone could not do the justice of describing her face. It was like she was a creature not of this world.

'Jacobo . . . finally, you have come home.' The sound that escaped from her lips was like a freshly forged metal bell.

'Do I know you?' I asked quietly, unsure and doubtful.

'Oh, why are you being so cruel to me? Don't pretend that you don't know me. It hurts,' she hissed.

A rush of breath escaped from me as I gasped from what I had just witnessed when she spoke. The woman's tongue was of black colour, and there was a missing gap between it. She had a forked tongue just like a snake.

'Don't act so surprised. I've missed you, you know? I have been waiting for you all this time.' The woman appeared right in front of me, her hands smoothed my face, her eyes looked into the depths of my soul.

And I felt exposed.

The venom of the wasps stirred under the depths beneath my skin. Then, she said, 'Oh, well, I guess this is just a short visit. But I am happy to see you here after all.'

'What are you talking about? Who are you?' I said.

The woman laughed, but it sounded more like a hiss, and she started to walk in a circle around me, her hands never left my chest, and that was when I realised that I was fully naked, though there was no shame between us, just pure rawness of familiarity. I kept turning and turning in order to follow her movements. Her fingernails were long, dragging along my chest, but they didn't draw blood.

'Who are you?' I asked her again.

She smiled, running her forked tongue along her teeth.

'You should go back. There is someone coming.' The dark ring around her grey eyes expanded until all I see was a black hole in front of me, swallowing me whole, then spitting me out.

'Jacobo!' Some other voice hissed. I flinched, and my eyes threw open. And it was no longer the woman's midnight eyes I was staring at, but some uncanny shadow on the floor.

It took me a second to realise that it was my own shadow, but because of the candle hinges on the wall that were casting a shadow directly upon my head, as if I possessed two horns.

'Jacobo!' A voice hissed my name again. I turned toward the origin of the sound, and I could see that I wasn't in the working room anymore, but in a dark corridor in the master's quarter with Flor's face and a dimmed orange light floating in between the darkness.

'Flor?' I said.

'I could not sleep, then I thought . . .' Flor held her breath as if she tried to keep her words in, 'Then . . . I heard unfamiliar footsteps and a murmur, like you were talking to someone, so I came out to see.'

'I don't remember walking here. I was—I was in the working room.'

'You must be sleepwalking . . . I have been calling you since before you stepped through the double door.'

'I had . . . this peculiar dream . . .'

'As I said, you must be sleepwalking. Now, you should go back to your room before Agnes or someone else sees you.'

Flor waited for me to go to her, but my feet remained rooted to the ground.

'Jacobo! Let's go!' Flor whispered loudly.

Once I walked out of the master's quarter, I was standing in the corridor of the women's quarter. I thought I must have walked all the way from the attic to here. If Flor hadn't found me, or if I hadn't woken up, I don't know where I would have found myself.

Flor stopped at the door near the stairs which must have belonged to her. 'Off you go before someone else sees you,' she said.

'What is it about me that I am forbidden to set foot inside the master's quarter and everyone else can?' I said with defiance.

Flor's eyes went wide, 'Shush! Lower your voice. You don't need to shout.' Flor looked reluctant before she said in a low whisper, 'If they catch us, both of us and Andrea will be in trouble!'

'Why would Andrea be in trouble, too?'

'He is my brother. If anything happened to him, I could not stand it, you see? And he would go wherever I go. So, if I am to get fired, he would not let me go alone.'

'He seems to care about you a lot.'

'Did you think that we were lovers?'

'No. I was just curious because Andrea doesn't seem to be friendly to anyone except you.'

'I suppose so. But if you get to know my brother, you'll see that he is the kindest person I have ever known.'

'Yes, you can say that because he is your brother.'

'You are the only son, aren't you?' she said, her brows furrowed.

'Yea,' I said.

'Well, that also explains why you would think that people

who share the same blood as you would be nice to you, when in fact they could be so . . . cruel.' Flor's voice became low, and it took her a second before she spoke again. 'Anyway,' she said, 'neither you nor Andrea can set foot inside the castle because Don Vicenç does not like it. He prefers . . . only women, you know what I mean? But women cannot work in a stable. So, that is why he hired my brother. I was surprised that not only did he accept you, he also allowed you to stay under his roof. To be honest, I still don't know the reason behind it.'

'That still doesn't explain the reasons why he forbids me to talk to anyone or ever set foot inside the castle,' I said.

Flor snorted. 'I happened to be around when Señor Martín went to ask if he could get you to work as his assistant because he needed help. Of course, Don Vicenç refused at first, but Señor Martín vouched for your talent, saying that your talent will bring more money to his pocket. Then, as you know, Don Vicenç agreed for Señor Martín to get some help, but on one condition, that is for him to never set eyes upon you . . . And as for the reason why he forbids you to talk to the others, it's that Don Vicenç usually has his own ways, but I believe he prefers his. . . belongings . . . untouched.'

'It seems like you know him well,' I told Flor.

'Let's just say I know him enough.'

Flor's eyes became unfocused for a second before they shifted away from my face. 'I think you'd better leave now. Watch your step. The wind is quite strong today. It must have blown off all the candles.' Flor whispered.

'Yes, I will. Thank—' The door was shut before I could finish my sentence. What did Flor mean when she implied the other people in the castle were Don Vicenç's belongings. I was sure that she used that specific word.

After Flor was gone, I was left in complete darkness. I wondered where the soft glow of the moon had gone. Then, with the humidity came a strong wind, I knew that it was going to rain. I hadn't noticed any sign of wind and rain when I was working in the attic. On the contrary, it was a rather quiet and windless night. I must have fallen asleep there for quite some time. It was quite odd, for I had never fallen asleep while my brain was so focused before.

After I got into my room, I found my way into my bed and laid in complete darkness. The wind whirled outside, casting a whooshing noise as some of the breeze tried to slip in the gap between the window. It reminded me of that woman's humming tune in my weird dream. And as I closed my eyes, I saw the darkness of the woman's midnight eyes swallowing me under once again.

# Chapter Twelve

I flinched, awoken by noise from a deep sleep.

I'd had the dream again, of a beautiful woman who looked almost identical to Delilah except for the darkness of her eyes. She had come to haunt me with her beauty and her charms. She had taken me to the highest sensation of bliss. But every dream ended when I was awoken by a noise.

A noise!

Someone was in my room.

I was alert with all the sense of reality now. I quickly sat up on my bed and rubbed the drowsiness off my face. Agnes was standing near the cupboard, laying something out on the other bed. When she noticed my movement, she looked my way. 'Ah! Look who is awake. You sleep like a dead person. You didn't even hear when I knocked or when I walked in,' she said.

I couldn't believe Agnes knocked before she came in. She was looking at me now as if she was looking at a mistake. She might have been right, for I must have overslept again. The angle of sunlight that penetrated through the window reminded me that it must have already been late in the morning. I knew what Agnes must have been thinking; that I was a disappointment to both Martín and Don Vicenç; an ungrateful lazy boy.

'Change into this, will ya?' she said. 'Be as quick as you can, and meet me in the kitchen right away!' Agnes pointed to a pile of clothes on the bed nearest to the door, and then that was it, she shut the door and left without saying anything else.

The truth was, I didn't want to wake up from my dream. But what could I do? My hands clenched on a stained white bedsheet, agonising that the dream had been transformed into reality against my will. I was sweating, all the heat excreting from my body.

I knew I had to get out of bed.

Looking over the open window, where the morning breeze normally entered, I could see that today the window shutter laid still; not the slightest movement could be detected. There was no sign of a strong wind from last night.

I walked over to examine the clothes that Agnes had told me to change into. They weren't like the ones that I had usually worn but much more luxurious. It included a black doublet with elegant gold embroidery trimming on the edges. The inner shirt was white with a golden button, reaching up to the ruffled collar.

I quickly rinsed the sweat off myself with a bucket of water before I put on those fancy clothes.

I pulled up the breeches, and they fitted me perfectly. I could not tell what material it was made of, but it felt so smooth against my fingers. The colour was the same as the doublet, black with gold trimming. I finally pulled on the white stockings.

I remembered how Delilah praised me for the way I looked the day before. Confidence was building up within me. Placing a hand on my jawline, my cheekbone and my nose, and I thought to myself that they were well-formed like what I had seen on

Delilah's face. I ran my hands through my hair, adjusting the fussy brown curls into place, then looked at this strange clothing. I found that somehow, it fitted me quite well, much better than I had expected.

After I was done changing, I went down to the kitchen. Agnes was waiting for me with different pairs of shoes. And all of the maid's eyes were on me, then whispers and giggles followed.

'What is the meaning of these fancy clothes? What is it for?' I said.

'It's the master's business, and I have no intention of getting involved. But aren't you glad to be wearing these?' Agnes said as she widened her already bulging eyes. I averted my gaze away from her face as I was afraid to witness her eyeballs coming out of the sockets. 'Well, I have to say, you look quite like one of the master's guests!' she continued. 'Now, try on these shoes and see which ones fit you. Be quick, time waits for no one!'

'Uh . . . right, Señora,' I said and did as I was told. The several pairs of shoes on the floor were the ones I wished I had, but it was just a wish. When I picked them up, I took my time putting those leather shoes on my feet. They fit perfectly. Now, seeing them on my feet, it felt like another one of the small fragments of my dream had been scratched out from the list.

'Those fit you well?' Agnes asked.

'Yes, Señora, but to whom do these clothes and shoes belong?' I asked curiously.

'They are from Don Vicenç, of course, when he was younger.' Agnes said, looking at me speculatively, 'Right, you look like a son of a baron. Now, follow me, come along.' Agnes went straight through the big wooden door that connected to the master's quarter. I followed her. I tried to contemplate the reason behind my current situation. Was I being summoned because someone had caught me sneaking inside? Could it be Delilah who had summoned me?

It was my first time stepping inside the master's quarter with an invitation. I was met with a wide corridor similar to the one I saw yesterday on the first floor. The whole way was lit with torches along the wall. Curiosity consumed me again when I saw that the torches inside the castle didn't have a lot of smoke like the ones my mother used back in the hanging town.

'Those torches, why don't they have any smoke?' I asked.

Agnes turned her head slightly my way; her feet continued shuffling slowly along the smooth cobblestone floor. I had to watch my steps, or else I would have been ahead of her by three meters by now.

'If that's what you want to know,' Agnes snorted. 'Don Vicenç only uses oil from whales. They eliminate smoke. I believe that you have not heard about such things before, well, that is for a master only and not for the likes of you.'

I rolled my eyes at her choice of tone and words as if she thought that I was stupid. But her answer did surprise me.

A whale? How interesting to be able to think about how a human could hunt a large sea creature and discover that its oil could be used to light a torch? Don Vicenç, even though I had not met him, had managed to impress me no end.

As I walked after Agnes, I started to wonder about me being in these clothes again, but my curiosity subsided when we finally turned out of the corridor to the right. I was mesmerised by the scene; it was a familiar space that I had seen yesterday—a vast area with high ceilings and a foyer on each floor, but in the daytime, the windows on the stone wall allowed enough sunlight to penetrate. I could see everything much clearer now—all the details and the colours of every corner of this place. In the hall, eight tall carved columns stood opposite each other on either side of the wall. Ribbed vaults were formed on top of the columns, covering the whole hall with intersecting diagonal arches.

Large framed paintings were placed on the wall. One of them showed a larger than a life-sized portrait of a man who stood proudly with a long elegant cloak of deep purple that piled up next to his feet. His long dark hair was drawn in so much detail that I could see each strand of his hair down his shoulder. Another painting that caught my attention was of an angel with white wings, holding a wooden string instrument in his hand, hovering over a man in his bed-chamber.

There were also smaller paintings of different faces looking at me everywhere I walked on.

We came through the hall to another corridor with tall vaulted ceilings, where I hadn't reached from my little adventure the night before. It led to another open space where chatters were echoing through, and I could see that the sound came from the room further inside, as one of the tall wooden door panels, where Agnes was directly headed, was left open. From afar, I could see that the room was the one that I had been searching for; a library.

A tall bookshelf lined the wall. All the books were stacked from the floor to the top of the ceiling. I was awestruck by the size of the shelves and the amount of books. I wondered how long would it take to read all of them and what different contexts I would find there.

When we reached the door, Agnes stepped in first. There was a group of about twenty men and women gathered inside. Some of the men and women noticed her presence, but no one heeded her any attention. She signalled for me to follow her, and I did.

Stepping inside the large library, I found out that it wasn't just a mere library, but it was a gathering place. And at the table in the middle of the room, I spotted Delilah right away, as her beauty shone out from the rest. The red dress that I saw her wearing the other day had changed a shade darker. It had a squared neck that still showcased her full bosom and bright red jewellery on her neck. The colour matched her skin and hair deliberately well, for the shade polished the colour of her white skin and dark hair.

The nearer I walked closer to her, the more she shone, like the midday sun. But Delilah didn't pay me any attention as she was talking to the group of men and women who sat around a long table located under a portrait of a very elegant man and what looked like a dead white bear as a carpet under his feet.

Groups of people were scattered around the room. But the group that caught my attention the most were those who sat at the same table as Delilah. These men and women were dressed in their fine clothes, but as I paid closer attention, the most elegantly dressed were the people who sat at the head of the table.

My attention shifted to Delilah again. She was talking to a man next to her. Upon whatever topic they were discussing, the man made Delilah laugh. She pressed her hands upon her lips, her eyes wide with eagerness. Then, she addressed another man, who sat on her opposite side. Though I could not see the man's face, I'd remember his figure and his hair any day, for he had wavy soft rustled curls in chestnut colour like mine. He was the same man I had seen making love to Delilah, the same man who drew a passionate expression to her face.

Delilah's gaze still lingered on that man's face. And the picture of them making love came back into my mind. I wanted to walk inside and strangle him. My glare still lingered at the back of the man's head for a second when suddenly his voice boomed out with a sense of pride and authority, 'Oh, ladies, then I can show you what you are bound to love later. But first, try this orange juice. I got them from Valencia recently. The taste of it, hmm . . . not at all pungent, it's sweet and hides a subtle unique aroma. Shall I take it and turn it into a new scent? And gentlemen, you will love this drink. It's called the aroma of Montserrat. You will taste fifteen different herbs in this beverage.'

I was looking back and forth at all of the people in the room when finally, the best-dressed man who sat at the head of the table spotted me. He stood up, and I could see that even though he was of some height, he was large and round in his middle, and his elegant doublet could not hide that fact.

'Vicenç! I believe this is the young man that did me an honour,' he said with a low bass tone that echoed through the room.

The man who had his back towards me responded to the name that had just been called out. He turned towards me, his face was grim, but once our eyes met, his eyes widened in surprise, his brows raised a little before his facial expression fixed to the first time I set my eyes on him.

Don Vicenç, my master, and the same man I had seen in

the throes of passion with Delilah. The same man I wanted to strangle the life out of just a second ago.

# Chapter Thirteen

At last, I had come to face to face with my master.

Don Vicenç got off from the chair, and in that split second, I couldn't help looking Delilah's way. My gaze locked with hers. A tiny satisfying curl played upon the right corner of her lips before she was distracted by the man next to her, who leaned in and whispered something in her ear. My attention switched back towards a tall built man, my master, who was now walking towards me. He possessed dark and complex features with an elegantly styled moustache and a beard as stylish as his outfit. His eyes remained on my face as he strode nearer and nearer. His gaze was intense and unwavering. No smile escaped from his lips. Had he caught my misbehaviour of last night? Did he know what I had seen, that I had sneaked into the master's quarters? My first natural reaction was to step back, but I stood my ground and kept eye contact. I must confess that I was scared of the possibilities of what my master was going to do. But then, a smile curled upon his lips, and his hands extended in welcoming gesture.

He reached where I stood, and once he grabbed hold of my arm, he squeezed it and whispered so only I could hear, 'If you still want to remain under this roof, do as I say.' I didn't know exactly what he meant, but surely, I wasn't prepared for any of this.

Don Vicenç ushered me towards the round-bellied man. I looked back at Agnes, who started to retreat slowly, her head still bowed, her presence totally forgotten and dismissed.

'Count Alfonso, may I introduce the person who sculpted your beloved and magnificent sculpture? He is a distant cousin of mine, you see, who arrived just last night, and he will be staying with us for a while. Right? Jacobo?' said Don Vicenç.

I bowed at Count Alfonso in a gesture of greeting I had learnt from my mother.

Don Vicenç's hands grabbed my upper arms once again, and I could feel the pressure upon them. When I didn't answer his question as I was still processing the words that he had just been saying and upon my silence, Don Vicenç squeezed a little harder.

'Yes, mas . . . uh, Don Vicenç,' I said as I had just realised that my master wanted me to play along with him.

'Come, Jacobo, meet our companions,' said the round-bellied man whom Don Vicenç addressed as Count Alfonso. 'I am quite jealous of Don Vicenç to have such a talented cousin like yourself. And I suppose you will grow up to be even more charming than him.' He then looked at my master. 'I am afraid you have a rival at last! I would be careful with this one.' Count Alfonso laughed loudly at his own joke. Other people in the room looked my way and gave a subtle nod.

I looked over at Don Vicenç whose expressions I could not read. His eyes were intense. I had never met anyone who possessed an air of authority around him, who, if he wanted, could command you to jump out the window, and you would

142

not disregard his command. But then, after a second, a smile touched upon the corner of his lips before it changed into a grin, exposing a row of straight white teeth. He said something to Count Alfonso then laughed, but at the moment, my head was still buzzing with Don Vicenç's previous words, addressing that I was his distant cousin, even though his eyes contradicted his every word.

My eyes set upon Don Vicenç once again, which when he wasn't looking my way, I took the time to observe, and observe I did.

My master was a very handsome and charming man.

A man can be handsome, but if he lacks charm, the good bone structure will do him no good, as after you get to know him, you might discover that the man was nothing but bland and lame, who was just lucky to be blessed with good looks. But for Don Vicenç, not only that he possessed a great bone structure, but he also possessed an exceedingly great amount of charm. He had this particular dignified air; he was so bold of every movement, so sure of what he was doing, and so proud of knowing that he knew how to exploit these authorities and charms of his.

His voice was the thing that attracted me the most. It told the story of a powerful man whose demands had always been answered. It sounded like the voice of an older man with years and years of experience and maybe a lot of cigars along the way, but it convinced us of the hardship he had been through and the wisdom he had acquired through all those years.

But Don Vicenç was far from old age. Seeing him this close, there were no lines of ageing that ran along his face. He was young but mature. He must be no more than thirty-four at most. He had a tall and manly frame. I remembered from when seeing him shirtless; his back was muscular and lean, his hair was the same chestnut colour as mine, and it was messy and unruly with subtle untamed soft curls.

'Young man,' Count Alfonso's voice called for my attention. I looked at him, and I could see pride shining in his eyes. 'Or might I just call you a man already, as you will be fully grown in less than a year! I do believe that you really have a great future ahead of you, you know that? You see, I never thought to pay that much for artwork, but with that sculpture of yours? I must say that I have never witnessed anything like that before. It's like the horse has a life of its own. The excitement reminded me of the time when I was young, maybe the same age as you are right now! Oh, those times were the best of my life, I'd say,' Count Alfonso said with a tear brimming in his eye.

I knew what he was feeling, as the sculpture of mine reminded him of the most exciting feeling he had ever had in his life. It dragged that distant memory of his to the surface, and he was feeling that particular excitement and wonderment all over again.

'Oh, Alfonso, and what about me?' said a petite woman who suddenly appeared by Count Alfonso's side. 'Am I not in those moments as well?'

'Oh, of course, my dear, Helena. I was just implying the feeling of excitement I had when I was younger, you see. When you believe you can conquer the world, and it was true.' Count Alfonso chuckled in his low tone.

Count Alfonso's wife, looked up at him with a satisfied expression.

'Jacobo, meet my wife, Countess Helena,' said Count Alfonso. Then, this woman, Countess Helena, stepped in front of me and extended her right hand towards me. At that moment, Don Vicenç's presence was upon me again, hovering over my head, but before he could say anything, I gave Countess Helena's hand a quick kiss, suddenly remembering a paragraph in one of the books which The Cid bowed to the queen and her ladies in waiting as a gesture of greeting and respect. I heard Don Vicenç whisper, 'Well, Martín has taught you well, hasn't he?' But the comment was only for me to hear.

'Don Vicenç, introduce us to your cousin,' a pretty voice caught my attention, and as I turned, my eyes caught sight of two women who possessed the exact same face as if I had been hit in the head and the blurriness of my sight made me see one object as two. But this wasn't the case. The women's similarity was so much so that it became unnatural to me. Apart from a slightly different shade of their dress, I would never be able to tell them apart. The one on the right had a dress of mauve colour, while the other wore a shade lighter.

'Ladies, this is Jacobo,' said Don Vicenç with a questioning look. 'Jacobo, these two ladies are Lady Amelia and Lady Cecilia.'

The woman with a mauve colour dress, Cecilia, was going to utter something, but a snort that came from Delilah's direction stopped her short. However, Cecilia regained her senses and extended her hand towards me. I quickly kissed the hands of both Cecilia and Amelia.

Cecilia smiled at me, and before she could say anything else, another woman's voice cut in. 'Well, well, who do we have here?' And it was the voice that I had dreamt of, a voice that I longed to hear, a voice of Delilah.

'And here,' said Don Vicenç, 'is the star of every gathering, Lady Delilah, and the gentleman next to her is Don Bernado, her husband.'

I wasn't aware, at all, of the presence of a man next to Delilah, but when Don Vicenç said that he was her husband, it confused me. I switched my gaze back to Delilah, and she stared at Don Vicenç, then back to me. I was lost in her beauty, but also, at the same time, lost in confusion. Didn't I just see her making love to Don Vicenç the other night? I was sure of what I had seen. And the look that she had given Don Vicenç a few seconds ago made my blood boil.

Delilah extended her hand towards me. I took it and gave a gesture of greeting, but on the inside, I felt agitated by jealousy. She must have had no idea that I had witnessed her and Don Vicenç committing adultery the other night.

Through our quick touch, Delilah gave a little squeeze of my hand, her finger grazed softly across my palm, a gesture that only I could see and feel. I caught her seductive gaze, and the corner of her lips curled up a little. My skin burned, and I shivered upon her touch. At that moment, I thought to myself, if I had to commit adultery, it would be worth it with Delilah. But our touch lasted a few seconds, and everything crumbled when Delilah averted her eyes towards Don Vicenç once again.

I could not help but feel sorry for Delilah's husband, for I didn't know if he was lucky to have such a beautiful and charming wife or if he was damned to have such a beautiful

146

and charming wife. Although, when I looked at Don Bernado, I could not be so sure if the man was too stupid or too naive to know that his wife was unfaithful, or he might be both because as I was looking at him, I saw he had not the slightest idea of his wife's gaze lingering on Don Vicenç.

'Shall we all take a seat?' Count Alfonso said.

Don Vicenç delayed me behind the group as they dispersed to their seats, with his hand on my left shoulder, he said, 'I'd prefer you to not say anything stupid. As a matter of fact, I'd prefer you not to speak at all.'

Don Vicenç signalled to me to take a seat on an empty chair beside Delilah's husband. I wanted to make my dissatisfaction and irritation be heard, but I knew better than that, so I just kept my mouth shut. I lowered myself down next to Delilah's husband. He had the scent of Delilah. It was very faintly in the air, but it was there. It reminded me of the other night when Delilah's presence was so close to me. She had looked into my eyes and allowed me to inhale her scent. I told her that I worked for Don Vicenç. Did she know that I was a servant and not really Don Vicenç's cousin? If she did, it didn't matter, for she didn't say anything to contradict Don Vicenç's word. I remembered she also told me that she would meet me again soon, but I didn't know that it would be this soon and under these circumstances. But what did it matter now? Delilah was a married woman, and her husband was right beside me. Above all else, her lover was my master.

Delilah . . . my sweet dreams crumbled instantly. She was married and owned by a man on my right. What was his name again? Bernado?

So, this Bernado man must have all of Delilah to himself, every night and every day, making love to her whenever he wanted.

'Jacobo?'

A voice caught my attention, and it was Don Bernado who was talking to me. 'Yes?' I said.

'Count Alfonso has just asked you a question. Are you well? You look a bit . . . um, lost?' Don Bernado's baritone voice dragged me out of my head. My eyes snapped at his features. He was just an ordinary man. What was it that made Delilah interested in him? I understood why she would seek Don Vicenç as her lover, but Don Bernado was just plain and uninteresting.

'Oh, please, excuse him,' Don Vicenç announced loudly for everyone to hear. 'If he's somehow forgotten his manners, it's because my cousin here is obsessed with his work, and he hardly socialises with friends of his age or even his own cousins.'

'What a waste of youth, young man!' said Count Alfonso. 'You could be an expert in every kind of fun and a star at every social gathering. But I see, you don't talk much. We are all friendly faces here.'

'Indeed,' Delilah looked at me and smiled.

I caught Don Vicenç's eyes landing quickly upon Delilah's face. I was envious of this man. How a person could have everything he wanted. How was it possible that God preferred this man over the rest of us, for Don Vicenç had the perfect face and an exceeding amount of charm. He also possessed the most magnificent place a person could ever wish for. And Delilah was in his clutch.

Once I let my envious thoughts slip away and I was composed, I looked up and saw the twins gazing at me. Their look gave me a chill, and it felt uncomfortable, especially from the one in the mauve colour dress, Cecilia. Did they know or sense what I was thinking? Did my expression give away my true feelings?

Luckily, Don Bernado repeated his question and averted my attention.

'Um . . . I'm perfectly fine, Don Bernado. Might it be because I have not eaten? My cousin is right. Sometimes I'm so focused on work that I forget to eat.'

'Oh! Then you must get something to boost your energy, Jacobo,' said Don Vicenç from across the table. 'You are young. We can teach you a thing or two, but first of all, the heavenly tasting drink from God himself.' His voice caught my attention, and I was attracted by his movements. He reached out to take a small bell on the table. Slightly, his wrist flicked like a violin player finishing his last suspenseful note, the flared sleeves of his white shirt swishing from the movement. The bell rang twice in a clear note. Then, he dropped the little bell back and placed his arm around the chair's backrest next to him. That was when my gaze shifted to the twins. They were staring at me again, but it wasn't like the way Delilah stared at me or like the other maids did. They were staring at me curiously, but it was as if they could not place in their heads an unsolvable mystery of whatever they saw in me. I had to avert my eyes, as I was getting uncomfortable by having the same but different lady looking at me in such a manner. Did they really know that I was just a fraud and not really a cousin of Don Vicenç?

And Delilah hadn't paid any attention to me. That made my

irritation triple. I could see from my peripheral view that she was talking to her husband, looking in my direction but not looking at me. I cast my glance away, not wanting to see how she had ignored my existence.

My gaze shifted to the twins again, expecting them to be looking at me the same way they did, but their attention had shifted to Don Vicenç. I took my time to observe both of them. They had the same hair colour, dark blonde with a glimpse of red. They must have been considered pretty in their own way. Looking closely at them, one thing that made Cecilia stand out from her twin was her freckles that spread across the bridge of her small nose and her shapely cheekbones, and they spread lower to her neck and then her chest. I had to avert my gaze, trying not to imagine where those freckles ended. Cecilia was a lovely woman, but she didn't attract me the way Delilah did, for I had never felt that way about anyone, and Delilah was so close to me, yet so far away. I didn't understand how could that short meeting could eat up at me, destroying me by yearning for her touch and her attention.

The sound of heels clicking on the stone floor stole me away from my thoughts. I looked up and saw Flor walking in with a tray in her hands. Her head was bowed, but I could sense a shifting of mood in her as her feet stumped harder on the stone floor while she approached the group. Don Vicenç gestured her to put the tray that held two jars and mugs that I knew so well because I had made them, and Martín had painted them in a shade of red.

As Flor put down the tray and arranged the mugs on the table, nobody paid any attention to her but me. I could see a slight tremble in her hands, but it wasn't from nervousness or fear, it was all from anger. Her hand trembled because she was squeezing the mug so hard that her nails turned white from the pressure. She took her time placing the cup on the table, and still, no one paid any attention to her, except now, Don Vicenç and me. He was looking at her and gave a subtle sign with his hand for her to leave. She was upset. I could clearly see that.

When she finally walked towards the door, her head bowed lower, and the harsh footsteps, defying movements were all gone. Flor walked away slowly, but before she exited through the door, she looked back at us one last time, and that was when she saw me observing her. She quickly averted her eyes, but it was too late, for I saw her eyes brimming with tears. And somehow, I knew the reason for her misery. Flor was heartbroken by witnessing someone she had fallen for, but that someone was with another person and was out of her reach. I knew because I felt the same way when I had caught a glimpse of Delilah with a man who was her husband, and her lover, who was my master.

# Chapter Fourteen

I sat there, dumbfounded, looking at a married woman whose aura reeked of danger, but I still yearned for her touch upon my skin. How was I supposed to know that she already belonged to someone else? How she had treated me the other day was as if, she too, longed for me. But then maybe I had allowed myself to deliberately think of what she might want, even though it wasn't what she really wanted?

I tried hard to recall the exact moment that had passed between us the other night. Even it was just a few seconds, it felt like an hour, a passionate hour. I recalled the images in my head, of her white bosom, of her cry when Don Vicenç, a friend of her husband, plunged into her. Did she like to be treated that way?

What devilish game was she playing?

Everything at that moment felt a bit like a blur to me, like there was a big jar made of glass covering my head. I could hear and see people talking, but the meaning had been blocked out by clear glass. Slowly, the bubble of doubts, confusion and irritation surged through, and I was drowning in it.

I wasn't quite sure whether Count Alfonso had suggested that we move to another room for a different activity, but when I saw a crowd of people moving towards the door, I followed suit.

Suddenly Cecilia was next to me, crossing her arm in mine, leading me towards the group. 'Come, Jacobo. Walk with me?' she said. 'So, I didn't know that Don Vicenç had a cousin.' She smiled at me innocently.

'I just arrived, not long ago,' I said, trying to make something up. 'We are not usually in contact, but—'

'You can tell me the truth, you know,' Cecilia whispered low in my ear. 'I know you are not really his cousin. But that is not a problem. We can still be friends.'

Her words confirmed my suspicion that this woman knew more than she should, something her blue eyes and innocent smile could not hide.

'Amelia and I also work for him,' she said.

'What kind of work?' I couldn't help but ask, as I thought they were more of his lovers.

Cecilia burst out laughing. 'Not exactly what you are thinking. We are not courtesans. But if I tell you exactly what I do, you mightn't want to befriend me.'

'What are you two whispering about?' Amelia's presence was before me. I looked down at her and still felt disconcerted every time I looked at the similarity they shared. Apart from the freckles on Cecilia's face, another different thing I noticed was that Amelia's eyes were green, while Cecilia's eyes were blue.

'I am just trying to make a new friend,' Cecilia replied to her twin.

Amelia's face showed that she wasn't happy with her sister, but if I was right, she didn't show her dissatisfaction. Amelia turned to smile at me, but with doubts that she was trying to hide, 'Come with us, then. We're going to play a game of fate.'

We arrived at another large room with many circular tables scattered at every corner. Each person started to spread out and take their seat. Cecilia and Amelia guided me towards Don Vicenç, whose table was located at the far end of the room. The guests seated at his table were the same; Count Alfonso and Countess Helena; Delilah and Don Bernado. Amelia approached Don Vicenç and sat next to him. The table was already full, as there were six seats available at each. I was about to move towards another, but Cecilia stopped me and said, 'We'll watch and wish for the best of luck for Don Vicenç and Amelia, shall we?' So, Cecilia and I sat behind Don Vicenç's seat, on the chairs that were placed against the wall, so I was facing directly in Delilah's direction.

They played their cards in pairs.

At first, I didn't know what the game of fate was until I understood the stake of losing. People were betting away their fortunes, and whoever was unlucky could lose their coins and so much more.

I didn't understand how could they be betting on their fate when they weren't fully themselves. They kept on drinking, and the more they drank, the more reckless they became.

Later, they invited me to play with them, but I refused, as I literally had nothing to wager on, which Don Vicenç knew, and he found an excuse that he would prefer me to watch and learn, and I might be able to join the group later on.

'It's truly Don Vicenç's lucky day!' Cecilia told me in excitement, 'Look! he won almost every round!'

My mood couldn't be matched with Cecilia's, as I wasn't really paying attention to anything except Delilah. Sometimes when I glanced at her, I caught her looking at me, but she swiftly looked away as if I just happened to be in her eyeline.

I kept on glancing at her, and she knew it. Though whenever she managed to win, her husband would give her a kiss, and that was when she kept her eyes lingering on mine. And as I had caught her looking at me, I was quite sure that she didn't completely disregard me. I started to hate her game, as I was burning up with anger and jealousy.

If that was what Delilah wanted, I could play the same game as her.

Other people's games went on and on, and time ticked by slowly as ever. I felt the pictures of every second pass by like everything was moving through the density of water.

The maids, whose faces I could not recall, came in one after another to refill the blood-red contents after the sound of a bell upon a flick of Don Vicenç's wrist.

After a lot of wine flowing through my veins, the bitterness inside me eased up a little. It was replaced by something else, something more confounded and confiscated, some hidden satisfaction I had just discovered. My head felt woozy, and I was feeling much braver than I had ever known, and some aspects of life weren't important to me anymore, like the woman in front of me, Delilah.

The bitterness I felt inside when I saw her with her husband was no longer my concern. I wasn't paying her as much attention, even though something in her had snapped, and suddenly from ignoring me, she was staring at me from across the table like she could have strangled me if she had been given the chance.

And the reason behind her bitterness? It was because right now, I had Cecilia sitting on my lap, whispering something in my ears. It was just her opinion about the game, but I liked Delilah to believe that she was saying something else, something more private. I played my game by turning to Cecilia and breathing in the soft vanilla scent in her hair. She smelled nice, I had to admit, but just for a second there, I regained what was left of my consciousness and flicked my gaze to Delilah; her eyes didn't falter away in another direction. She was looking at me looking at Cecilia and smelling Cecilia's scent.

I loved the way Delilah's gaze lingered on me. It gave me power, knowing that I had the upper hand. I could see that Delilah was now calling for my attention as she kept her eyes on me, but I hadn't given her any. I wanted her to yearn for it even more when her satisfaction hadn't been fulfilled. I suppose this was the first time she wanted something, and she could not get it. And I could see it in her eyes that she hated me for not giving her what she wanted, and she hated Cecilia even more, as Cecilia reminded her of her own insecurity in which her youth was slipping away, and she had to give in to younger girls even though their beauty couldn't be compared to hers.

I felt Delilah's hatred seeping out of her every pore. If her hatred was a knife, it would have stabbed me a million times. But Delilah had hurt me, so I wanted to hurt her back. That was why I didn't stop whatever game I was playing with her, using Cecilia to drive Delilah to her limit.

Everyone around the table was behaving more raucously, too. They were all laughing and shouting a little louder than they used to. Don Vicenç lifted Amelia onto his lap and continued with his card game. Count Alfonso's hand was also slithering up Countess Helena's bodice before both of them got lost in an intimate kiss. Don Bernado was trying to talk sweet words to Delilah as if he could sense she was in an extremely bad mood. He tried to kiss her, but she urged him to focus on his cards, as they were losing a lot of coins.

I observed Don Bernado and tried to understand the reason why Delilah chose him as her husband. I could see that he was even older than Don Vicenç. He wasn't large and round in his belly like Count Alfonso, but he didn't possess any grace or charisma, and his hair had already turned grey. One thing that he might have won over Delilah's heart was the fact that he seemed to have a lot of coins in his pocket, even if they now belonged to my master.

Don Vicenç won almost every round and had gained quite a fortune from a servant's point of view like myself, but for him, it was just a tiny thing that he spared for fun.

'Vicenç, Vicenç, I have never seen you this lucky before. I'd say your cousin here is truly your lucky charm! Don't you think? Well, I'd like to demand a rematch tomorrow!' said Count Alfonso with a low chuckle, in harmony with his wife's soprano laughter.

'I believe the same thing, Vicenç,' Don Bernado added, 'I have never lost more than one-third of my pocket playing against you, but now it's all empty.' He threw a red velvet bag on the table, and it didn't make a sound, whilst before, from looking at it from afar, I could feel the heaviness of the contents inside the bag as well as a reassuring sound of fruitfulness.

After listening to other men praising his luck, Don Vicenç laughed. 'I believe my cousin here is my lucky charm, indeed!' he said.

Another thing that assured Don Vicenç that I was his lucky charm happened when a red-faced Count Alfonso suggested I make another sculpture for him. He didn't request anything in particular, although if I could succeed in bringing out another emotion from him, he swore that he would pay triple the price for it. Upon hearing that, I was happy as I wouldn't have to be secretly working on what I wanted to do, and it would also mean that I didn't have to be making the same endless kitchenware any longer. Don Vicenç seemed to be unrecognisably happy as his lips curled into a smile that reached his temples. I had witnessed something in his eyes that he had never given me before, a deep satisfaction of one human giving to another and not of a master giving to a servant. There was equality there, between him and me, even if it was just for a few seconds.

After a few moments, he stood up from the chair and told everyone loudly that it was time for him to pay back a little from all the coins he had won. Don Vicenç called out for more wine.

And wine we had.

I drank and drank until I was on the edge of not knowing what was right and what was wrong. I was beginning to slip away, and that was when Don Vicenç approached Cecilia and me. He whispered in our ears, 'Dear lucky charm of mine, I believe you deserve some reward, don't you?' Then, turning to Cecilia, he said, 'Celia, I believe you could make my cousin here happy tonight?'

Don Vicenç grabbed my shoulder. 'By tomorrow morning,

you will be a real and respectable man.'

Even if I was naive, I was no fool. I knew what Don Vicenç's game was. It was because I was useful to him. He wished to buy my loyalty just like he had with Martín. But even so, I could not detach myself from this alluring new experience.

I was lost in the sensation of being in control, to feel like I finally had power over something. And that wine! They made my bad habits grow by a hundred times.

The fault must be the wine.

When one of my feet had stepped over the line of good conscience, and before I went further across the line of not knowing right from wrong, Cecilia led me out of the room. I hadn't noticed where I was heading and when exactly I had left the room, but I would follow that vanilla scent wherever it led me. Cecilia's cold fingers intertwined in mine. And along the quiet castle, our footsteps echoed loudly. I realised that we were half walking and half swaying, me rubbing my shoulder along the stone wall to keep myself straight. I managed to regain some sense, as the quietness along the corridor knocked upon my conscience.

As we turned the corner, an extremely bright torch glared directly into my eyes. Instead of seeing a usual orange glare, I saw red.

'Can you believe that he uses whale oil so that his torches won't create smoke?' I said as the image of a huge whale being hunted in an open red blood sea popped into my head. Maybe that red wine had reminded me of blood after all.

'Well, can you believe that we have reached my room safely and without tumbling head over heels?' Cecilia chuckled.

We came to a halt at the wooden door decorated with wrought iron in a shape of an eight-pointed star. Cecilia pushed the heavy door open and led me in. The room smelt like her hair, vanilla scent flowing in the air everywhere.

'I think that you ignored what I said,' I told her.

'And I think that you are drunk,' she answered. 'And I can't believe you just talked about a whale?'

I snorted, 'I believe so.'

When the breeze of the wind blew in from the gap of the window, the vanilla scent grew even stronger. I looked around to find the source of the smell.

'I love your scent,' I told her.

'What do you smell? I believe everyone gets something different out of it.'

'It's soft, mild and sweet, like vanilla.'

'Oh, so you are the first that really gets that. I'm curious.'

'How many men are you referring to?'

'Does it matter to you?'

'No.'

'Then, come, Don Vicenç said there is so much more for you to learn. And he wants you to be ready for what is coming, and I know that you have never experienced it.'

'How do you know that I have no experience.'

Cecilia chuckled, her eyes never left me, 'I don't need to be a genius to know that you have never had an experience with a woman before.' She started to approach me. Her hands slowly unravelled the strings at the front part of her dress. 'Now, tell me you aren't curious?'

'I'm not,' I slurred.

'Oh, of course. But you can't take your eyes off me.' I looked at the freckles on her chest that ran down further along the unravelled strings of her dress.

'Don't you belong to Don Vicenç?'

'I belong to no one,' Cecilia said as she walked closer. 'But he pays me well. Oh! You have such a wicked master! Don't you know that? But I must confess, I do love his wickedness.' Cecilia stopped right in front of me and placed her soft hands on my face. 'Now, now, I know you are wicked in your own way. I can feel it in the air, in your presence, like I can breathe it in.' Cecilia inhaled whatever she was saying that she can smell. Her eyes closed, and she took her time to concentrate.

When she popped her eyes open, her blue eyes shone a little darker, 'There is something about you that I cannot put my finger on yet.'

She slowly continued to undress in front of me. Her corset showcased her womanly figure. Slowly, she let loosen her corset, and I could see that her freckles ran only to the upper part of her chest. The skin on her breasts was milky white, contrasting to her nude coloured nipples.

'I can sense the darkness in you. Do you know why we are with Don Vicenç?' she said. 'It's because he has this energy in him that we love. Something dark, something uncanny.'

'I am not anything like him,' I said

'Oh,' Cecilia chuckled as she pushed me down on the bed and kneeled between my legs. 'Yes, you are. Definitely! You just don't know it yet. Our superstitious feelings are never wrong, you see? There is a darkness in you, Jacobo.'

'What are you talking about? Is this some kind of witch-craft?' I slurred.

Cecilia laughed. 'Come now, aren't you curious about your future and the greatness that is coming your way? I can get a glimpse of your future if you like.'

Cecilia pulled a small knife out of nowhere. She grabbed my hand and cut it lightly across the middle of my palm. It drew a spot of blood. Then, she pulled my hand to her face and sniffed the blood before she licked it. Her eyes closed, and her lips mumbled something as if she was in a trance. A minute or two passed when Cecilia spoke again, this time in a language that I could understand. 'Yes, I was right,' she said. 'You will gain something that none of the mortals could ever dream of get-ting. But that comes with a price. Oh, and it requires a sacrifice. But I am not sure if you are willing to pay for it.'

Then, her eyes wide open, looking down at me, her lips red as my blood trailed upon them.

'Now, aren't you curious about me?' she laid her hand on my hair and pulled me into her. I ran my hands on her soft skin and curves, leaving a trail of blood.

Cecilia whispered softly in my ears, 'Let yourself be free.' Her sweet voice pierced through my senses. She slowly planted a kiss on my lips. Our wine breath tingled, and I had never im-agined her lips could be so soft against mine.

That night, upon the soft bed of Cecilia's room, and upon her soft lips, skin, breasts, and her body, I was hardened, shaped into a man like Don Vicenç had promised I was destined to become.

162

# Chapter Fifteen

I stirred in the middle of the night. I did not know how long I had fallen asleep. The candle was out. Looking out the window, it was dark outside, the dawn of the day hadn't touched upon the horizon yet.

My head hurt, and my temple was pounding in a rhythm of my own heartbeat. I was still in the soft bed of Cecilia's room. The wild woman she was a few hours ago had disappeared, moulded away into a delicate and innocent girl who slept soundlessly next to me. Her bare white skin with trails of freckles shone out from the moonlight. Looking at her now, she looked so harmless with her eyelashes brimming upon her soft white face and her long dark golden curls spread across her back.

Cecilia had loved it when I lost myself in her. And she kept on telling me things I didn't really understand.

'I know who you are . . .'

'Let yourself be free . . .'

It might be that she had had too many cups of wine.

And when I let myself go completely, her voice went high-pitched, and she seemed as pleased as Delilah making love to a man who wasn't her husband.

After removing a strand of hair off her face, I quietly slipped out of bed and quickly pulled up my breeches. With boots on, I grabbed the fancy doublets and buttoned-up black shirt off the floor and left the room.

My footsteps were quiet across the stone floor of the castle, like a lynx that was aware of a larger predator nearby. Finding my way back to my room was easier than expected.

In the quiet of the night, I could hear the wind howling through the small gap in the windows. Or was it that usual wailing I kept hearing hidden somewhere behind the wall? Maybe I was too tired, and maybe the wine had pulled me beyond my limit, and maybe that was why I kept hearing things that weren't there.

I yearned for a personal space where I could reflect on what I had done in order to keep my good conscience intact. Finally, I reached the stairs on the master's quarter that would lead to the exit of the women's quarter. I didn't want to go through the kitchen and risking meeting Agnes who might be getting a cup of water.

I ran up the stairs and went directly to my bedroom, not bothering to keep my footsteps quiet anymore.

Sitting on the bed, cradling my head in my hands, I tried to reflect on everything that had happened. A minute passed, maybe five? Maybe ten? But I felt . . . nothing . . . empty on the inside, no guilt, no regrets even though I did happily do things with Cecilia for my own pleasure and not just to spite Delilah.

But what made me angry was that I had allowed Don Vicenç to easily buy me off when he didn't even have to sacrifice a thing. He wasn't playing a fair game at all.

The wooden door of my room creaked loudly, and my head snapped up to the intruder. I wasn't ready to face anyone, but the person who came in was Flor. Her face was puffy and red like mine, but from crying and not from the shame of being someone's easy prey.

'Jacobo . . . I—'

'What are you doing here?' I said, my voice sounded rougher than I had intended.

Flor flinched a little, but she didn't retreat.

'I just wanted to talk to you,' she said.

'What is it? And at this hour?'

Sensing that I wasn't in a good state of mind, but I was willing to listen to what she wanted to say, she told me, 'I heard your footsteps. I—couldn't sleep . . . I won't take much of your time.'

Flor tried to close the door, but the creak made an antagonising noise. She tensed, and I knew she didn't want anyone to discover that she had come to my room at this time of the night. 'I thought Agnes gave you oil to fix that hinge on the door,' Flor whispered.

I raised my eyebrows, indicating to her that no one had given me anything. I got up from the bed and went to the bucket of water, splashing fresh and cool water on my face, hoping to gain part of myself back. I turned back and found Flor sitting on my bed.

'I suppose you had fun?' Flor said quietly, but as the room was quiet, I could hear her voice clearly. I didn't give her an answer, just kept staring at her, waiting for her to get to the point where she had decided to come and talk to me. Seeing her in her nightdress and not her usual maid outfit, she looked even younger. She could not be much older than me.

'Well, Jacobo. I came here to ask about Don Vicenç,' Flor

said.

'What about him?'

'Do you know that . . . that he . . .'

'Yes?'

'I mean . . . who are they? The two women next to him?'

Flor's question made me able to connect the dots in my head. Flor was crying because of someone, I recognised the look in her eyes, and now that she had come to ask about Don Vicenç, it must be the master that she was falling for.

'Him? Do you mean our master?' I emphasised the word despite knowing the answer, but she didn't respond; instead, her face started to pout like an angry child. 'And I suppose the two women you mentioned are the twins that sat next to Don Vicenç,' I said.

'One of the twins must be Don Vicenç's lover. Is she? What's her name?' she asked.

I wanted to tell Flor that Amelia was just Don Vicenç's plaything, but his real lover was the other woman, his friend's wife.

'Amelia,' I told Flor just to stop her from asking the same question for the third time.

Did Don Vicenç manage to fool everyone? like he did with me?

The idea made me angry, not with Don Vicenç, but with myself and with Flor, who was so stupid and naive that she had fallen for him. Don Vicenç managed to pull on our strings like we were his puppets. I wondered what Don Vicenç had offered Flor to make her fall for his trick like I did.

I had a tingling feeling building inside me—of why could I not be like him, to be able to exploit charms to get whatever I wanted, to get people to like me and to be respected.

I turned to Flor. She was still sitting on my bed, eyes losing focus. 'Amelia . . .' she mumbled to herself, staring at nothing. Then, her eyes snapped back up to my face. 'Did he ever mention how long she is going to be staying here?'

'No, he didn't. I wasn't in a position for him to tell me any of his private matters.'

'But why is he dressing you up like you are one of them? What did he say?'

'I don't know.'

'Do you know anything at all? Tell me about him, please. How did he act with her?'

'Why are you so concerned about him?'

'Oh, please, just tell me anything.'

'Don't tell me you are in love with our master,' I said.

Flor's eyes changed from pleading to anger. 'Oh, you don't know anything. You have no idea! So do not look at me like that. I have had enough of that disdainful look.'

She must have sensed that I wasn't happy with her tone or that she was the one who had come to ask for help.

'Oh, please, Jacobo. If you know anything about how long they're going to stay. Just please tell me.'

'What did he promise you?' I said.

'What?'

'What did he do to make you fall in love with him? What did he promise you?'

'What are you saying?! He didn't promise me anything!' Flor frowned, and it seemed like she was about to cry. 'In fact, he—he said that he loves me, that one day, I . . .'

She stopped short at what she was saying, so I told her what was on my mind, 'That one day he will marry you? And take you for his wife? And end your miserable life as a maid?'

Tears escaped Flor's eyes, flowing down her cheeks. She raised her voice, 'Oh! Look around you. You are not in any higher position than me. You can't presume that by dressing like them, they will accept you into their circle.'

'At least, I am not pining after any of them,' I said. My words sounded cold and hypocritical. Of course, I wasn't moping after Delilah, I just dreamt of her and wished that it was real. What I said must have hurt Flor, for she stood upright and wiped her tears away. She defiantly looked my way, 'I didn't know that you could be this cold and arrogant. You look and talk like one of them now.' She left without any back glance, and this time, without fearing anyone would hear, she let the door slam shut.

I felt horrible as the words that Flor had said were true. I wasn't one of them, and they had accepted me just because Don Vicenç said I was his cousin. And when that role was over, I would be put back in my place.

But why did Don Vicenç have to introduce me to all of that lavish life? Why did he plant that knowledge in my head? Had I been wasting my youth away like Count Alfonso said? Had I been missing all the fun? I didn't know what the middle ground was anymore, and since I had been introduced to all of these new tastes and temptations, how was I supposed to swallow and accept the truth that when the sun rose, I would have to go back and live the same life?

I looked around me and realised that I was in a small room with a tiny window, crammed with two empty beds and an empty cupboard. I sat on my bed, cradling my head in my hands, pulling at my hair . . .

Again, the door was thrown open with a loud creak.

'Have you come to insult me again, Flor?'

'Well, well, I didn't think you would be expecting someone.'

My head snapped up towards the voice I knew so well.

Delilah stood by the door.

'Delilah? What are you—'

'Don't call me that. I am your master's guest and not one of your kind.'

'Then, what are you doing in the servant's quarter, Señora Delilah?' I made sure that her marriage title was well heard.

'Nobody has ever treated me like you did! No one can ignore me! No one!' Delilah looked frustrated with her bloodshot eyes. But her beauty seemed to grow fiercer with her temper.

'You have your husband to take care of that,' I said.

Delilah glared at me with her dark beauty. Approaching me, she said, 'Where is she? Did you just fuck her?'

'Who are you talking about? Flor or Cecilia.'

At my words, Delilah slapped me across my face. My face stung, but it also woke up my excitement. I glared back at Delilah's face, and she seemed perplexed by her quick reaction. But she didn't lose her determination to get an answer from me.

'Did you fuck Cecilia!?' She shouted.

I kept quiet but continued glaring at her. Her eyes sparkled with jealousy. I knew that look so well now as it shone in mine whenever I saw myself in the reflection. I didn't want to tell her what had happened between Cecilia and me, but something about her anger made my blood boil with excitement.

'Do you wish that it had been you?' I said.

This time before she could slap me again, I grabbed her hand mid-air, and when she tried to hit me with another, I pulled her other hand toward me. Her slim hands were fragile compared to mine. She tried to pull back but lost her balance, and she stumbled into my chest. And when she looked up at my face, I saw tears brimming in her eyes. I had no idea how I had planted a seed of desire inside her, just like she had planted inside me.

But her next words stabbed me directly in my already wounded ego, 'Good! Because as lowly as you are, you could never have me anyway.'

I slowly let her go, and before she could leave, I didn't forget to tell her, 'Fine, I don't need to be in your stupid game anyway.'

Delilah stopped at the door, her hands trembled. A second later, she left without a backward glance.

The insult and the disregard that Delilah had thrown my way was another reminder for me to face my reality.

# Chapter Sixteen

Another day, another knock upon the door. Another knock upon the door meant more reckless behaviour.

Had I overslept again? Wasn't it just a few minutes ago that I had just fallen asleep? I could have sworn that I hadn't been sleeping more than twenty minutes at most, but even so, the fact that somebody was at the door, trying to demand something from me, was something that I could not get rid of. Drowsily, I looked at the origin of the noise, but the room was still quite dark. I realised that it must be extremely early in the morning.

'Jacobo.'

I heard a raspy voice whispering my name. In this dim light, I could not tell who stood at the door. Then, the footsteps approached. I peeked through my half-closed eyes.

'Boy, are you awake?'

It was Martín.

What did he want from me at this hour of the day? Curiosity still didn't win over my sleepiness. I'd had no rest at all after a long day of losing control of my body and mind. But the old man didn't leave and still persisted. Slowly, I got up and groaned from the pain in my head. I rubbed the sleepiness from my face. Nonetheless, it did me no good.

'Uh, Yes, Señor Martín. Is there a problem?'

'I—I just wanted to talk to you before you leave.'

'Leave?' I said loudly, then sat up on the bed. Now, that sentence managed to gravitate every sense in me.

The pain and sleepiness were slowly slipping away. Had Don Vicenç decided to dismiss me? The realisation hit me at that moment, and all of the sleepiness had miraculously disappeared. I felt blood surging up all over my body. Was it because of Delilah? She must have said something. Or was it because I wasn't supposed to sleep with Cecilia? Or did Don Vicenç not think that I was useful to him anymore? I thought I had just provided some money and was becoming his lucky charm. Millions of questions and possibilities sprung out of my numbed brain.

'Shit!' I swore loudly, cradling my head in my hand.

'Hmm?' said Martín.

'Sorry, Señor. I'm—just . . .' I didn't know what to say. At that moment, I was just telling myself that I would have to leave this all behind and go on to search for somewhere else to work.

'Well, then Don Vicenç did not tell you about it yesterday?'

'No. He was quite happy to hear when the count wanted to buy more sculptures. I don't know what made him change his mind.'

I got out of the bed and went straight to where the bucket of cold water laid and splashed it on my face.

'No, boy, no. Don Vicenç isn't going to dismiss you. He is leaving for Barcelona today, and he told me that he is bringing you with him.'

I turned to Martín, a drop of cold water glided down my face and my neck.

'So he didn't decide to let me go?'

'No.'

'You have no idea how bad I felt just now,' I said.

'Well, I managed to get you out of bed, didn't I? The only thing that would lead you to think that he is going to let you go is because you know that you must have done something wrong. I am curious about what you did to make you think that you are in trouble.'

'Nothing at all, Señor,' I said quickly, ignoring the white lies that had quickly fallen from my mouth.

Had I done something wrong? I might have, on Martín's terms, but on my terms, I was as innocent and clean as the new white, spotless bedsheet that had miraculously appeared on my bed last night.

'Well, then,' said Martín as he turned to leave. 'I'll leave you to do whatever it is that you have to do, then meet me in the workroom after, all right?'

I looked at the old man innocently before I told him, 'Of course, Señor. I'll be there right away.'


Entering the workroom, I had almost forgotten that weird smell existed. However, I felt like it had been a week since I'd been in the workroom. Those wines and luxurious lifestyle must have played with my sense of time and my being. Another thing I found strange was that Martín wasn't in his usual seat but rather in my corner. He was sitting on the floor with his back turned to me.

'Good morning, Señor,' I said, but Martín didn't greet me

back as usual. 'Uh . . . I'll just open the window,' I told him. Still, he didn't respond. It must have been the sound of the creaking window or my movement in his peripheral vision that snapped him out of his trance. He looked at me, but his eyes were vacant and doleful.

What was happening to Martín? He seemed like a lost soul when just a minute ago he was all right. My brows furrowed as I observed him. He was mumbling something before turning back to what he was getting himself lost into. My eyes traced back to the object he was staring at, and then, I caught sight of a sculpture of a woman in the corner of the room, in front of my usual seat, the one that Martín couldn't tear his eyes away from.

That sculpture! I knew who it was right away. It was the woman I'd seen in my dream.

Now that I had seen the figure, a flash of vision entered my mind. It was like I was in a dream, some kind of trance when I spent time making this sculpture under the darkness of the night, when I let all the new emotions that I felt seep through my fingers; those of envy and hatred; and all of my desire and longing for Delilah. The surge of all the emotions, of the strong feelings that I had ever felt, ran through my fingers and flowed into this sculpture. It was like I had given life to her.

Another flash of memory entered my mind; I was looking into the woman's pit dark eyes, listening to her sound, watching the swaying of her hips as she skipped her devil dances around me. Her forked tongue running along the point of her sharp teeth while she whispered in my head, 'You have unleashed me at last.'

I blinked, and all the images were gone. All of my attention shifted back to Martín, who was still staring blindly at the sculpture.

'Señor Martín?' I called out. He slowly turned to the sound of my voice, but his eyes were still out of focus.

I extended my hand and placed it on his shoulder and gave a little squeeze. Then, the old man's eyes started to look into mine. There was something that had changed in his eyes. Those eyes . . . they were full of guilt and shame, far beyond a place that I could reach.

'Oh, Jacobo,' he said as he stood up. I let go of his shoulder, and my hand fell naturally back to my side. I watched him walk slowly back to his usual seat at the table full of unfinished porcelain. He sat there for a minute before he finally uttered, 'The—the figure, you—you made it?' The shaking in his voice was so apparent.

'Yes,' I said in a pressing tone, walking towards him.

Then Martín turned and looked at me with great alarm. He grabbed my arms and shook, 'It—she—she reminded me of all the sins I have done. Jacobo, please, I was blind. Oh! So blind. It wasn't God's plan! It was the plan of a devil all along! But there is still time! Everything is not yet lost! I am so sorry.'

Was that a tear? Running down on his face? Was he crying?

'If I asked you not to go with Don Vicenç, would you listen?' Martín pleaded. 'Would you listen to me if I told you to leave this place?'

'Why? And then what?' I said, surprised how this topic had come up. 'I still have no idea why Don Vicenç decided to take me with him. But isn't that a magnificent chance for me? I met Count Alfonso yesterday. He wanted me to make more sculptures for him. I think I am going to present him with this new work of mine. He will want to buy it! Did you know that he said he would pay triple this time if I could capture his emotions again! And I thought you believed in me, that my skill would—'

'I want you to leave! And get away from him! I have done many deeds. Some things I'm not proud of. But I had no choice. With you, I think I do, and it might not be too late for—'

'Too late for what?'

'For saving you,' he told me, his eyes widened, and there was a huge crease between the space of his eyebrows. His face . . . it was like he was asking me for forgiveness.

I felt extremely uncomfortable.

'Saving me?' I said.

'Yes . . . Saving you from your own fate.'

What was happening to the old man?

Martín kept squeezing my arms, 'I am so sorry if I dragged you into this. That wasn't my intention. But I can see it now. I have tried to keep you out. But seeing this sculpture. . .' His body started to tremble. 'It—it told me that you have already crossed the line.'

'Señor Martín. Are you all right!?'

'Don't you see it? It's a sign of sin!' He raised his voice and suddenly pulled me by my arm, dragging me towards a small wooden door that had always been locked. He tried the handle, and as it should be, the door didn't bulk. Instead of backing off, Martín pounded at the door.

'AHHHHHH! The devil! I have done the devil's deeds!' He kept pounding and shouting. I was too shocked to be able to do anything.

The main door burst open just in time, and Agnes rushed in, 'What in the world!' she said as she quickly rushed and pulled Martín away from the door. Agnes grabbed hold of Martín's body with the power I knew she possessed, and when I tried to approach, she shouted at me, 'Leave! Master is looking for you! And on your way down, tell anyone you see to come up here and lend me a hand, would you?'

'Are—'

'Leave! Now!'

I hurried out of the room, but after me, Martín's voice echoed along the attic, 'The devil! He made me do it!'

The shouting of the old man shrieked down the whole corridor, and I had to run down to get away from that beastly haunting sound.

The old man had finally gone mad.

I ran down the stairs as fast as I could, still processing what had just happened. The wailing sound of Martín made my skin prick. I hurried through the kitchen door. There, I saw two of the maids that I had never seen before and another one that I remembered, though I had forgotten her name.

'Jacobo? Aren't you supposed to be using the master's door by now?' said the one I knew, and the other two smiled.

'Agnes needs help right now. She asked me to ask all of you. She is in the attic.' I said. I knew Agnes didn't specify how many people to help her keep the old man tame, but as of now, I was in no mood for a jest or sneer.

'Oh, girls, follow me.'

And off they went.

I let out a big sigh as if the breath would take away the confusion, then, after a second, I recalled that Don Vicenç was looking for me, so I swiftly left the kitchen, trying to locate him. In the master's quarter, I was thankful that Martín's wailing didn't reach this part of the castle.

It took me several minutes to reach the library, but I didn't find Don Vicenç there. The whole castle was still quiet, and I supposed that all of the guests must be in their rooms as it was still early in the morning. I wondered why Don Vicenç was awake at the same time as the servants.

Walking out through the corridor, I had no idea where to locate my master, and the idea of checking on Cecilia tempted me, but I knew that I had to wait. I was about to go back to the kitchen, but as I walked past one of the doors, I heard my master's voice at last. He was arguing with someone, and that someone's voice caught my attention because it was Flor's.

I knew her insulting words quite well as they rang in my brain from time to time.

'I thought you loved—' Flor's voice emerged behind the door.

'I do not take other people's leftovers!' said Don Vicenç.

'What could you possibly mean?'

'I know what you did. You let Jacobo touch you, didn't you?'

'What? What are you saying? No!'

'You went to his room last night! Don't think I don't know what everyone in this place does!'

'I went to see him to ask about you! You never come and see me anymore. And you forbade me to come and see you! What

178

was I supposed to do? If I hadn't sneaked in today, would you just leave without saying any word to me? How could you possibly be like this? I thought you said you loved me!'

'Well, I did, but not anymore.'

After Don Vicenç's words died down, the room went quiet.

A moment before the storm.

Then came another wailing of the day.

'How could you! Is it because of that bitch?'

'Keep your voice down, woman! For God's sake.'

'Why? Are you ashamed of what you did then? Sleeping around with me? You know what? You can never get rid of me! Because I am pregnant with your child!'

The shouting ceased, and the room went quiet again, but a few seconds later came a sound of objects falling to the floor, then a muffled sound. A second later, the door swung open, and by some miracle, the wooden door obscured my sneaking presence.

I saw Don Vicenç pulling Flor out of the room. One hand on her mouth, keeping her from screaming and another dragging her away.

I could hear Flor's muffled sound. None of it made any sense.

Don Vicenç pulled Flor into one of the rooms at the end of the corridor. I didn't follow them.

In the dark corridor, I stood rigid on the ground, thinking to myself, what on earth was happening on this morning.

# Chapter Seventeen

I left the castle that afternoon quite unexpectedly and in a rush.

In the morning, after the incident with Flor, I went straight to the kitchen, expecting Don Vicenç to come and find me, as I didn't want him to suspect that I had been spying on him.

There was no one in the kitchen when I entered, and I felt thankful because I was still in no mood for talking, jesting, sneering or even flirting with any woman.

I rested my tired body and confused mind on the stool near the table in the middle of the room. On top of the table, there was a loaf of bread which distracted me away from the thoughts in my head. Even though I was still confused about what was happening with Martín and Flor, and even Delilah, I would not let hunger get the better of me, so I devoured it like a starving person who hadn't eaten for days.

A moment later, the large double doors from the master's side swung open. I still remember Don Vicenç quite clearly when he found me, for his face was raw with joy and satisfaction. I knew he was scheming something inside that beautiful head of his, and in his hand, there was the sculpture of a woman I had made.

I tried to act as naturally with him as I could. I smiled at him and didn't ask any questions even though in my brain, there were thousands of questions that needed an answer. I wanted to ask him about Martín since he must have gone into the attic to find the sculpture, and he must have noticed a big change in Martín's usual self. I wanted to ask about Flor. And I wanted to know what he was going to do with the sculpture? And what was his plan for me? But the only thing I did was keep smiling and keep my mouth shut.

'There you are!' said Don Vicenç, 'I am leaving for Barcelona right now. And you are coming with me. Do not worry about clothes, I have plenty. Leave all your old belongings here. Now, follow me.'

His words didn't resolve any questions that were floating in my head but instead added more. Why would he want to leave for Barcelona at this hour? What about his guests? And Delilah? Would I ever see her again?

Don Vicenç turned, and when he found me still standing on the same spot, he raised his voice, 'Did you hear what I just said? Follow me. Quick!'

I was on the move again, with a belly half full and a nagging pain in my head.

I had no idea why Don Vicenç was in such a hurry. But I didn't stop to ask him. He reeked of too much power, too much audacity and too much authority for me to dare contradict his words and commands. I feared him, and at the same time, I wanted him to accept me, so I tried to please him. Deep down inside of me, I wanted his favour in exchange for recognition and respect like a real artist. And of course, I'd like him to treat me fairly, for if, as he said, I could make a lot of sculptures, I would be recognised, and I would surely not have to work my life away in that dark and smelly attic anymore. He'd said that my talent would be known to the whole world. It only seemed fair if Don Vicenç treated me like I deserved, so I did whatever he'd told me to do.

We, Don Vicenç, Cecilia, Amelia and myself, left the castle before the other guests were awoken. Don Vicenç forced all of us into the carriage. Amelia and Cecilia seemed to be half awake. Shadows formed under their eyes. Amilia was massaging her temples while Cecilia was yawning. However, both of them didn't protest under any circumstances.

Before we were to leave, Don Vicenç left a note to his guests, saying that he had an urgent business matter back in Barcelona and that he would see them all again in a few weeks at the same place, same time. He extended his sincere apology in his note and told Agnes, who came to send us off, to prepare anything that his guests should require. Don Vicenç also told her to send a message to Itzal, 'Make sure Itzal does his job well and tell him to come to see me after it's all done.' Those were Don Vicenç's exact words. Agnes nodded, and on her face, it shined with pride as if she had received a message from the king. She managed to smile at me like I was one of her masters now, and I wished I could unsee it. I quickly looked away, just to cast my eyes anywhere else that wasn't her, and at the main gate of the castle, I caught sight of Andrea, but as I was about to lift my hand in a farewell gesture, his eye caught mine, and from the carriage, I could see his face was sour with hatred.

I thought his crooked nose suited him better when he had

that expression on his face.

I tried to imagine the new life that I would have in the new city that I only heard about, telling myself that it was going to be my chance to work on what I loved and be recognised by it. We left in the grand carriage with four white horses of Don Vicenç's. I cast one last look at the peculiar castle behind me and reflected on the changes in me from the first day I set foot there.

'What's the reason for us leaving so soon, Don Vicenç? Aren't we supposed to leave next week after the ceremony?' Amelia, who was sitting in the opposite direction of Don Vicenç, spoke up a few minutes after we were on the main road.

'Just a change of plan. Nothing you two should worry about,' Don Vicenç answered with a wave of his hand.

The twins looked at each other and shrugged.

'I am happy that Jacobo is joining us, though,' Cecilia said with a smile directed at me.

'Oh, aren't we all?' Don Vicenç added, but he didn't turn and look at me in the eyes.

The carriage kept moving, and I wondered how much longer we would have to sit there altogether. I could sense that Cecilia was still looking at me. And when I glanced at her, our eyes met. And the picture of her soft freckles that ran all over her skin came flooding into my head. Then, I thought of Delilah. Would her skin be as soft as Cecilia's?

All of a sudden, Cecilia stopped smiling as if she could sense the changes in my thoughts. There was a shadow of sadness underneath her eyes, and Cecilia blinked it away before she looked away from my face and out of the window.

When we finally reached Barcelona, it was late in the evening. I was hoping to get out of the carriage as soon as possible. Throughout the whole journey, Cecilia refused to talk or even look at me. Amelia tried hard to get Don Vicenç's attention but failed miserably as Don Vicenç kept looking out of the window. From the reflection, I could see a dark shadow on his face. And he wasn't simply just staring outside the window. His eyes were moving to the left, then to the right, as if he was deep in thought about something in his head.

Once the carriage passed the stone wall that surrounded the city, I looked out of the window. I saw what I'd expected from a big city; lots and lots of buildings, twice the size of the ones in the hanging town. It surprised me when I didn't feel so excited to see the big city, to witness something real and not from the drawings or from my imagination. I should have felt some thrilling sensation because it used to be one of my biggest wishes. But I didn't. The wonderment inside me was numbed by an unknown reason; maybe because I had already tasted and experienced something far better than this, or maybe I had embedded all the excitement into the skittish horse sculpture.

But even if I were that same boy, who first left the hanging town, I still would have been disappointed. The city was dirty. The street was narrow. And where had all the colours gone? Everywhere I looked, all I could see was faded colours. The once bright bricks and sandstones on the buildings, streets and walls were now covered with dust and dirt. It was almost as if I was looking at a painting painted in black and white.

All around us, people were minding their own business,

walking swiftly with their heads down as if they were dealing with some tricky business.

Even though it was late evening and the sun was still lit up in the sky, the tall stone buildings blocked out the strong sunlight, making some corners of the street look even more gloomy than they should. As the carriage slowly travelled through the narrow street, I looked up at the facade of those tall buildings, and they reminded me of Don Vicenç's peculiar castle, for it had the style of its own, the mysterious feeling from the unknown shadowy corners of small alleys, the gargoyles that were watching you wherever you went like those paintings on the wall of the castle.

We zigged zagged through the small street until we reached a big plaza. In this part of the town, it was busier than the area we passed before. People were selling poultry, fruits and ailments like the market that my mother used to go to on the weekend, but the size of the tiny market in the hanging town could not be compared to this place.

The carriages moved further into the maze of the buildings until the area where the street was wider, and that was where the carriage started to slow down. Finally, it went past a large wooden door and came to a halt inside a square patio.

We got off the carriage and took a few steps up the stairs where it led directly to a grand wooden door. Through it, I was met by a grand apartment fit for a grand person like Don Vicenç.

Amelia and Cecilia went straight to their room and left me in the hall with Don Vicenç. A second later, the main entrance opened, and the servants carrying our trunks came through. One of them was holding a wooden chest with a golden latch. I had a clear idea of what lay inside.

'You idiot, give me that chest!' said Don Vicenç. He walked towards the servant and snatched the chest from her hand. 'Bring the rest of my trunks to my room and tell everyone not to enter my private chamber!' He told the woman servant, who looked like she was going to burst into tears. 'Now!' he shouted, and the servants hurriedly dispersed to do as they were told. Then, I was left alone with my master.

Don Vicenç turned towards me with the wooden chest still in his hands. The angry face that was shown to the servants just now melted away into a grin. 'Now, my dear, Jacobo. That's the room where you are going to be working and staying,' he said as he pointed with his head to the door not far away from the main entrance.

'But first, let me make something clear to you.' He continued with the grinning and incongruous intense eyes. 'You are not going to mention the woman sculpture to Count Alfonso or to anyone. Instead, you're going to make a new sculpture for him. So, I believe it's a good time for you to get to work.' And just like that, he walked away down the corridor and disappeared around the corner. His footsteps landed heavily on the floor, followed by a loud bang and a noisy bolt on the door.

I didn't know about my master's nature until then. It was clear to me now why we'd left the castle in a hurry. Don Vicenç was afraid that if Count Alfonso saw the piece, he would want to pay for it and because the money that he was going to offer would be high enough to tempt Don Vicenç into selling it, but Don Vicenç didn't want to be in that dilemma of greed, that was why he'd told me to never mention that particular piece to the count.

I was glad to have a luxurious chamber of my own, and on top of that, I was assigned to do what I loved. And my first week in Barcelona was spent inside my own room, trying to create another piece of soul out of myself.

I attempted to create another woman sculpture, but it was all in vain. I could not recall how many female sculptures I had attempted to make, however, each and every piece of them laid scattered in the corner of the room, ignored, unworthy and incompetent.

As my room was near the main entrance, I could hear constant knocking on the door by a great number of people all seeking out for Don Vicenç. It was always Amelia or Cecilia who went for the door and told whoever came that Don Vicenç was out of town for urgent business and he would be back soon. But I knew that Don Vicenç had never left the apartment. He spent most of his time in his private chamber just like I did, but as I was busy creating another sculpture, I didn't know what he was doing in there all by himself.

Once, when Cecilia and Amelia weren't in the apartment, when I was working in the quietness of my room, I could hear voices coming out of Don Vicenç's room. He was talking to someone, but there was no one else inside. His words were spoken repeatedly, 'Mine, mine, mine, and I shall not cease!'

The only time Don Vicenç came out of his private chamber was to set his eyes on my attempts at a new woman sculpture, and every time he did, he would go a little mad.

'This is not it! When I look at this piece, I feel nothing! You have wasted my entire week trying to make a useless replica of it!' he said. And as if Don Vicenç himself sensed that his mask of good nature had been slipping, he tried hard to calm himself and fix his tone with me. 'Now, Jacobo, why don't you go out with Cecilia and let her entertain you?'

With Don Vicenç's words, Cecilia had to take me out. However, when I managed to get on her good side, Cecilia's cloudy mood with me was lifted and the sun was shining upon her again. She took me out on the streets of Barcelona, to different street stalls, trying different food and strolling around the street like a young couple. I knew Cecilia to be a very cheerful person, but she tended to sulk easily if something or someone offended her, and I could also sense that she liked to hold a grudge. So, I tried to keep on her good side.

Cecilia taught me to enjoy another part of life apart from the sculpture. A little stroll in the morning with her over the past weeks helped me clear my brain. And after the outing with her, I would continue on with my work. Sometimes Cecilia would come and sit with me just to keep me company.

And when Don Vicenç did not force me to make another woman sculpture, I felt life spring out of me again. I let myself loose into the new feeling, emotion and inspiration. I made many new pieces of sculpture for Don Vicenç, and in all of them, I had implanted a little of me within. And this time when Don Vicenç came into my room, he nodded with a gleam in his eyes. 'Yes! When I look at these, I can feel something at least. Even if they are not the masterpiece like the one you made before, they will do,' said Don Vicenç one evening.

I had managed to make a few sculptures that resembled the curiosity, happiness and fun that shone from Cecilia's eyes.

After Don Vicenç was satisfied with my sculptures, he emerged from his room after a month of inactiveness like a snake waiting for a meal to digest. And he was on the move again. With my sculptures, he was ready to search for prey in the form of a rich man that would agree to give him an unimaginable sum of money in exchange for my sculptures.

And I was back to creating more pieces for Don Vicenç.

# Chapter Eighteen

'What are you doing?' Cecilia asked as she stepped into my room one night without bothering to knock.

Cecilia and I had developed a deeper relationship other than only the temptation of the flesh. However, our little stroll in the city every morning had ceased, as Don Vicenç wanted the new sculptures to be made as fast as possible, for the ones I had made earlier were all sold for a large sum within a few days.

'Does Don Vicenç need something?' I asked when she entered. Cecilia didn't come to visit me as often anymore, as she was always busy with whatever she was doing for Don Vicenç. For the whole past week, I had mostly been left alone in the apartment with my work.

'No, I am just here to see you,' she said.

'Is there a problem?'

'No? Do I always bring problems whenever I come and see you?'

With eyebrows raised, I answered, 'Sort of.'

'Oh, please, speak the truth. You do enjoy my company,' said Cecilia with hands on her hips. 'Don't you miss me or feel curious about my whereabouts after all?'

Cecilia's sulking habit made my lips curl in a smile. And when she sensed that what I had said earlier wasn't my intention, she came to me and gave me a quick kiss. 'Don Vicenç went out with Amelia. So I am alone.'

'Why didn't you join them?' I asked.

'Oh, I told them that I didn't feel well. I'm just tired,' she said.

Cecilia went to an armchair and dragged it near the table where I sat. She lowered herself on to the seat and sighed. Her small feet swung back and forth under the pile of her skirt. 'My work is draining all of my energy. Besides, Delilah will be there, and she is the last person I want to see.'

With Delilah's name mentioned, my curiosity piqued. I hadn't had a chance to see her since the last meeting in the castle. A small tick in my body gesture must have revealed what I was thinking to Cecilia. I turned and looked at her.

'Oh! Dear Jacobo, you fell for the wrong woman, you know that?' she said. I didn't answer. However, she must have also read the expression on my face.

'Don't look so surprised. I think if anyone paid enough attention, they would see that you couldn't stop looking her way. But you see, she has been unfaithful to her husband for who knows how long. The way she looks at all the men. I can even tell which men she has slept with. And I saw the way she had looked at you when she could not take her eyes off of us. She wanted your attention!' Cecilia emphasised the words as she leaned over and placed both of her small hands on the armrests.

I could not say that Cecilia was wrong, for I knew that it was true.

'And I was glad that Don Vicenç gave me permission to approach you that day,' Cecilia continued, 'You should have seen her face when you walked out of that room with me. I'd trade anything to see such emotion on her face again. She must be very angry, you see? that she had lost your attention to me, to a person she has a low opinion of.'

I placed the pen that I was holding on the table and completely turned around to face her. As Cecilia knew that she'd managed to capture all of my attention, she stood up from the armchair and walked towards me. Even when I sat on the chair, my height almost reached hers. I tilted my head up and looked into her blue eyes and freckled face.

'Oh, Jacobo, she knew that you wanted her, too, and that was why she wanted to make you jealous. But I must say I was afraid that you would refuse to come with me, as you were falling head-over-heels for her. I must also say that maybe you are the first person who denied her,' she chuckled.

'You knew?' I asked, surprised by how much Cecilia could read through all the situations.

'Of course, I paid enough attention. But you can thank me later.' Cecilia shrugged as she started to walk back and forth in her short steps. 'First, you don't want anything to do with her. And, second, if Don Vicenç knew that you have messed with what he thinks is his, you wouldn't be in his house today. He wants everything that belongs to him untouched.'

'That is the second time I have heard about that about Don Vicenç,' I snorted.

'And it won't be the last time, I can assure you that,' said Cecilia.

'But Delilah does not belong to Don Vicenç. She is married

192

to someone else.'

'I suppose she is the only one for whom Don Vicenç overlooks the fact that she is already married. Well, I am not surprised. With a face like hers, if I were a man, I would also want to be with someone who looks like that. But I think her time is running out,' Cecilia turned and looked at me with her round blue eyes. 'She is getting older every single day. I can't imagine the day when she can't use her beauty to get what she wants. Oh, and I wonder when Don Bernado will find out that his wife has been unfaithful all this time. But I doubt he will. Don Bernado is quite dull. I can't find anything interesting about him except his big pouch and his big crotch,' Cecilia giggled.

'You don't seem to get along with her,' I said.

'Oh! No, no, not at all,' Cecilia's voice raised, and she suddenly stopped pacing and went back to sit on the armchair, facing me. 'But our relationship wasn't like this at the beginning, you see.' Her tone was back to normal as she kept on telling me about her history with Delilah. 'I used to admire her beauty, her charm and everything about her. I used to think to myself that if I could choose to have a new face, I'd definitely choose hers. But after we got to know her, Amelia and I, that is, our opinion completely changed. She treated us like we were less than dirt. She called us names. As I said, Delilah is the only one who truly knows that my sister and I are not really daughters of any Viscount from France like Don Vicenç told everyone. Actually, like you, we are just ordinary people. No title, no fortunes. We work for Don Vicenç like you, but we just have a different task.' Cecilia tilted her head to one side but kept her intense blue eyes on mine.

I raised my brows, surprised by the truth that Cecilia had just told me. 'You mean Don Vicenç also dresses you up?' I asked curiously.

'I mean, you could see it like that, but you see, these clothes are all mine,' she said while looking at her pale blue gown that I thought suited her well. 'I chose every gown myself. But Don Vicenç was the one who paid for it,' she giggled again.

'But anyway,' Cecilia continued, 'Delilah suspected us because she seemed to dislike us from the beginning. We weren't sure why, but now, we are sure that she was just jealous because she thought Don Vicenç had taken a new interest in us and not her. She caught us by surprise. What she did at the time was come to us with a piece of letter, telling us to read about the latest gossip. She asked us what we thought about it. Of course, because we could not read and we didn't know Delilah came with a plan. I remembered her friendly face changing into a sneer after she confirmed her suspicions. She told us, "I knew you two were frauds. You aren't one of us, and you never will be. I will find out what trickery you two used against Vicenç. I will find out what rat hole you came from." We were surprised that such a beauty could spit so many foul things. I didn't know that her ego is bigger than Montserrat, and I didn't know jealousy could drive her to hate us that much.

'But Don Vicenç must have dealt with her, because since that day she has left us alone. I mean, in a manner in which she refuses to acknowledge our presence. For me, since that moment, my dislike of Delilah never disappeared. But Amelia is not like me, somehow, she learns to forgive. Still, I wonder what Don Vicenç had told her that made her agree to have us around.

But you know Don Vicenç by now. He also does whatever it takes to get what he wants.

'Aren't you curious why he told everyone that you are his distant cousin?' she asked.

'I am actually,' I said, 'but I kind of guessed. Because he didn't want to be associating with the likes of us?'

'Yes, and by saying that you are his cousin, the value of the sculpture you made increased. And nobody can prove that you are not actually his cousin, and you two do look alike. Everyone will believe what he said. But he could not tell others the truth about our origins because he can't be seen or known to have associated with the lower-class, and not that he cares, as long as we work well for him. So that is why he needs you.

'And your sculptures saved his reputation, too. They diverted everyone's attention away from Don Vicenç's inexplicable behaviour. He was supposed to lead a religious ceremony. You see, we are all strong religious devotees and that day when he left the castle without telling anyone, it upset everyone as they think that he upsets God. It caused such a stir in our group. You must see that was why he never left his room and had been telling Amelia and me to tell the others that he was away. But after he got those sculptures of yours, he managed to save his own reputation.'

I contemplated Cecilia's words. Whatever she had told me so far made sense. First, Delilah seemed to possess the character that Cecilia had just described. I had experienced it once. Her jealousy, her game, her insult and her temper. And as for Don Vicenç, I hadn't any idea that Don Vicenç was a strong devotee of God. He didn't look like one to me. But that must be because there were many sides of Don Vicenç that I still didn't know about.

'Well, I hope I am not interrupting you. I can see that you are not working, but what were you doing?' Cecilia asked, interrupting my thoughts.

'Just trying to write a letter to my mother. Since I didn't have any free time before, I hadn't managed it.' I thought about how easy it was this time to seek paper and ink. They were inside the drawer of the desk I was sitting at.

'I didn't know you could write,' said Cecilia in some sort of shock.

'Why does everyone keep asking me that? Is it such a wonder that I can?'

'Oh, there are still many things that I don't know about you. I cannot write, nor can I read. Well, I suppose if I could read, I believe your handwriting would be quite beautiful. It's more like what I have seen from the book, and not as messy and all over the place like Don Vicenç's handwriting. So? What are you writing about?'

I almost rolled my eyes at her supposedly nosy habit, but I told myself that she meant no harm. It was just who she was, a little nosy, a little of everything.

'I'm writing to tell my mother how I am doing. Where I am and how busy I've been. You know, those kinds of things. I sent her a letter once back when I was at the castle, but there was no reply,' I told her. And before she could press me further about the topic of my mother, I changed the subject. 'Celia? You said that you couldn't read or write. Why is that? Your mother didn't teach you?'

196

'Oh, we don't know who our mother is,' she said, and I was surprised by her answer.

'So, you said you were born in France. Tell me about it? Since you are bored, I'd like to know,' I told Cecilia. I wondered how her life had been before she met Don Vicenç.

'Of course, if you want to know. We are friends after all,' said Cecilia with a gleeful smile on her face. In the moment before she started to speak, she got off the armchair and started to walk back and forth around the room like she was nervous recalling her past.

'Amelia and I,' eventually, she spoke up, 'we were raised in a religious orphanage in Paris. We didn't have the privilege of learning or the privilege of being loved by our mother or father. We had another mistress once, before everyone, before Don Vicenç. It seems like a lifetime ago, but to think about it, it has just been ten years. When we were ten years old. I remember it well because it was the same date as my birthday, the tenth of January, and the same day I stopped begging for God's help. He seemed to turn his back on us.

'Our headmistress used to say that we were lucky to be alive inside the gates of an orphanage, where we could receive the blessings of God. I didn't think so. I waited and begged him for too long. It was all fruitless.

'We thought we would always end up in an orphanage. Disregarded not by our parents, but by everyone who came and went but didn't choose to take us with them. However, one day, there was this woman. Her hair was black like a raven. She always dressed in black too, and it made her green eyes so intense. They were a shade of emerald.

'Mistress Sabine, that was her name. She was the one who got us out of the orphanage. I'd remember her exact words. She told our headmistress that she was looking for a specific girl, "I want a girl with blue eyes, dark blonde hair, and with freckles on her face." That described me all right. Then, the headmistress brought my sister and me out. She told Mistress Sabine, "If you want this one, you have to take the other, too." The headmistress seemed to want to get rid of us.'

I listened to her attentively as if I was seeing everything through her eyes.

'Mistress Sabine was surprised that we were twins, but, of course, she agreed to take both of us. We were so happy that finally we got to leave the dark and smelly place of an orphanage and escape the devil headmistress. But our new place wasn't any different. It was dark and gloomy and strange . . . at first. But at least we knew that the Mistress loved and cared for us. I really believed that she loved us.

'When we arrived at Mistress Sabine's place, we found out that she was a religious person, for she always prayed and lit a candle that reminded me of a vanilla cake we had once in the orphanage. She showed us to our own room. Even though it was small and gloomy, I was happy to have something of my own. You must remember what having something of your own for the first time feels like? I started to think that God had answered our prayers after all. For a second, I felt guilty that I had abandoned him. I told the mistress so, but she said it wasn't that at all, God, who answered my prayers. It was another god that we have to thank, another god that told her where to find me. It was a sign given to her by her god in her dream. That was the reason why she found us and took us out of the orphanage.

'She taught us everything we know, but not exactly how to read or write like your mother did. It was more about salvation.

'I understood later on why Mistress Sabine was looking for us. It was because we could sense something in people, something out of the ordinary. And that was our gift, and Mistress Sabine knew this. She was a spiritualist and not just a simple religious person.' Cecilia raised her voice. 'I still remember the hopeful look on her face when she told Amelia and me that we would lead her to the true saviour, who would liberate all of those who believe and free us all from this polluted world!'

Cecilia paused and lowered herself back on to the armchair. She took in a sharp breath before she started to talk. Her voice was low. 'But around six years later, Mistress Sabine died. She was hanged. Three policemen came to our place at night and tore everything down. They thought Amelia and I had escaped, but we were hiding in a secret hiding place. We could see everything that they did to the mistress. Those policemen . . . they raped her, but the mistress, she wasn't afraid of them. When those people saw her laugh and unafraid, they . . .' Cecilia's eyes shone with terror, 'they beat her and took her away. They must have tortured her, for the day when she was hanged, we were there, but we could not recognise her at all, except her long raven hair.

'The policemen must have known about us. We could not stay there, or else we would end up like the mistress. We fled Paris, out of France, with a goal in our hearts that we would avenge our mistress, and we would not fail her mission. We came to Barcelona, and since then, we have tried to find our liberator. We never went hungry here, for there were always men who took us in, and they feed us well.' Cecilia smiled dryly and avoided my gaze.

'But since we got here,' Cecilia slowly got up from the armchair. 'We have been given a sign, and at last, I thought I had found the one we were looking for. Don Vicenç, that is.' And slowly, she approached. 'I was quite sure that he was our true liberator until I met you.' Cecilia stopped right in front of me.

'What do you mean? A sign? From who?' I asked, looking straight into her eyes.

'Of course, from our god, the devil,' nonchalantly, she told me.

# PART THREE

A flood of guilt is gushing through my veins
A droplet of shame is wringing out of my heart
How did I ever come to understand
That I once had a heart as big as the ocean
And a soul as high as the sky?
My soul is screeching in a different note of sorrow
And in the hollowness of my mind,
I know where my fate lies.

# Chapter Nineteen

My first year in Barcelona passed by like a current of water rising with the tide. The wings of pigeons fluttered. The winds blew. The sun rose and set so many times I lost count. And too many things happened in the course of time.

And my nature, of whom I once was, had changed on a whim. I wasn't the same person, though I could not say what it was that had changed me. But it happened so slowly, like rust corroding my heart that used to be made of iron.

And Don Vicenç's nature came to change as well. The day when he emerged from his room, there was a shift in the shadow on his face. It was like he had discovered a new purpose. And that disdainful look that he had been trying hard to hide when he looked at me had also disappeared. Don Vicenç truly treated me like I was his own class and his own kin.

Words from Count Alfonso had spread among the high class men about my sculpture, and among the women, words spread about Don Vicenç's charming and handsome cousin, and those words were also passed onto me. I was invited to every social gathering. Countless invitations started to pour in.

Don Vicenç and I, together, we attracted women of all classes and status, the unmarried and the married ones, whose integrity was like a wisp of smoke being blown away by a strong wind.

He also introduced me to the gentleman's club, a privileged and hidden place inside a dark gothic courtyard, a place full of beautiful women in a poppy field cloud. I would smoke away my senses to the unknown of the night and wait for whatever fate would come in the morning. I started to become reckless in that way.

We threw these secret wild nights almost every week. And those who attended were to wear a mask that would disguise their face, but I'd remember them, standing stiffly next to their wife at another social gathering anywhere. I didn't know what lies they had to tell their wives in order to join this secret party almost every week.

One secret gentleman club also happened to be one of Don Vicenç's properties. Inside the hidden courtyard of the building lay a vast elegant room, where men of his status would secretly come to enjoy time off from their wives.

Don Vicenç told me once to look at those men with an invisible chain of shame hanging around their necks because they had to hide men's true nature from their wives. Why can't they take as many women as they want without feeling guilty and having to hide their doings in secret? My master said it was because of the mistake they made by getting married.

I used to agree with his words. I thought if I had to hide and bear the shame and the consequence of doing what I liked to do, why would I wrap my neck with a chain and be ruled by something intangible. And I thought of the man I never knew, a man who I must call father, a man who deserted me and my mother to whatever cruel web of fate had been drawn upon us.

One thing that I might have truly respected Don Vicenç for was the ability to never let himself fall upon the ambiguity of recklessness. Even when he had spent nights in the gentleman's club, enjoying time with countless courtesans, he would never let the deeds of the past night overshadow his version as a respectable and hard-working man. And men did respect him because of his responsibility. He was the centre of fun and a star among the lords and counts. He knew very well how to keep those people entertained, including me.

My master was good at what he was doing and as wicked as Cecilia used to tell me. He knew how to buy people's hearts and keep them all at bay and at his mercy.

Another wickedness of my master wasn't revealed to me until later. He had this particular thing about him that he loved to have his women use the perfume he created before he went to bed them. It was the same smell that I had smelt before, particularly in the master's quarter on the third floor back in his castle. But then, for me, it was somehow a sign to differentiate the women who had been with Don Vicenç and those who hadn't. I would remember the smell well, and then I would remember their faces.

Don Vicenç was a man that every free-spirited woman wanted to be with. And then there was me. As young as I am, I attracted a different age of woman, a daughter, a niece of all the upper classes, and without knowing who my true parents were, they were blinded by the wealth of Don Vicenç, believing my root of parentage was as well a wealthy one. Don Vicenç introduced me with his last name, I was Jacobo Velasco, and a second cousin of his brother's wife, and my parents had passed away, so he had taken the matter of raising me. 'You are like a son to me,' he'd once said. And I thought until the day I was no longer of use to him, he would cast me aside. But that day didn't seem to be coming in the near future, as I was making him more money than ever with my sculptures.

There were many men, ranking from barons, viscounts, and lords, who wanted to hire me personally and commission a sculpture, of which the payment would provide me with a fortune if I had accepted. And Don Vicenç must have been aware that if I had known of this news, I would have made my own decision by leaving him for a new opportunity and leaving him empty-handed. He was afraid that someone would take away his prized possession, his money factory, and all of the efforts he had made into telling lies about my true identity, all the efforts of feeding and dressing me up as his own kin would go in vain. But Don Vicenç wasn't a person who would give up any of his belongings. So, he decided to take another gamble with me by allowing me to partake in the decisions on the matter of his land and business in such a way that it would take my mind off making my own decision for myself. And I had done a very good job at it. He taught me, and I learned everything, from dealing with a matter of making serious business decisions to enjoying the pleasures of the night.

Don Vicenç taught me about his business as well. As I was a quick learner, I learnt his way of business quite fast. He mostly dealt with land and collecting money from people. But his business with art such as ceramics, porcelain, sculptures, perfumes and paintings were his passion. He told me once that even if he did nothing his whole life, he would still earn money from all the land he owned, but he wanted to trade, especially in the matter of arts, as he said that it made a great deal of money.

'One can never have too much. I shall cease at nothing.' That was what Don Vicenç said.

Collecting debt and overdue rent was another thing that Don Vicenç was good at. Once he had seen that the money from this land or whatever else that the money had to be collected from, he would send Itzal and his men to go collect a debt at every doorstep of every part and every port of Spain. As such, any overdue debts were paid in full.

Don Vicenç's cousin, a representation, a mimic, his right hand or whatever they called me, I stood in the spotlight of the new light in my era. I was known and respected by word of mouth. Not only because of my skills and my looks, but because I was a quick learner, and I possessed an ability to shine like Don Vicenç.

The enchantment of being known and respected in the new world of an upper class society consumed me, and by being known came another seed of temptation, another kind of rust slowly creeping up my iron heart without me knowing it: pride.

I was accepted among men of high status. We dined and conversed. Don Vicenç taught me upper-class manners, and I learnt them quite quickly, for it was nothing but the words and words alone that came out pretentiously, but on the inside, we were depraved.

We did nothing but fill our lives with luxury. We drank, we gambled, we had more women than we had ever yearned for.

Days went on, and each and every day passed by like this.

As I had been drowning in a world of illusions, there was the thing that pulled me deeper into hallucination, laudanum and opium.

And I had been drawn into the delusion of Don Vicenç's words with the amount of opium. I would lock myself up in a room—my own room in Don Vicenç's apartment—and set myself to work again. My mind ran a thousand light-years onto the images hidden deeply in my brain, images that burst with new feelings. And I easily became addicted to that state of mind.

Like a father or a dear cousin, Don Vicenç said he was to me, he still kept me in chains with all of those addictions.

I would keep on smoking and working for days and nights, and that was when I'd prefer to have Cecilia come to visit me. She had become my grail of nostalgia. Whenever I had been too wild and lost, seeing her reminded me of who I was before, of that boy lying on the soft mattress in her room, feeling the soft skin of a woman for the first time.

And Cecilia knew me. She really knew and saw through me. She didn't judge who I was and who I was becoming. On the contrary, she loved it even more when I slowly shed a little of my old self, little by little.

# Chapter Twenty

Lavish!

Everything was so lavish!

Everything was lush and colourful. I couldn't recall this room having so many colours. The red, blue and gold popped out in my eyes, along with the shadow from the flickering of candle lights that swayed like they were enjoying their sinister dance.

My visions were moving so slowly, zooming in and out. Then suddenly, the burning lights were too bright. I kept rubbing my eyes, but all of the effects didn't seem to cease.

I was sitting alone in the privacy of my own room, smoking away my good sense of self and replacing all that was left with hallucinations.

But I could see that everything wasn't just an illusion after all. Like the exquisite opium pipe in my hands or the bottle of laudanum on the table. Or this golden legged chair that I was sitting on, or the golden trimmed clothes that I was wearing. Everything was so valid and solid that I could touch and feel. I looked around and absorbed everything around me, and I thought to myself, how far I have come, to be living in such a grand place, and to be experiencing all that I have.

I used to feel envious of Don Vicenç, of how he spent his

life in his grand castle. But now, I was living the life Don Vicenç was living. A sense of satisfaction filled up my insides. I was proud of my achievements and enjoying every minute of it. I had made it here all by myself.

I thought back to the moment when Don Vicenç and I were at a social gathering. Not only did I look like one of the people from the upper class, but I also talked and acted like one of them. I was proud of the person that looked back at me from the reflection when I looked into the mirror. I was so proud of the man I had become. I was everything that Don Vicenç was, if not better. I remembered how all eyes were focused on me wherever I walked. Every person in the room, you name it, was looking at me like they used to look at Don Vicenç. And I knew it was a look of fascination. I'd remember that kind of look anywhere.

A new feeling was overwhelming me. And it had called unto to me for me to unleash it. I started to form a new figure that resembled myself, a man with a great sense of pride.

I was fuming drunk. My ears rang. I faintly heard a banging noise on my door. I focused on the sound—it was still there—I hadn't imagined it after all. Stumbling on the tools on the floor, it took me a moment to finally reach the door. When I unlocked it, the door swung open, almost crashing into my nose. My sight was still blurry when I looked at the shoes in front of me, then slowly, my eyes trailed up to the man who was standing in front of me. My focus was coming back intact. But the piercing sound from outside of the room made me cower.

'Don Vicenç . . .'

'Yea, I've been banging on your door for a while. I thought

you were dead, drowning in all this smoke!' said Don Vicenç before he strode off to open the tapestries and the window. A freezing rush of air came in, melting away all the smoke and my blurry visions, and I noticed that it was late in the morning.

'Ah, I see that you are working on a new piece,' said Don Vicenç after the cloud of smoke had cleared. He leaned over the table, trying to look closely at the form of the sculpture.

'Yes, but it's not done yet,' I said as I approached him and took a seat, giving a sign that he was interrupting my work time.

Of course, Don Vicenç didn't take any notice as he kept staring at the new sculpture. 'I can see that it's a figure of a man, from the look of it. Surprise me again this time, will you?' He had a look of an enthusiastic child. 'Oh! I can't wait to feel whatever the sculpture is going to make me. Then, we'll see who'll be the lucky one to buy it. Or might I keep it myself . . .' He completed the look with a mischievous grin.

I sighed, feeling annoyed by his words as I thought I was making this one for myself as it resembled me, my pride, and who I had become, and someone was just going to take it away.

'Yes, we'll see. When I finish with it, that is,' I said, my voice and expression never gave away what I was truly feeling inside.

'You haven't had any sleep, I suppose. Look at your face. Why don't you go get some sleep for a couple of hours? We have a long day ahead of us.'

'Are we going somewhere?' I asked.

Don Vicenç placed his right hand on the table and laid his whole weight upon it. I stared at his golden ring with a colourful diamond on top. 'Not exactly,' he said. 'Didn't I tell you before that we will have guests today? It's the last day of the year! And we are to celebrate!' The diamond ring hand formed into a fist as it pounded on the table. 'I have so many devotees to entertain. And this year, I expect you to join us.'

I tilted my head up and found Don Vicenç staring down at me.

It surprised me that Don Vicenç had asked me to join his religious ceremony, as he had never done so before. In fact, he had never mentioned any of it to me. I knew about it from Cecilia that Don Vicenç and everyone in his close group of friends was involved in this religious group, a cult with the belief that all of the devotees would be deliberated on a judgement day. And through a conversation with Cecilia, I also had connected the dots that they were worshipping some higher being or a devil, who they called their god.

Even though Don Vicenç had included me in his group of friends and business, one thing that he didn't allow me to be a part of was this religious group of his. If I had read between the lines, it was because he didn't fully trust in me, because their practice was against the law of the church. If anyone were to find out, all of them would end up in a noose, like Mistress Sabine.

Truthfully, I couldn't care less about this cult, but I was curious enough to witness whatever that was going on.

'Yes, Don Vicenç,' I told him, and with a nod, Don Vicenç left me on my own once more.

All these past months, I had forgotten the time and the date, and above all else, my birthday, which was the 31st of December.

With my mother, we didn't only celebrate the end of the year but also the day that I was born. The last day of the year, the day of the end of the old thing and the start of the new beginning.

The thought led me back to the moments I spent with my mother . . . Why hadn't she replied to my letter? I thought the last time I wrote to her, I had made sure that I had the return address.

I scrubbed and searched through the drawers in search of paper and ink.

I could not believe that I had forgotten this little gesture of writing to her. All these times, I had not spared her any thought. All of the light that she had given me was blinded by temptations of pride, of ego, of lust, of fun. My mind was elsewhere, travelling and exploring its own capacity, even so, it had never settled upon my mother, and that was why I never wrote to her. And when the thought was lost among the thousand new things in my head, writing to her was just not the top priority anymore. Sometimes, I would remember that I should write to my mother, but then the task became more like an obligation, and it wasn't from a pure desire of letting her know that I was well.

However, at some moment in time, like right now, when I'd remembered the time that I spent with my mother, a pure desire of letting her know that I was well or letting her know that she was in my mind came up again.

I glared at the white paper and black ink on the table and a pointed pen in my hand. Carefully, I dipped the pen inside an ink-pot and started scraping a short message to her.

*Dear mother,*

*I am sorry if I have not written to you often. I have been busy and was taking in everything that is going on in my life. Oh, mother, you would not believe me if I told you about all of it. You won't believe how people in Barcelona are with my sculptures and that I have met a gentleman who has taught me all about the world. He is my master, Don Vicenç.*

*But, above all else, I hope that you are well. It's the last day of the year today and my birthday. I can't believe that this is the second year that I am not celebrating with you. I think I am no longer the boy you remember. I promise you that next time, I am going to celebrate it with you.*

*I'd like to tell you everything in this letter, but it'd be too long. So, when I am back, you will have to stay up the whole night to listen to what I have to say.*

*Until I see you again.*

*J.*

I kept it short and simple because I could not tell her every single achievement or every experience that I had had. I wasn't so sure if she'd believe me if I did. But then everything would be too long and take too much time to get everything down on paper. Also, I told myself that I could not mention anything too private, as I wasn't so sure if the letter would reach her unopened or if it would ever reach her at all. At that moment, I just hoped that it would. For there was no exact address at where to reach her, but I had to take my chances. I specifically addressed on the envelope to anyone in the hanging town to pass it to a lady with red hair, who lives in the hut in the wood, and that she comes to sell herbs every weekend at the market.

To get the task done, I slipped quietly off to my room and

found that the apartment was busy with servants, men and women I hadn't seen before. Every one of them was buzzing here and there, preparing the apartment for the guests. I stopped one of the servants that I remembered seeing before and told her to make sure that she post the letter. I placed some coins in her palm before I slipped back into my room.

Now that the little task had been lifted off my chest, I thought, it'd be better to really get some sleep to keep my good senses and upper-class manner intact before meeting Don Vicenç's guests.

I awoke again to loud footsteps and noises outside of my door. I quickly freshened up and went out.

Guests were moving everywhere around the apartment. Tonight, only Don Vicenç's closest circles were invited, but still, the number of guests in the apartment must have been more than twenty. There was no problem with the space being too cramped because the apartment itself was enormous. There were too many rooms than the four of us could ever use. Some of the rooms in the apartment I had still never set foot in, and that would include Don Vicenç's private chamber. Amelia and Cecilia had their own room, but I believed Amelia must be spending most of her time in Don Vicenç's. So, that made many of the rooms in the apartment deserted. However so, right now, guests were roaming everywhere. Most of them I knew well from the previous outings. I spotted Delilah and Don Bernado among the crowd, as well as Count Alfonso and Countess Helena, dressed in their usual best.

'Here is my man! The star of the party,' said Count Alfonso, who approached me as soon as he spotted me. He placed his heavy arm over my shoulder. 'You have truly captivated me. Truly! You wouldn't believe it if I told you that I spend most of my days in my art collection room.' His voice was bravado, and his squeeze was firm.

Count Alfonso continued complimenting and praising my work as well as sharing the same disappointment over and over again that he had not managed to win an auction for any of my sculptures, as some Lord from France had outbid him.

More lords and ladies arrived, and I excused myself away to search for Don Vicenç. I had no intention of doing so, but I did wonder why he hadn't shown his face to his so-called devotees. And this so-called last day of the year party hadn't been going long, but guests were already starting to get drunk.

Food and wine were being served by the servants, both new and old faces. And a supply of wine never stopped flowing in the dining room, it also followed the guests into the salon where they talked, then to the gambling room, where triple amounts of wine washed over their good senses.

I quietly slipped away from the crowd again. Tonight, I didn't quite feel like associating with anyone. Being on my own with a little peace was all I asked for. The noises outside were impossible to block out. I lit the opium and decided to continue with my unfinished sculpture. I had only just sat down behind the table before the door of my room was thrown wide open. Cecilia walked in. She always knew where to find me.

'You forgot to knock again,' I told her. Cecilia ignored my comment and closed the door. My gaze followed her small frame as she approached me. She was wearing a beautiful lilac pastel gown.

Cecilia stopped next to where I sat.

'So,' she said, her head slightly tilted to one side, her hands were on her hips.

'So?' I said after I was sure that she wasn't going to say something else after her 'so.'

'Please tell me that the reason you are hiding here alone is not because of Delilah,' she finally announced. Her eyes narrowed.

'The reason I'm in my private room is that I seek my privacy,' I said, making sure that Cecilia caught my sarcastic tone.

'So you no longer care that she is here? You have gotten over her?'

'What do you expect me to say?'

'Say that you have completely forgotten about her.'

'I am in no mood to discuss her or anyone tonight,' I said and dragged in the opium I had lit before.

'Then, are you open to a discussion about the amount of opium and laudanum you have been taking?' Cecilia said as she placed her small hand on my cheek for me to look at her face.

'That is why my work comes out so well. My state of mind is at its best,' I told her with a smile.

'No, you don't need that thing to justify how good your work is.' She removed the strand of hair that fell over my forehead. 'Just be careful, will you? One of these days, you won't be saying those words. Can't you see that it's getting—'

'Oh, please,' I said, cutting her off. How could she lecture me when she enjoyed it when I shed my good conscience. 'Don't

217

worry about me. You should go enjoy yourself. Do you know that Don Diego could not take his eyes off you?' I said.

Cecilia lifted her brows in surprise, 'Oh, so you have noticed after all. But Don Diego must know better . . . Anyway, you don't mind him then?' She cocked her head to one side.

'Should I?' I asked, turning away from her slightly as I blew out a cloud of smoke.

Cecilia's facial expression changed. She took the pipe from my hand and threw it on the table. She then slowly bent down to look me in the eyes before she planted a soft kiss on my lips. Cecilia still smelled like vanilla. Her lips lingered on mine, and I responded to her kiss. It was full of hunger, but after a while, her kiss felt different; the sensations from the touch of her lips shifted to yearning and longing.

But, of what?

I stopped kissing her, but I didn't push her away. Then, I saw her long lashes flutter open, and her blue eyes were looking at me sadly before she slowly pulled away.

She stood upright, and the glimpse of sadness in her eyes turned into annoyance. 'Maybe you should care about what I'm going to be doing with Don Diego after all,' she said as she stomped away and out of the door.

I took a long breath. I knew she was upset. I knew what that kiss meant, what Cecilia wanted.

She wanted to be loved.

But how could I give it to her if I didn't even know exactly what love was? Was it the same kind that I had given to my mother? Or the feeling I once had for Delilah? My feelings for Cecilia weren't the same as any of those. I knew that I liked to have her around more than her sister. But when her kisses asked me for more? I could not give her what she wanted. I preferred the same Cecilia, who enjoyed my kiss and my body without any expectations, and Cecilia who didn't judge me. Now, she was making me uncomfortable by trying to destroy what we had between us.

Had my heart completely been eroded with rust?

I put away the opium as it was having an effect on me, and I could not think straight when I needed to. I stood up off the chair and looked out the window. It was so dark outside. Tonight, the moon was completely hidden by the thick amount of clouds.

I heard the door click open again.

'Cecilia, you have to learn how to knock now. And I'm really in no mood to talk about whatever you want to say,' I said without turning around.

'This is the second time that you have addressed me by another woman's name. And I am not so pleased about the name you just called me.'

I turned around. It was Delilah who stood in front of the door.

'What are you doing here?' I asked.

'What about a friendly face who just wanted to say hi?'

'Now you are calling me your friend? Am I not your lowly humble servant?'

'Oh, dear Jacobo, don't be so bitter. Why do you still remember my silly words I said years ago?'

Delilah's walked towards me and stood in front of me. She extended her hand to feel the side of my face. I looked down at her beautiful face. But the effect that she used to have on me was gone. Her touch no longer burned my skin. My heart didn't beat as fast, making me forget to lose all my senses in the world. And she smelled too much like Don Vicenç's stupid perfume. I pulled slightly away from her touch. And Delilah's face changed instantly. I knew that this time she no longer had power over me. But Delilah still wanted a taste of me, and she wanted to get my attention.

'Don't be so bitter,' I told her. And with a temper like Delilah, she hit my chest with her fist. I grabbed her delicate wrist and pushed her against the windowpane.

'What does that woman have that I don't?' said Delilah.

'Everything, but I like your temper though,' I told her, and before she could open her mouth and insult me, I kissed her. Finally, tasting the first woman that had awoken my desire.

We fell under a spell of lustfulness. I discarded all the words that Cecilia had warned me about dealing with whatever that belongs to Don Vicenç or the pleading to be with anyone but Delilah.

# Chapter Twenty-One

Delilah slipped out of my room silently as she didn't want Don Vicenç or her husband to know about what had happened. All of the evidence of our lustful deeds where Delilah scratched and bit me was hidden beneath the fabric of our clothes.

As the night went on, the guests of all ranks started to mingle with one another inappropriately. They were all drowning in wine or opium or maybe both until a few minutes before midnight when everyone, in unison, started to walk towards the reception room.

I followed the crowd as they entered the room. The servants that were busy walking back and forth along the hall were nowhere to be seen now. Suddenly, everything was quiet. Only the shuffling of footsteps against the wooden floor could be heard. I was surprised at everyone's behaviour, from drunkards to tame and solemn creatures who would do anything that the master told them to. I was the last to enter the room. It surprised me that the large reception room that used to be elegantly furnished had been all cleared out. All pieces of furniture and paintings were gone. Tapestries at the windows were drawn, leaving the flickering candlelight to find all the trouble lighting up the room.

Everyone was gathering in a circle now. And between the gap of skirts and doublets, I could see the objects that they were surrounding; there was a small round table in the middle of the room and beside it—a metal cage with a large curved horned goat.

I had no idea how and when that curved horned goat ended up in the middle of Don Vicenç's reception room. Everything started to get interesting. No one had paid any attention to me, so I stood near the entrance and watched.

Suddenly, all of the men and women started to hum in low tune. First, it sounded like a sob, but when the humming got louder and louder, it became more like a chant with a disturbing melody. Then, at one point, everyone seemed to be lost in a trance. And that was when Amelia and Cecilia walked into the middle of the circle. In their hands, a shiny metal glimmered. I wasn't prepared when both of them stabbed the goat's neck at the same time. The creature cried in terror and thrashed in pain, but there was nowhere for it to escape. Two knives stuck out from each side of its neck. The twins chanted in unison as they brought a large bowl to hold the goat's blood that spurted out of its neck.

The chanting of the disturbing melody never ceased when the twins, one by one, used the goat's blood to draw an eight-pointed star on everyone's forehead.

I watched everything in awe. I knew that Cecilia was involved in a dark cult, but I had no idea it would be like this.

Then, after Amelia finished drawing on the last person's forehead, the loud chanting stopped, and they all went back to humming in low voices again.

Right at the moment, I heard footsteps approaching from outside of the room, and the last person who entered was Don Vicenç himself. He wore a large cloak that trailed after him, and on top of his head was the head of a goat, the same type that was now lying dead on the floor. Its horn curved backwards, and the pointy end ended just above his shoulder.

People parted for Don Vicenç to pass, and the circle was formed again. I could see Amelia approach him, and out of the same bucket that was filled with goat's blood, she drew the same eight-pointed star on his forehead. Upon one of the lines that Amelia drew, Don Vicenç announced, 'Blessed by love . . .

'Blessed by appetite . . .

'Blessed by abundance . . .

'Blessed by relaxation . . .

'Blessed by passion . . .

'Blessed by encouragement . . .

'Blessed by dignity . . .'

I knew it was the deadly seven sins that the Bible talked about. But the words that Don Vicenç used were distorted and used in totally opposite meanings.

And upon the closing of the last corner of the star, he said, 'Blessed by eternity.' Then, Don Vicenç raised his voice that was full of confidence, 'Greetings, my devoted fellows. Another year, we have accomplished what was expected of us, and together, we are moving closer and closer towards our goal.'

Everyone around started to mumble in agreement.

'What are we without faith?' Don Vicenç continued. 'What are we without an anchor with the willpower that guides us and gives a purpose to our lives? Of those who are lost shall find no purpose. They have nothing to wake up for. Each and every day would go by meaningless, until one day they would ask themselves, where has their time gone?

'But for us, we are blessed with guidance! We have been chosen to fulfil the wishes of our god.

'What do we live for if not for faith and the belief that we are achieving the purpose that has been given to us? We know that each and every day, that task is more fulfilled.

'We embrace our human appetites while others blindly tried to deny all those blessings. Why do we have to deny and suppress our pure desires? We must enjoy what our body and our mind yearn for. We know what we want, and we know who we are . . . All these urges were given to us by god. We are blessed by love, appetite, abundance, relaxation, passion, encouragement, dignity . . . and he wants us to fulfil . . . and when everything is fulfilled, my dear fellows, we are also fulfilled, then we fulfil our life with god's commands. And he will bless us! Every day, every minute, and every second, we are walking closer to the hall of eternity.'

People around him started to hum and sway left and right like they were possessed.

'The stronger our willpower is, the more successful we will be. And tonight, the urges of your nature will be stronger, and you shall be set free. You shall embrace it and fulfil your needs because tomorrow, you will feel anew and afresh as if you have been reborn from your own flesh.' Don Vicenç finished his speech, and from inside of his cloak, he pulled out a sculpture, my woman sculpture. And once the base of the sculpture thudded on the surface of the table, everyone gasped in unison, and all the humming stopped.

An uncontrollable murmur began. Don Vicenç slowly shed his large cloak, and underneath it, he was fully naked.

Men and women of every rank and age went hysterical as they rushed forward towards the woman sculpture. Some people started to mumble something as if they were talking to someone. They were lost in some kind of trance, and at the next moment, without awareness, I saw them all kneeling around the figure while they started to undress themselves. It was a picture I could not get out of my head.

All hands were roaming over each other. Their voices started to moan in unison. They started kissing and groping. They were all enjoying themselves so greatly that I had to look away. Their clothes were fumbled alongside them on the floor. To the right, Count Alfonso was lost in his trance of having some woman's lips upon his body. And everyone else was lost in their unaware desires.

Amelia and Delilah were kissing Don Vicenç. Their bare backs were smeared with the goat's blood from Don Vicenç's hands.

I was confused and felt oddly sick in my stomach.

All of a sudden, a woman's voice next to me said, 'Look at what you have done to them.'

I quickly turned towards her. She was unaffected by this unusual dark magic. Then, I could see in her eyes something I recalled but could not put my hand on.

The woman started to run her tongue along her teeth. The gesture I had remembered except that her teeth weren't sharp and her tongue was of human's and not black with a slash in between. 'Look what kind of power you have unleashed,' said the woman, her voice a tone lower than the voice of a woman.

I looked carefully into the dark pit of her eyes.

'It's you . . .' I said, confused and beguiled. 'Am I dreaming? Was all this a kind of hallucination?'

'Oh, far from it. I am of your own flesh and blood. I am of the deepest and darkest part of your soul.'

'What kind of macabre thing are you doing to them?'

'I only enhanced their existing desires . . . I did them no harm. Can't you see that they seem to be immensely enjoying this?'

I stumbled back to the door as the woman approached, her eyes pitch black, her lips curved into an uncanny smile, a smile that only appeared only on her lips, but her eyes showed no emotion.

'I have been bored, you know. That man locked me up and kept me to himself. But, well, how could I complain? He has been feeding me with all of his delicious sins.' The woman licked her lips and smiled. 'And now he has brought all of these people to me. I could burst into flames with all of this immense magnitude of desire. I bet you can feel all the energy inside you, too . . .'

I looked from the woman to those people. Her dark gaze was exploring me. She walked towards me, her gaze unwavering, her pace uncannily steady. She was floating nearer and nearer until her pitch-dark gaze swallowed me whole once again. My visions became black, like I was standing up too fast from a chair. When the blackness faded away from my eyes, the woman was no longer there, and instead of looking at her uncanny smile, her face was replaced by Cecilia. But I wasn't looking at Cecilia. She was lost in a trance, and slowly as if she didn't know me, she started to walk towards the sculpture, undressing the rest of her remaining clothes. I knew then that the sculpture, that woman, or whatever kind of dark witchcraft it was, must be the cause of it.

I stepped over those debauched people and the pile of clothes. Looking directly at the sculpture, I wasn't sure if it was a trick of the light, but the lips were curling into that uncanny smile.

I felt a pang of unrecognised energy that filled the air of the room, and instead of losing myself like other people, this energy filled me, like a satisfaction when I was moulding a sculpture and pouring my soul into it.

Slowly, I stepped closer to the sculpture, careful not to touch the muddling people on the floor. And once I reached it, I held it up from the table and quickly slipped the sculpture out of the room, straight into my own. I didn't know why I had done it, but it was like the energy was a part of me. And it made me feel content and fulfilled.

Once I reached my room, I didn't bother to light the candle. I placed the figure on the floor as I was still trying to understand what it had done to those people, and on the contrary, what kind of fulfilment I was feeling. It was like I had everything within my grasp, within my fingers, and I could have everything that I wanted.

But what did I want? And can it be achieved? I thought about what I could do with that kind of power. But somehow, it scared me.

I remained motionless in the corner of the room, looking at the woman sculpture on the floor. I was tempted to destroy it. Would destroying it destroy part of me?

In the quietness, all the noises outside intensified. A moan of pleasure ceased only once it was replaced by a mixture of shouting and a howling and a mumble, echoing along the hallway and right in front of my room.

'How could you do it in front of me?!' A woman squealed.

'What? You were just kissing Marquess Cristobal in front of me!' came a voice of another man.

'Oh, you insufferable man! You did that behind my back, didn't you?'

'I—I, no, I mean, I don't know what was going with me, and with you, too, and everyone else! Maybe we had too much to drink, or maybe it was those poppies!'

'Excuses!'

'What about you and Cristobal? And where is that sculpture? I would like to see it again.'

'Right, the sculpture! I have never seen, no, I have never felt anything like that before. . .'

Then came more muffled footsteps and more voices penetrating from behind the door.

'What is that sculpture? Where can I get one like that?'

'I need one of those. Oh, I would pay any price.'

'It's Don Vicenç's cousin! Jacobo! He made it!'

'Oh, Don Vicenç. Here you are. We all would all like to see the sculpture again. Where has it gone?'

'Please, Don Vicenç, I would like to commission your cousin to make one for me.'

Then came the booming voice that I knew so well, 'Gentlemen, I will be informing all of you once the new pieces are done, and we will have an auction. After you all have a glimpse of the new sculpture, the new symbol of our group, I assure you that the new piece that is to come will not disappoint. Right now, I must talk to my cousin. Please, be patient, Marquess, Count, you will get your hands on yours soon.

I took another glimpse at the woman figure on the floor.

Footsteps trod back and forth past my room. And I could hear the front door open and shut for the thousandth time. Finally, my own door burst open by the force of Don Vicenç.

'Where is it?' Don Vicenç's voice boomed with command. He scanned my room in the darkness until he spotted what he came for. He took a quick step towards the sculpture and grabbed it from the floor. Eyes shone with fury, he said, 'I'd better make one thing straight. Do not touch my stuff if I haven't given you permission. Do not ever try to steal anything from me. Be sure to remember that.' He pointed his finger at my face.

Before Don Vicenç was about to leave my room, he looked back at me, and his eyes had the look that I knew so well; it was the look of judgment and disdain, the one he had given to the beggars along the streets of Barcelona. 'And by the way, the party has ended, so you'd better finish that figure of yours before sunrise. Make as many as you can, and give the piece that you are done with to me first. I do not care about the amount of my opium you take in order to get that head of yours flowing, but if you cannot finish the work, you will not be allowed access to any of my opium and laudanum! Do you understand? And be quick! Time and money wait for no one!'

His words cut me inches deep because, at that moment, his intentions and his plan were becoming clearer to me. Don Vicenç knew too well about the poppies and addiction. That was why he never let himself become bound by it. But for me, he wanted to have that power over me, to chain me under his authority. With the money that he had given me from the sales of my sculpture, even if it was more than a wager of unknown servants, I could not leave him and expect to have the same lifestyle, and Don Vicenç must have calculated his every move in dealing with a stupid boy like me. At that point, I'd never complained about any money he had given me because I had no need of using any coins as whatever I needed, I already had.

Sitting in the dark, I recalled the power that I felt from holding the sculpture in my hand, and I knew right away what I needed to do. I needed to get rid of Don Vicenç before he could get rid of me. Before that time came, I would have to calculate my move and wait for my time to strike back. I needed to be more careful when dealing with Don Vicenç now, as I could not let him have the upper hand over me anymore.

I would let the devil sculpture eat him alive, destroying him from the inside out.

# Chapter Twenty-Two

The past few days, I had been resisting the urge of sucking in the cloud of opium that called me to quench my burning thirst.

As I couldn't sleep, I came to sit by the window and second by second, I watched the sun slowly unveiled its light upon the shadow of dawn. Everything was quiet, but inside my head were a thousand voices, murmuring their way through. I tried to breathe and seek a quiet corner in my brain.

A shuffling of skirts could be heard along the hallway, and what came next was the whispering voices of Amelia and Cecilia.

'We have sworn to Mistress Sabine. Without her, we would still be rotting away in that orphanage. Get your senses back,' said the voice that I knew belonged to Amelia.

'But, it's different. I love Mistress Sabine, but she is dead. I think I—'

'And what is it that makes you lose your focus?' Amelia hissed in a sharp tone at her twin sister.

'Because . . . oh, because you are not the one everybody disregards. Because of my ugly freckles, men don't like me. Everyone chooses you over me, don't they? And why would they bother to choose me when there is a better version of myself standing next to me all the time?' Cecilia said in a distressed and sarcastic tone. 'Only Mistress Sabine was the one who chose me over you and—and Jacobo did, too. He even preferred me over that woman, Delilah! Maybe I want a different path in life, a life where I could make a family and have children.'

'Are you mad? Listen to yourself!' Amelia hissed. 'Our life is far from normal. We have a purpose. Oh, don't tell me that you are falling in love with that man. You can't let whatever you feel towards him block our path and our plan. We have found our saviour who will get rid of all the non-believers and avenge the death of Mistress Sabine! You told me that yourself, every day.'

I remained as quiet as possible and kept on listening to their angry whispers.

'I am not so sure anymore, Amelia . . .'

'How do you even know that he loves you back? You talk about family, but you are not even sure that he wants you!'

'He chose me over that woman, didn't he? And he does not think that my freckles are ugly!' Cecilia protested, her voice raised.

'Of course, because he is enjoying the pleasure your body gives him,' Amelia said mockingly.

'Don Vicenç doesn't think so. He never calls me to him. He only calls you. It's because he doesn't want to look at my freck-led face. And I'm tired of moving around. I want to settle down. You know that Don Vicenç won't keep us around forever.'

'Why would you say that?' The mocking tone from Amelia was still apparent.

What followed was Cecilia sarcastic tone, 'Oh, Amelia, you tell me to not be blind, but you must know that a person like

Don Vicenç lies all the time. I know he tells you that he loves you, but—'

'Oh, shut up! You are saying this because you are jealous of me!'

'No! I tell you this because I know that he is telling you that he loves you, but when you aren't paying attention, he slips away with Delilah! Of all women in the world, it has to be her, who insults and scorns us.'

They were almost shouting now. I didn't have to keep still for them to not hear any movement from my room any longer.

'Oh, please, Celia. I didn't know that you will go this far with your jealousy. I have always known that it's the worst thing in you. But you, my dear sister, you are letting it into your head. And that man, Jacobo, you are letting him fool you. You are blinded by a love that doesn't even exist,' Amelia said scornfully.

'And you think that the so-called love between you and Don Vicenç is real?' Cecilia threw back the scornful words. 'Now that I have told you he is fucking that woman, you can find out for yourself because she will be here with him again soon!'

'Oh, shut up and leave me alone, won't you? And come to your senses!'

I heard footsteps stomping away heavily. Then, a curse word came from Cecilia. Her footsteps were pacing back and forth and came to a halt right in front of my door. They stayed only a few seconds before I could hear them retreat.

I thought to myself, were women's hearts supposed to be so vulnerable?

The late morning that day and just like the late morning of the days before, Don Vicenç received an exceedingly large amount of calls from his friends, requesting to see me, and of course, Don Vicenç told all of them that I was sick and was unable to meet anyone.

Some of them had come to offer large amounts of money to buy the woman sculpture, and to which, to all of the offers, Don Vicenç had bitterly refused.

In the late afternoon, when Don Vicenç knocked upon my door, I had to let him in.

Amelia and Cecilia trailed in after him. They went to sit at the end of my bed while Don Vicenç strode off to open the tapestries, then he turned and looked at me. Don Vicenç stood directly in the middle of the window, blocking out the extremely bright light from the sun that shone in behind him. To me, he appeared like a dark shadow in the middle of a pure white canvas. And apparently, his bitterness towards me had recoiled into his good nature once again.

'Count Alfonso just left,' said Don Vicenç. 'And he just offered an unimaginable amount of money for you to create a special sculpture like that woman sculpture especially for him.' His eyes glowed with greed. I was still contemplating his words when Don Vicenç continued, 'Why do you look so dull? Don't tell me that you are still vexed about what I said the other day. You know, sometimes people get angry,' he said with an unnatural chuckle.

But I knew that this was just Don Vicenç's pretentious self, and he knew that I knew it; for a smart person like Don Vicenç, he could see the burning hatred in my eyes that I tried in vain to hide. I wondered how much pride he had to swallow in order to say those words to me.

'It's not about that. I am just unsatisfied with my work. I wanted to get the best out of it. So we won't disappoint whoever that pays the highest price,' I said. Then I realised that Don Vicenç didn't have any problem because the lies just came out too easily.

There was a hairsbreadth of a pause before Don Vicenç said, 'And I believe you are done with the recent sculpture?'

His shadow form walked closer to me.

'Oh, yes, I want to see, too.' I heard Cecilia said with a clap.

'We all hope that you won't disappoint us,' Amelia added in, 'You must know the stir you have caused over these past few days. We were unable to rest because of the guests.'

I turned to look at the twins who were now on their feet. 'Oh, yes. I finished it this morning. It's specially made for Don Vicenç. I'll show it to you,' I told all of them.

That afternoon, I had permanently shattered the mask of my master, the one that he had worn to face me all along. When I pulled off the white fabric, it exposed a half a meter-tall plaster sculpture of a man with a sense of pride and triumph, capturing a large serpent in his hands, holding it up in the air victoriously. But its face was of an ugly beast, baring its teeth aggressively to every onlooker.

Since Don Vicenç said that he was going to take away the sculpture I intended to make for myself, I hid that one and made a new one for him.

'What is this sick joke?' Don Vicenç approached me, grabbing my shirt. He was no longer a dark shadow that seemed to loomed over me. Up close, his face was turning red, matching the dark maroon doublets he was wearing. He pushed me against the wall. 'You think a low scum like you could insult me?' he shouted. His eyes were full of hatred, burning stronger than the one in mine. But I could not stop chuckling at the resemblance I saw between my master and the beast right now, for their eyes were wild and bloodthirsty.

Don Vicenç's hands that grabbed my shirt were trembling with anger. I was sure that he was going to use his force on me, but he let go of my shirt and went straight to the sculpture. With the metal tool next to it, he picked it up and started to smash everything down with full force. He didn't stop at the sculpture, for his anger was spent on the table, chair and everything he deemed worthy to release his wrath on.

Amelia and Cecilia were protesting and shouting for him to calm down, but it was no use, as one object after another, Don Vicenç smashed everything into pieces. I watched with contempt in my eyes, oh, how I loved to see him get so affected by a little bit of mockery.

Amelia was crying now.

I was sneering.

Don Vicenç kept on smashing.

Cecilia rushed towards me, 'Please, Jacobo, leave, leave.' But I told her no. I could not miss witnessing part of Don Vicenç's true self, and if he was going to direct his anger on me, I wasn't going to just stand around and let his madness pour over me. I was going to fight back. I was the same size as him now and younger. However, the situation didn't come to that; Don Vicenç came upon the original gentleman sculpture that I had hidden among the rubble of useless woman sculptures, then his wrath subsided and evaporated into nothingness. His face was serene. The only evidence of the man he was before was all the broken pieces of furniture and scattered plaster, clay, and stones.

Don Vicenç adjusted his clothes and hair with his right hand, whereupon his left was my sculpture of a man of pride. Everything in the room was quiet now, except the sound of Amelia's sobs. Within a second later, Don Vicenç walked out of the room without looking at my face. Amelia, who was crying earlier, swiped her tears away with the back of her hands before she went after Don Vicenç.

I was still smiling when Cecilia came to me and adjusted my crumpling shirt. 'Oh, Jacobo, this isn't funny at all. Are you out of your mind? I thought he was going to hurt you. Why do you provoke him so?'

'Wasn't it you who told me that you would trade anything to see the face of—'

'This is different!' Cecilia cut me off, 'and you know it!' she said with apparent anger, but her voice was of a whisper. 'You are lucky that his greed surpasses his anger. And you don't want him to ruin your face and break your nose like that stableman back at the castle.'

'What stableman? Andrea?'

'If that's the stableman's name, then it's him.'

'What did he do?'

'Who?'

'Andrea, what did he do?'

'Oh, now you are worried about the stableman?' said Cecilia as she pointed around the room. 'Look around you. How are you going to sleep in this wreck tonight?'

'Never mind about that.'

Cecilia looked at me as if I was joking, but the look on my face must have told her that I wasn't.

'Tell me about Andrea,' I said.

She eyed me speculatively before she said, 'I just heard from Amelia that the stableman, I mean, Andrea, was having some relationship with one of the maids, you see. And he planned to take the maid and his sister away from the castle. His sister works in the castle, too. You must know her.

'Yes,' I told Cecilia because I knew she was talking about Flor.

'But, then, I suppose Don Vicenç found out. And not only that Andrea was messing with his maids, but he wanted to take both of his maids away. And by now you must know that those maids weren't just maids, but they were his . . . I wouldn't call lovers; they are more like his property, I would say.

'After Don Vicenç found out, he got so angry that he beat the man up. Broke his nose and part of his face. But I don't know why he is still there, though. And why he didn't leave or why Don Vicenç still keeps him.'

I snorted with the knowledge of the true reason why Andrea had such hatred towards me. It was because his hatred toward Don Vicenç must be so great that he would hate anyone on good terms with Don Vicenç. And Andrea must love Flor so much that he sacrificed his own pride to stay where she was and tried in vain to protect her. I wondered about Flor, as the last thing I heard was that she was pregnant with Don Vicenç's child, but Don Vicenç had not set foot in the castle for almost two years. The baby must be at least a year old by now. I hope Don Vicenç had enough decency to let her and the baby stay in the castle even though he didn't seem to care about the baby at all. He was drowning in greed in this city.

'Oh, please, can we talk in my room?' said Cecilia. 'I cannot stand it here. All I see is Don Vicenç's anger repeating in my head. And I want to show you something.'

'If that's what you want,' I said as I walked to the door. 'After you, then?'

I realised that since I arrived at this apartment, I had never entered Cecilia's room before. It was she who always came to mine.

Stepping into her room, a familiar vanilla scent touched my sense of smell. The thick tapestries were drawn, obscuring the light from the outside, dimming everything in her room.

'I'm going to let more light in,' said Cecilia as she walked to the window.

'Never mind. I quite like it like this,' I said, following her footsteps. As I was curious where her room overlooked, I peeked out through the tapestries, and upon the courtyard, slowly moving out through the main door, was Don Vicenç's carriage.

Where was he off to now?

'I am going to light some candles, then,' Cecilia said as she walked to a small table where a bunch of candles laid together with strange-looking objects and some blackish twigs. I looked at Cecilia; after she lit all six candles on the table, she put the blackish twig on the candle flames. The smell was of vanilla, the one I had smelt in her hair before, and the same smell that had lured me to her.

'Now, I see the source of your smell,' I told Cecilia.

'Oh, yes. They all like this sweet smell.'

'They?'

'Men and devils all together. And it helps me think straight, too! Like with you and opium.'

By now, I wasn't surprised by the fact that Cecilia was involved in Don Vicenç's religious occult that worshipped devils. She told me once she was working for Don Vicenç, but I didn't have an exact idea until now. I understood the story of Mistress Sabine and the unusual behaviour she had shown me before. I understood the reason why Mistress Sabine was hanged; it was because the church knew that she was associated with witchcraft and black magic, and the only punishment for that type of activity was death. And now, Cecilia was following her mistress's footsteps.

Cecilia must have sensed something wrong in me, and that was why she had shown interest in me since the day we met. But I was sure that she didn't know about my ability to unleash the darkness inside of me.

How did I end up involved in all of this? How did I manage to have that kind of power? What was my role in this whole story? Questions swarmed into my head.

'Our master is a dangerous man if you cross him,' Cecilia's words caught me off from my thoughts. 'There are more things that you don't know about. He is more dangerous than you think. You have no idea when people start to come to him but asking to see you. I could see it in his face that his patience with you is wearing thin. And the situation after today . . . I think you should go back to the castle and stay away from him for a while.

# CHAPTER TWENTY-TWO

Amelia and I could try to talk to him and make things better.'

She lowered herself to sit at the end of the bed, and I did the same.

'What else did he do? What wicked things has he done that I don't know about?' I asked.

'Oh, Jacobo, there are many more things that you don't know about him. You see, he has been very good to you these past years. I would say he likes you as well. But before that, back in the castle, I know one of the reasons he kept you away in the attic is because there is a place, a hidden place. Its entrance is in Don Vicenç's private study. I have only seen part of it, but I know that's the place where Don Vicenç committed his wicked deeds.'

'And you know about these wicked things?'

'Not exactly . . .' she said. 'But I know there are things that he's hiding within the castle.'

'Why are you telling me all this? You work for Don Vicenç, aren't you supposed to be loyal to him?'

'Because—because everything is changing,' Cecilia said without looking at my face, then reluctantly she added, 'and I was given a sign at the last ceremony.'

'What sign? Don't tell me a sign from the devil.'

'Yes, a woman devil with a black tongue and midnight eyes. And that is why everything is changing. Our theory before must be wrong.'

'What?' I said, surprised that Cecilia could also see her. 'What—what theory are you talking about?'

'Of course, that Don Vicenç is our liberator. I have talked to Amelia about it, but I didn't tell her that the sign actually pointed to you. I just told Amelia that maybe it's not Don Vicenç after all. But she refused to listen to me because she believes that everything points to Don Vicenç. But if Don Vicenç knew about this . . .'

Cecilia's face went so pale, and her blue eyes shone with fear. 'Oh no, Jacobo, the prophecy . . .' Suddenly, she got up off the bed and went straight to the small table and lit more incense. In the small corner of her room, she mumbled in a weird tongue that I could not understand. Everything was too bizarre for me to raise a question or to ask what she was doing.

Cecilia held up a knife on the candle flame before she slit her hands, and waited for the blood to drip down into a small black bowl, then she came to me.

'Drink it.'

'Are you mad? And what prophecy are you talking about? Is there something that I should know and you are not telling me?' I said. 'And I'm not going to drink your blood!'

'This is a matter of life and death. Do as I say. If I speculate this, soon, Amelia will, too. And you don't want her to find out before I do.'

'Find out what?'

'Drink it!' Cecilia persisted.

I could feel that Cecilia was serious and she was scared. I did as I was told. The smell was strong and metallic. When Cecilia saw that I had drunk it all, she took my hand and slit it before I could protest.

'Ow! This is the second time you've done that without telling me.'

'It's not a big cut. It will heal.'

She waited for my blood to flow inside the bowl. It was a second before she was going to do the same thing as I did with her blood when the door clicked open, and the person who entered could not be anyone but Delilah.

'Oh, am I disturbing something?' Delilah's voice echoed through the sudden quietness of the room. Upon seeing Delilah, Cecilia placed the small black bowl that contained my blood on the table next to the door, then her small frame went straight to Delilah. 'Why are you here! This is my room! Who told you to come here uninvited?'

'Oh, don't look so surprised,' Delilah said with a chuckle. 'I came here to see him, not you! Vicenç is meeting my husband and Count Alfonso. So, I took the liberty to come to see a dear friend of mine. We have been getting to know each other for a while, isn't that right, Jacobo?' Delilah addressed me, but I didn't answer. Still, Delilah's voice echoed through the room. 'I went to his room, and it was quite a mess. I heard his voice from this room. Of course, I have no idea that this room belongs to you, and I didn't know that you were here as well.'

It was true that over the past few days, whenever Delilah came to the apartment, she never forgot to slip into my room. We would enjoy the temptation of the flesh and lay together for a while before she had to leave. I did it just to spite Don Vicenç. I didn't think of Cecilia's feelings.

Cecilia turned back to look at me. Her face was full of anguish, and her lips trembled. The anger that had built up in her just now was gone. She retreated from the door without looking at me.

'I want both of you to leave,' said Cecilia.

'Celia?' I called out her name and tried to approach her. But she turned away, and her voice was of a whisper when she said, 'Please, leave.'

'I think she wishes to be alone. Should we at least fulfil her wish?' Delilah's sweet voice was becoming cloying in my ears.

I walked to Delilah, grabbed her arm, and led her out of Cecilia's room.

'Oh, you should have seen that woman's face. I knew that she was here, that is why I came. I can't get past the way she looks at me when she walks everywhere with you.' Delilah told me with a mocking smile on her face. I grabbed her arm harder and pulled her towards the exit. 'What are you doing? Now, you are hurting me.'

Upon releasing her, I said, 'I think you should be the one to leave.'

Delilah's face showed a sign of surprise, 'Don't tell me what to do. And don't tell me you are going to go back to that little witch bitch.'

'Just shut up and leave!' I told Delilah once again, and her surprising face slowly turned into malice.

'I will wait for the day when you fall from your grace and go back to being that lowly servant again.'

'And you, too. Let's see when your beauty fades, which will be soon. And that is when you will have no one. A person like you is not worth half of Cecilia. And soon, everyone will realise that.' I walked away from her as I had no further wish to deal with Delilah. The feelings crumpled when I thought of Cecilia's anguished face in my head.

I realised that temptation I saw in Delilah wasn't worth losing Cecilia's friendship at all. I wished that it wasn't too late.

As I stepped into Cecilia's room, she was standing at the same spot with her back to the door.

'Cecilia,' I called out her name, and when she heard my voice, she turned to face me. There were tears all over her face. But the look of anguish was gone; instead, it was replaced with anger and malice.

'Cecilia. I—'

'You said that you are not wicked and cruel? You should rethink. And please, if you don't go for your own sake, then go for mine. I don't want to see you anymore.'

Cecilia's sorrowful face was too much for me to bear. I knew that I was no longer welcome in her life.

Guilt filled me. And I was ashamed of my thoughtless deed.

# Chapter Twenty-Three

I paced back and forth inside my destroyed room. Outside my door, I could hear Cecilia's quick steps leaving through the main entrance. I felt a flood of guilt gushing through my heart and droplets of shame wringing their way out. I was disgusted with myself, of the man I had become. How did I ever think that I had a heart as big as the ocean and a soul as high as the sky?

With a troubled heart and mind, I left Barcelona that day. I took a bag of coins and left everything behind.

There was no point in staying at Don Vicenç's place when I fell out of his favour, and I had also betrayed the only one person who truly loved me. It was too late for me to tell Cecilia that I was sorry for what I had done, and that I was sorry for her friendship that I had taken for granted. If I hadn't been so engrossed in using Delilah as a tool to get back at Don Vicenç, I would have seen into Cecilia's heart and understood her feelings.

Even though I didn't love Cecilia like a lover, she had taught me another kind of love, of which I had never known its existence. Cecilia had taught me what friendship was.

But now I had lost my only friend.

Thinking back to her sorrowful and teary face, I felt tremendous regret gnawing in my chest. I had done the only thing that Cecilia could not forgive, betraying her with the person she hated the most in this world. I realised that the longing I used to feel for Delilah wasn't at all love, but a blinded lust, whose claws had come back to gouge my heart and played their dirty trick on me.

I thought about the last kiss Cecilia had given me, the longing that yearned for more than just my body and goodwill. Cecilia's good feeling of herself for me had grown into a garden of love, but it must all be wilted now.

Oh, how she must have hated me, for I knew that hate that was sparked from love was the strongest hate of all, for it didn't burn out of only bitter hatred but also regret and malice.

I suppose I had learnt my lesson the hard way. And I suppose the only person left in this world who loved me with unconditional love was my mother.

That late afternoon, on horseback, I thought of my mother. Did I also take her love for granted? Almost two years passed since I had left town without seeing her. Even if I did write to her, it was only one-way communication, as she hadn't replied to any of my letters. I didn't even think of going back to see her because I was drowning in my own pride and ego and other black holes of emotion. I had been led astray. But the love of my mother was a twilight in my soul, which had prevented me from being sucked into the black hole of evil, and shown me that everything else wasn't truly dark and lost.

Under all those layers of my corroded heart, a tiny part of me still had a sense of right and wrong. There was a strong conviction in me that still believed in all of the goodness in this world. The deliberate sense of goodness that had been nurtured and grown and all of which was taught to me by my mother. But I also believed that there was a seed of evil that had been planted within me since I was a blank slate. I wasn't as innocent as Adam, whose fault was never in his hand, instead, only blaming Eve for eating from the forbidden tree.

I was like a spinning coin with two sides, waiting for the moment when it ceased to spin, and wondering whether the side of vice or virtue was going to end up permanently on top.

After a short ride out of Barcelona, I brought the horse to a slow gallop as I spotted an inn ahead of me. I knew that if I was going to go for another long ride, I had to stop for some food and water. I hadn't been resting and eating properly for I don't know how long.

After a full meal, I continued on.

It would take me around eight to nine hours non-stop horse ride in full gallop speed to reach the hanging town. But with only one horse, I had to take several short rests along the road for the sake of the horse and my tailbone.

Nightfall touched upon the horizon of the purplish sky when I left the inn. During winter, the sun quickly shied away from the sky, leaving all but darkness behind. It was almost pitch dark along the road now, and the only light that was guiding me was a faint glow from the moon that came and went from time to time from the effect of the clouds that were passing by. I had to use all of my senses to keep riding north and not stray off track.

I took another rest along the road until a cold and humid

wind that carried a scent of rain touched upon my nostrils. Swiftly, I got on the horse and continued with my journey. I rode on, and the wind that was blowing across my face grew stronger each step the horse took me forward. The cold slowly crept under my cloak until it became unbearable. I gained speed in the hope that I would find shelter before the storm arrived. However, I couldn't see any glow of candlelight in the next few kilometres ahead of me.

All of a sudden, the world flashed brightly in front of my eyes, allowing me to see a crossroad not far away in front of me, and at the same time, it dragged my attention upwards. The faint glow of the moon was gone now; instead, there was lightning flashing underneath the thick dark clouds.

It would be another long ride until I reached the hanging town, and it would be impossible to endure the cold and the rain, and it was even more impossible to go on without a rest. The horse itself was showing signs of fatigue with saliva fuming along the corner of his mouth. However, when he heard the groaning sound from the sky, he became alert in an instant. His ears twitched, and his steps faltered. The horse knew what was coming. I had to reign him straight on the road, and with the encouraging words, I whispered in his ears, saying that it wouldn't be long until he would be in a warm place with food and water waiting for him. Then, he finally used his last energy to gallop ahead before the storm could catch us.

When I reached the crossroad, I'd decided to turn to the left, upon the small road that would lead me to Don Vicenç's castle. I wondered about people there, how they must be doing. And especially about Flor and Martín, as the last time I saw them, they weren't living under such good circumstances.

It didn't take long for me to see the silhouette of the castle that cast flashing light upon the midnight sky. But at the window of the castle, there was no light that escaped through the night. I thought all of the servants who must have already been in their quarter, resting their fatigued bodies.

The horse's gallops came to a halt in front of the big wooden door. I jumped down and led the horse directly to the stable, where he would find water and warmth. I also looked forward to finally finding my way inside as I yearned to rest both my body and soul.

Upon walking to the stable, I contemplated what to say to Andrea since I knew that Don Vicenç had ruined his face and taken away his beloved sister with lies and manipulation. Andrea must have also known that Flor was pregnant, as I remembered the conversation I overheard a lifetime ago. However, if Andrea refused to acknowledge me, I would understand his reason. To him, I must be someone who reminded him of Don Vicenç.

When I reached the stable, I didn't find Andrea there. Instead, the man that was sleeping under the coarse blanket near the small fire was someone else, who I had never seen before. When the horses in the barn neighed at the newcomers, the man jolted awake. He rubbed his eyes and looked towards me. The man removed his blanket and got off the hay that was his bed.

When I set my sight upon him, I saw he must have been around sixty, and his eyes were clouded by some kind of white smog.

'Who's there?' he said.

'Where is the previous stableman? Andrea.' I said.

The man walked closer to me. With clouded eyes, he observed and after he had seen the clothes I was wearing, he said, 'Oh, master. I'm sorry. Agnes didn't tell me about anyone coming here tonight.'

I realised that he wasn't completely blind after all.

'No. I didn't send any news.' I said, partly lying as I continued to pretend that I was the master of the castle.

'Oh, please, let me take care of the horse. Master should get inside before the rain gets him wet.'

'Where is Andrea?' I asked him again.

'Is that the name of the previous boy? I guess he is gone? But thanks to him, otherwise, I wouldn't have got this position. And thank you to you too, master, for giving an almost blind man a chance to work.' His smile exposed a few teeth that he had left. He nodded once before leading the horse away.

Before I was about to leave the stable, I spotted Martín's cart. I looked back at the stable for Blanco. And there he was, a medium-sized black horse, jutting his head out of the stable. It was a good sign as Martín must still be working in the castle. I headed straight to the servant's entrance at the back kitchen. It was securely locked. But it didn't matter because I knew one of the locks in the window on the right-hand side of the kitchen was broken. I hoped that someone hadn't fixed it after all, like that hinge on the door of my old room. As I suspected, the broken lock remained unfixed. Winds were rattling against the loose knotted window. I gave a hard push, and the window gave away. Through the window, I went in, and my feet landed on the stone floor at the exact moment the drops of rain landed on the dirt outside.

All the light in the kitchen was blown out, except for a dim fire at the kitchen hearth that gave no warmth to the room, for it was as cold as a minute ago when I stood outside. I went to the small wooden door that led to the servant's quarter, and once I opened the door, a burst of heat swam into my face. The torches upon the wall were all lit, and the fire glowed an intense orange flame throughout the corridor.

The contrast between the dark and cold kitchen and the hellish light and heat of the corridor made me freeze on the ground. It was as if I was about to enter a gateway to hell. But after my imagination subsided, I suddenly felt thankful for the heat, for the cold outside was gnawing from the tips of my fingers through my bones.

Slowly, I walked in, through the corridor and up the stairs, passing the women's quarter. Here, the torches weren't as brightly lit as the corridor down below. It was just enough to provide heat and guide my way in the dark. I expected Agnes to burst through the door at any moment, but as my footsteps trod up the stairs, all the sound was obscured by the thunder and the wheeze of the wind that slipped through the crack of the window.

Along the stairway that led up to the third floor, the memory of a familiar scent hit me straight away. It was a scent I was quite used to by now, the perfumes, a lustful scent that Don Vicenç made his women wear when he bedded them. The memory brought me back to where my life had been strung by my master's hand. When Don Vicenç started to buy me off little by little, and even though I realised what he was doing, I had welcomed it with open arms. Those endless nights, where we would go out to the gentlemen's club with Don Vicenç and his friends. It was the part of my life that I could not forget, for I had sinned so shamelessly and without any regrets.

Further up I went, expecting Martín to be there in his usual seat and being his usual self, working until late at night. But upon reaching the attic, I knew that there was no one there because everything was completely dark, empty, and cold. I went back one level below to grab the nearest torch before going back to my old working room once again.

When I finally entered with the torch, the room glowed from the touch of the burning orange light, and through the small window, the lightning hadn't yet subsided. Everything I could see within the attic room was the same, just like the last memory I had. Martín's unfinished painting jars sat on the table and the dirty white sack that he used to carry lay on the floor. My first instinct when I stepped inside the room was to grab the sack and place it on the table where it had always been. But upon lifting it up, the contents inside of it fell to the floor. The metal tools rattled loudly. I cursed under my breath, and at the same time, felt grateful for the spiteful sound of thunder roaring its anger outside the window. I placed the torch inside the nearest empty jar before I went for the scattering objects that spilt out of the sack. With the burning light shining closely, the objects I was looking at on the floor caught my attention. They were weirdly shaped metal tools that I have never set my eyes on before. Were they supposed to be used for sculpting? I doubted it, mostly because if they were, I would have recognised them. These tools were definitely meant for a different kind of work. Some of them were sharp with a hook and another, a long curvy piece of metal with a grip at the end, attached to a double handle.

Curious as I was, I picked them up, and their weight felt heavy in my hand. I went through the sack, hoping to see more strange objects. Amongst everything else, I stumbled upon the knife that I had brought with me when I left the hanging town. I knew that it was mine because I had scribbled the letter 'J' on its wooden handle, and as expected, the letter was still there as clear as the day I had scribbled it. I thought that I had lost it, but why would it be in Martín's sack? I went through more things, and a piece of folded paper with a faint black ink caught my attention. Getting it out of the sack, I placed it near the fire to see it better. The faint black ink scribbled my name. It was my mother's handwriting. With extreme eagerness, I flipped open the letter.

*Dear boy of mine,*

*If you have opened this letter, you must have already found a secure lodging far away from your modest but loving home, away from my arms. I could never express a proper farewell without letting you know how much seeing you go affected me. I will never be ready to let you go, but I know that one day I have to be strong, and let you have an adventure of your own. I didn't know that the day would come so soon. So, my dear Jacobo, please have the greatest adventure of your life, but you must know that I will always be here whenever you feel like you need to regain your feet in the world out there. You must take care of yourself. You are my only boy, and I know of your nature, you are not completely white or completely black, but as your mother, I always believed that you would know the difference between vice and virtue. If ever, one day, you find yourself stuck in between, please think of me and what I have taught you, and* you *must know that, with me, you can always find my unconditional love to guide you.*

*Do take care of yourself. And do not worry about me. You know I will be fine. I had my adventure with you, and now it's your turn. I wish you all the luck in the world.*

*Lastly, if you find yourself in trouble, sell the bracelet. It should get you enough money to survive for a few months.*

*Your loving mother,*

*Rosinda.*

After I finished reading the letter, the first thing that went through my mind was how could Martín be in possession of my letter? It must be a letter that my mother wrote to me and hid in my bag, somewhere I hadn't been looking carefully, and for that reason, I never knew of its existence. She mentioned a brace-let, but when I went through the sack, I could not find it there. Abruptly, I got up, with a torch in my hand, I went straight to my old room, where my old bag must be located.

The door still creaked loudly to the motion as it swung open. I looked around my old tiny and humid room; everything was all the same. There was no sign of usage for the past few months, as the dust appeared on every surface of the furniture. I thought about the last time I had gone through my bag. It was the first day I arrived at the castle when I had emptied all the apples, then I had never been in need of it since. I went to search in the cupboard, and, there it lay, the leather bag made of a rabbit skin which I had caught in the wood ages ago, hidden underneath the rags that I once called clothes. Going through every pocket,

I could not find anything. I tried once again, this time flipping the bag inside out, and I finally found something out of the ordinary. There was a hole between the fabric and the leather, and upon pressing my hand against it, I could feel something inside. The content must have slipped inside the hole.

Once I managed to retrieve it, it was a dried leaf wrapped with hay strings. Underneath the leaf, I found the bracelet my mother had mentioned, it was made of gold and precious stones, blue and green.

I would have found this earlier if I had searched the bag thoroughly, but I had never thought that my mother would leave me a letter. I knew she wasn't a person who expressed her feelings openly, but thinking about her letter made me realise how much sacrifice she needed to make to implant a seed of virtue within me. She had raised me with everything she had, just to sacrifice everything for me to see me go and have an adventure of my own. And I had embarked on an adventure of sin with open arms, stepping into the line of immorality with a full sense of knowing that it was the wrong thing to do.

I had failed my mother. The sacrifice she made for me had gone to waste. I lived in sin. I betrayed my friend. I had no love or whatsoever for my master, who I at least was supposed to feel grateful for.

Outside, the sky was still weeping and howling as if it knew of my deeds. I went to sit on the nearest bed, trying to understand the reason behind Martín's doing. He must have thoroughly gone through my things. And the knife, I thought I had lost it as I could not locate it when Don Vicenç unexpectedly told me to leave everything behind and leave with him to Barcelona.

So, Martín must have searched my room once again just before I left the castle. Why? Did he expect to find more sculptures that he thought I must have hidden in my room? And he was acting extremely unusual the last time I saw him. I remembered he was looking at the woman sculpture just before he became delirious. The sculpture, the woman devil, it must have gotten a hand on him.

I started to trace and form an idea in my head about the sculpture I'd made. The darkness inside of me had corrupted people around me. I had let it slip out of the darkest and deepest part of my soul. I knew what the power of the woman sculpture had, that part of an evil I had let out; it would slowly corrupt and bring the worst out of whoever laid their eyes upon it.

I thought of Don Vicenç and his greed that had been enhanced after he had taken the sculpture. Delilah's pride and ego had gotten worse, as well as Cecilia's malice and jealousy. I would have to find out what had it done to Martín and other people.

Just when I was wondering where in the castle Martín could be, I heard a metal noise above my head, rattling loudly on the floor, louder than the sound of thunder and rain outside.

I thought Martín must have heard someone entering the attic, that was why he came to check, and he must have kicked the metal tools still scattered on the floor. I got up off the bed, intending to seek Martín out, and resolve the mystery behind his actions by asking him about his intention of keeping my mother's letter without telling me.

With the torch in my hand, I trod up towards the attic once again.

Upon going through the attic's door, the person who sat at

the table with my mother's letter in his hand was Don Vicenç.

# Chapter Twenty-Four

An orange flickering of the candle on the table made Don Vicenç's face glow in the complete darkness in the attic. His black outfit and cloak blended into the darkness of the night, making his head take on the effect of floating without the body.

I was surprised to see Don Vicenç here, for him to come all the way from Barcelona. Was the anger he felt for me so strong that he had taken a non-stop horse ride to catch up with me? Or because he wanted to punish me after he knew that I had decided to leave without his permission? However, the expression on Don Vicenç's face showed no glimpse of anger or any twitch that announced his irritation, for the emotion on his face was as if he was content to see me.

As I could not read his expression, I said the first thought that I had in my head, 'I didn't expect to see you here. I thought you were—'

'Martín?' said Don Vicenç, stealing the old man's name out of my mouth. 'No, he isn't here, and he must have not been here for quite a while.' Don Vicenç gave a low chuckle. 'Oh, what is it with people betraying me?'

He stood up from the stool, tossing my mother's letter on the table. He looked towards me then cocked his head to one side. 'Jacobo,' he said. My name on his lips was soft like a whisper. His eyes narrowed at me before he spoke up with his usual authoritative voice, 'Why have you run away? Why did you leave? Do you no longer want to share my dream?' Slowly, he approached. 'I didn't expect you to come back here, but news travelled fast. Honestly, I thought that you would go back to your mother at the hanging town.'

I contemplated Don Vicenç's words and the meaning behind them. How could he possibly know about my mother when I never had once mentioned her to him.

'What brought you back here?' I said. 'Are you going to take out your anger on me because of that stupid sculpture I made?'

Don Vicenç laughed his staccato voice, blending in with the sound of thunder. 'Oh, my dear cousin, my dear boy.' He walked past me towards the small wooden door and continued talking with his back turning towards me. 'You still don't understand, do you? This is a whole new thing. It has nothing to do with your stupid sculpture, but yes, yes, I would want to take out my anger on you because you are an ungrateful person!' Suddenly, Don Vicenç turned to face me. My breath faltered as the look on Don Vicenç's face was so sinister, like he was possessed by some kind of evil spirit. He raised his voice, 'Not only that you tried to mock me, but you also fucked Delilah! You knew that she belongs to me, and I hate it so when people touch whatever is mine!'

'But as I told you.' Don Vicenç's voice was back, again, to his usual tone. His sinister look changed into a serene one in a matter of a second. 'This is a whole new thing. Well, first, I am going to tell you a story, but it's not for the faint of heart,' he snorted.

'But let us see if you still have a heart at all after what you have done to poor, little Celia.' The sinister smile on his face was back again. My skin pricked from sensing something abnormal in the way Don Vicenç behaved.

'What do you mean? What did you do?' I said.

He chuckled and smiled, his eyes never left me. 'You'll see her sooner or later. Oh, but you asked what did I do? Oh, why? I should be the one asking you! For she was quite upset . . . very . . . very . . . upset that you . . . betrayed her!

'If you know her so well, you know about her jealousy, don't you? She must have loved you so much to keep such a secret from me. And the thing you did to her must be so unforgivable that it breaks her heart into thousand pieces for her to come to me and tell me what she should have told me once she suspected it.

'Oh, and don't look so guilty. You haven't heard the whole story. I bet after you hear this one, the one I owe you, you won't be able to live another breath.' Something in Don Vicenç's eyes shifted.

The sinister expression changed into something even more cynical. 'There was once this woman, who told me of a prophecy that I would die by the hand of my own flesh and blood. And it was a mistake to tell me that, because after I knew of the prophecy, how could I sleep soundlessly knowing that the little devil I created would come and take my life?

'Oh . . . she was my wife once, a pretty little witch who told me of this prophecy. And she wanted to challenge me. She told me of this macabre prophecy before she ran away . . . with that little devil still living in her belly.

'After she escaped, I searched high and low for her. But she was good at disappearing. Not even my best man, Itzal, could locate her. We thought she was dead along with the baby.

'But I have never forgotten her. The only memory I have left of my wife was my favourite scent of her. She made it with flowers and herbs that she collected from around the castle. Oh, she was the most beautiful woman to me. Her hair, red like a wildfire, her skin as white as snow.

'Yes, yes, you know who I am talking about, don't you?' Don Vicenç said, for he must have read the panic in my expression.

'Yes, it's Rosinda . . . and you . . . you are that little devil I have been searching high and low for.' Don Vicenç spoke with a steady and calm voice, but underneath his eyes the cynical look for blood was still there. His hand went inside his black cloak, and out with it was a pistol, which he cocked and pointed right in my face.

A smile slicked across his face, so sly and so cunning, a whole new expression I had never seen on his face before, and my heart sunk. It took me a second to fathom Don Vicenç's words, then what followed was an unexpected nerve that made my body go under an uncontrollable rise of impulse and a lack of breath. I felt like I could not breathe. My chest constricted, and my ability to think slumped into blankness.

Don Vicenç didn't stop talking. I looked at his face, that sly grin. His lips were moving, but his voice was muted. A second passed before I was back in my head again, before my senses started to make sense of my surroundings. Don Vicenç's voice rang in my ears again.

'Oh, my own flesh and blood.' The steady voice turned into a chuckle, the low humming from within his chest. It echoed through the quiet room. I looked outside, and there was no more flashing light outside the window. The sound of rain and thunder had subsided.

His chuckle turned into a snort, then into a high-pitched laugh that I could not fathom came out of his throat like a mad person. 'Oh, the god is just, after all, to send you right back to my doorstep,' he said in-between breathes, and when his high-pitched laugh ceased, his facial expression turned back into a sinister look as he stared straight into my eyes. 'Oh, and thanks to you, too. Now, I know where my little witch wife is hiding. Because of your stupid letter! Your indication of her whereabouts could not be any clearer, a hanging town, in a hut, deep in the wood.'

The room hummed with the voice of Don Vicenç's laughter.

'What did you do!' I shouted.

'To your mother? Or to my own flesh and blood?' Don Vicenç's eyes cast with shadow. He looked at me curiously. 'Well, well, well, I am going to show you now . . .' He went into the pocket of his cloak, and this time he produced a key out of his pocket. The metal reflected a burning light from the torch. He threw the key at my feet.

'Pick it up and open that door,' Don Vicenç pointed to the small wooden door with a jerk of his head. His eyes never left me, and his pistol steady. 'And give me that torch.'

I picked up the key, its surface still warm from the heat of Don Vicenç's touch. I had been curious about what was inside the room for a long time, how it used to call on me when I was working alone in the quiet of the night.

Slowly, I walked towards the door, towards where Don Vicenç stood. He grabbed the torch out of my hand and placed the point of the pistol right at my temple. The cold metal stung against my skin.

The lock gave way quite easily, and I tried to push the door open, but it was stuck. There was some white fabric in between the gap of the door, stopping the air from going in or going out. I gave a hard push, using the weight of my body, and the door sucked open as if the pressure of the air had been trapped inside. The smell that came out of it was horrid and unbearable, burning into my nostrils, but Don Vicenç didn't flinch or react to any of the smell.

'After you,' he said as he pressed the pistol harder against my temple, forcing me to do as I was told. I could not see whatever was inside the room, as it was completely and utterly dark. It was like the place had been sealed shut from every piece of light and air. The only thing that I could make out from within this room was a silhouette of tables and something on top of them.

When Don Vicenç walked in after me, the light from the torch started to glow and expose the objects inside.

It was a sight of utter horror.

There were rows of glass jars, carefully placed one after another. The contents inside were something white and wrinkled, floating in a yellowish liquid. I thought it was a rat without fur, but with a realisation that slowly seeped into my consciousness, I knew right then, the true nature of what these strange things were . . . stillborn human babies were floating inside these countless jars.

The sight made my stomach churn, for there were jars and jars, rolls and rolls of them alone on the table at the left side of the room. In front of these jars were white sculptures made in a shape of an angel. What an irony these sculptures were, for this wasn't a place for an angel, for this wasn't a place of heaven or earth at all, but of hell, the deepest and darkest part of all.

I cast my eyes to where Don Vicenç stood, cursed him for the things that he had done. There was nothing that could describe how I felt for this man. And he wasn't done tormenting every part of my soul. With a torch and a pistol he still in his hand, he moved further towards the middle of the room, and wherever he went, the orange flickered light exposed more sight of horror.

'Here are all my trophies, just to spite death in their faces,' Don Vicenç announced. 'Now, all of what was supposed to be my death are here. I can look them in the eyes and say that I have won.'

'What is this!? What have you done!?' I cried out.

Tears slid down across my right cheek when I saw the contents inside a jar at the end of the room. For the things I had seen weren't foetuses, but a fully developed baby, with limbs and hair, submerged and curled up in a yellow liquid. Their skin was all wrinkled and white except on their bellies, where dark blue cords were still attached, exposing the dark veins that ran along their stomachs. There were six of them altogether, and these ones must have been killed after they were born. Inside a small glass jar, their body and soul trapped forever within this small hellish room.

I gasped with horror, recalling the days when I spent my

time working beside this hellish room. The voice I heard that was calling to me must have been from these poor souls, urging me to set them free. I felt my stomach churn with a feeling far beyond horror. I felt lost, afraid and torn for all of them. And worse than that, the knowledge that Don Vicenç was my father disgusted me. The blood that ran in my veins came from this mad man.

Don Vicenç stopped behind the table at the far end, where fully developed babies were, and he started to talk, 'These ones belong to the women who think that they can escape me.' One by one, he started to throw the white angel sculpture to the floor right next to my feet. The white shards of the porcelain broke once it hit the floor, echoing like lightning outside the window just a minute ago. But when I looked at the pieces of the porcelain, there were parts of bones and skulls scattering on the floor.

My hands trembled with fear, disgust and anger.

Don Vicenç didn't stop as he was drowned in madness and malevolence. 'They think that they can hide my baby, my little devil. They think they can let them live without my knowing!? No! No one can!'

On and on, for what felt like an eternity, Don Vicenç continued talking and throwing the rest of the angel sculpture to the floor. Bones and skull broke free from their contents. There were six skulls all together. One of them bounced off the floor and stopped directly at my feet.

'Murderer!' I growled.

'They deserved it!' He shouted back at me.

I was going to lunge at him. I was blinded with rage and

hatred. I wanted to hurt this man so much so that I almost over-looked the fact that he had the upper hand.

What stopped me from making a stupid decision was a shuffle of footsteps outside the room. Agnes appeared. 'M—master?' she said, surprised as she saw the scene. But I doubted that she was surprised by the dead babies floating in a jar or the skull scattered on the floor, but the pistol that Don Vicenç was pointing at my head.

'Did you settle the matter?' Don Vicenç told the plump woman.

'Y—yes, sir,' said Agnes.

'Good, now, there is another matter I need you to settle downstairs. Itzal is busy tonight.' Don Vicenç grinned and looked my way before he turned back to Agnes. 'I don't think you want to stay and see what I would do to my son, do you?'

Agnes' widened eyes shifted to my face when she heard Don Vicenç mentioned that I was his son. Her face became pale all of a sudden. 'Uh . . . no, no, sir,' she stuttered.

'Then, leave and do as I just said!'

Agnes squirmed and ran out of the door like a frightened fat rat.

When Agnes left, Don Vicenç turned to face me again. He grinned with dead eyes. 'Where was I before that woman interrupted me?' he said. 'Oh, I do love to see your face when I tell you these stories. Ah, yes . . . I was telling you about your mother. She thinks she can outwit me, too!' He snorted.

'Did you know that I loved her?' His expression changed into someone in pain, but it was all unnatural to me. He acted like he was so absorbed in the story of my mother, the person he said he loved and the same person he wanted dead.

'Did you know that she was the one who made me go crazy? It all began the day I saw her. You see, it was never in my mind to imagine that I was going to be married to any woman after seeing my father cry from losing my mother when I was five. I knew at that moment that I was never going to cry and be weak like him. I would never let myself be attached to anyone.

'But my father made a promise to Rosinda's father, a physician, who once saved my father's life. My father believed that he owed this man his life. He offered him a large sum of money, but that man refused. So my father offered that I marry his daughter when she came of age. And that time, I could not protest because my father threatened to cut me loose if I didn't do as he said. I was about eighteen, and your mother must have been fifteen. And after I did as I was told, I made sure that my father signed his will and that after he died, everything he owned would be mine. He could not threaten to take away what belonged to me by birth! Then, a little four or five drops in his drink settled his and my fate. I made it look like an accident, of course. Everything was so easy.'

I drew in a sharp breath from discovering the fact that Don Vicenç had poisoned his own father. How insane could a person become? What was the limit to someone's insanity?

Don Vicenç kept talking, 'After that, I was left alone in a big castle with my beautiful wife. She was so beautiful, so innocent, and so naive. Oh, I owned not only her soul but also her body. You have no idea what her body made me do; that white skin, those innocent doe eyes. It awoke something in me. Whenever I laid my hands on her, that white skin would become red, then if

I pressed harder, the same blueish colour like those of her veins underneath her skin began to appear.'

'Shut up! You sick bastard!' I shouted. Anger was boiling inside me. I had never imagined how deep his psychopathic mind ran. His dark wicked thoughts were bottomless.

'Your mother once called me sick, too.' Don Vicenç snorted. 'But you have no idea how I cherished and worshipped her . . .

'But she betrayed me! She tried to send a letter to her father, saying that she wanted to leave me because I was mentally sick and that I had poisoned my own father. But Rosinda was wrong. I wasn't sick. It's the way I loved her.

'I could never let her leave me, don't you see!? I couldn't let anyone take her away from me. So that left me no choice. I had to get rid of both of her parents!

'And I wouldn't have locked her up if she didn't try to betray my love. She hasn't seen the love I have for her!' Don Vicenç looked as if he was in pain. 'Your mother is an ungrateful little witch! And she knows me too well. She knows how to get back at me. She told me that I was cursed, she told me about the prophecy. And then, she managed to escape. You have no idea how heartbroken I was. The only thing I had left of her was this smell, this scent she created. Years and years passed, she was still in my memory. She still haunted my night. I bathed every woman I bedded with Rosinda's scent.

'Oh, but after that, Agnes told me that she suspected that Rosinda was pregnant . . . because she had not bled. And all these things that I have done, it's all your mother's fault. All the blood is on her hands!'

Everything was too much for me to bear now, but Don Vicenç hadn't stopped talking. At that moment, I detested him, and I also detested myself just because I was connected to him. I began to think of all the possibilities of getting out of this situation. The only weapon that I could use to protect myself was Martín's metal tools. But Don Vicenç was always watching me.

When Don Vicenç started to move towards the right side of the room, with a burning torch still in his hand, my eyes followed his movements, and that was when I noticed a covered object in the right corner of the room. It was a little taller than the table. He must have seen where I was looking.

'Ah, that!' he said. ' That's my newest trophy, I haven't seen it myself. So, you'd be my first guest. But, first, I can show you these.' Don Vicenç pointed to the jars on the edge of the table with the torch. 'That little one belongs to Alba, and next to that was Flor's.'

My heart must have had stopped for a second there. Then the effect after that made my head spin, and my breath was becoming more rapid. I looked around me and suddenly saw the babies in the jar moving and crying for help. Their wrinkled bodies swam up to the surface and tried to escape in vain. Every single one of them cried with a screeching scream.

'Why do you look so pale, my dear boy, Jacobo,' said Don Vicenç, his voice caught my disturbed attention, and when I turned to look at him, the room stopped humming with that screeching, and everything became quiet and still. 'I told you this is not a story for the faint of heart, but you haven't heard the whole of it. Oh, how they scream when Martín takes the baby out of them.'

'What the fuck are you saying?!'

'Oh, dear boy of mine, little did you know, Martín was the one who aborted all these babies. He was such a loyal servant. Too bad, he too, betrayed me, and now he must live with the consequences,' Don Vicenç said as he walked towards the covered object and pulled the white cloth away.

What was underneath was a lifeless body of a little girl, floating inside the same yellowish liquid; her skin, once smooth and soft, were wrinkled. Her eyes, lifeless and staring at nothing in front. The little girl was Rosalia.

'You psycho bastard!' I shouted as I tried to charge at him. He fired a shot that grazed my head. My ears rang at the exploding sound of the pistol. Everything went quiet, but I could feel a warm liquid flowing down my temple. My right hand came out red after I ran it along my temple. There was something warm flowing down my temple, and when I touched it, there was blood on my hand.

Don Vicenç's mouth was moving with a word that I caught from my ringing ears.

'Next time it's going to be in the middle of your head,' said Don Vicenç with a terrifying calm expression. Then, when he started to continue on with his story, the calm expression suddenly changed into disgust. 'Rosalia was my daughter, did you know that? I lent her to Martín in order to keep his mouth shut and do whatever I told him to do. He always wanted to have a child, so I gave him one. The old man was a fool! Did he really think that I was going to let her live? I never intended to. I was just going to kill her when the time came. And what would be the best reason to take her back? Of course, when that old man betrays me.' Don Vicenç snorted. 'That letter on the table, the

271

old man must have been in possession of it before you left the castle. He must have known all along about who you really were, but he kept that from me. He knew! He knew. And he even had plans to let that woman escape with my daughter. That kind of tale would never happen. I always had my men watching over that girl.'

I recalled when Martín told me that Don Vicenç had given him something that he could not have, and that was why he was in his debt. Now, I began to understand how Don Vicenç had bought Martín's loyalty. Did Martín really believe that Don Vicenç would let the girl, who was his daughter live despite knowing about the prophecy? He was blinded by his own hypocritical action. He wanted to have a baby, but he kept killing them off one by one.

This castle must be cursed, for whoever stepped inside it would be damned. I remembered what Cecilia told me that there was a place under the castle. And Don Vicenç asked Agnes to settle certain matters down there. It must be the same place that Cecilia was talking about.

'I have let you live for far too long,' Don Vicenç's voice echoed in my head. 'But soon you will be following your brothers and sisters to hell. And after you are dead, I am going to place you next to that girl, or maybe, I am going to keep you in another form. I might have to hire the best taxidermist to keep you as you are right now. So whenever I look at you, I will see you as my trophy,' said Don Vicenç.

I wished with all my heart and begged for anyone, anything, and everything in my power to take this man away to hell.

Don Vicenç cocked his pistol. 'Goodbye, Jacobo, my flesh

and blood,' he said as he aimed the pistol directly at my heart, then fired.

# Chapter Twenty-Five

The last thing I heard was an explosion of gunpowder from the pistol. I braced for my death, for pain, for the last satisfying look on Don Vicenç's face before I was forever submerged into the darkness. But death didn't descend on me. I felt no pain, and I was still standing in the orange flickering room of death, very much alive. Don Vicenç had fired the shot as the smoke of gunpowder clouded over the room, but somehow the pistol had failed to do its duty.

The moment I knew that he had failed to take my life, I knew that I had to take his, for I could not let this monster take any more innocent lives even if he was my real father.

His fate had been set.

With smoke still obscuring our vision, I wasted no time to get a weapon, anything that I could kill this man with. I went for Martín's long metal tool with a hook on the floor next to the door, the one that he must have used on those women to abort those children.

When Don Vicenç saw my silhouette out of the cloud of smoke, looking straight back at him, his face changed from a sleek smile into fear. And out of the cloud of smoke, I lunged at Don Vicenç. His cry of horror rang through the room. He tried to brace for my attack and lift his pistol, but it was all too late. The hard metal landed in the middle of his forehead. I smacked him with all my force, aiming to kill. The blow cut Don Vicenç's head open, and blood streamed down his face. I kept on smacking him like a mad person. All the anger and hatred poured out of me into his face and his head. Don Vicenç lost his balance and fell to the floor, but I kept on doing my duty of taking this monster's life. I lifted the metal over my head, then swung it down with unimaginable force, making sure to hit him at the severe spot. The hook at the end of the metal scraped off the skin of his head and his blood-soaked hair. But I didn't stop. I had no love, no pity, no feeling left for this man. A surge of satisfaction ran up through me when the metal slammed into his flesh.

I didn't know how long I had been repeating the same action, but when I heard a cracking sound underneath the metal, it snapped me out of my anger. I looked down at what once was the face of Don Vicenç and chuckled. Half of his face was gone. There was only a scrap of flesh and blood, clinging to his skull. The metallic smell of blood was all over me, mixing up with the pungent smell of this room. I swept the sweat that was falling down my forehead, but it came out red. I looked over my clothes, and most spots of my black clothes were darkened by Don Vicenç's blood. Around me, there was blood everywhere, flowing under the table and under the glass where Rosalia was floating lifelessly.

So, the prophecy had come true after all.

I slumped down on the floor, panting, energies spent, but the madness within me hadn't subsided yet. It burned within my heart and soul. Looking around the room at all those babies and at poor Rosalia, sorrow seeped through me. I knew I had to set them free. With the metal tool still in hand, I swung it one last time, breaking the glass that contained Rosalia's body. The pool of yellow liquid flew out along with her body. I went for a white cloth fabric and covered Rosalia's pale body. I glanced around the room once more, the horror of what I had witnessed would never disappear. I knew what I had to do.

Walking over Don Vicenç's body, I grabbed the torch and the pistol from the floor. First, I lit the fire at Rosalia's body. The liquid that was soaking her body caught fire quickly, and in a second, the fire loomed over her. If I could not save her, at least I could set her soul free, along with the rest of my brothers and sisters.

I stood at the doorstep and watched as the fire quickly spread throughout the room. The heat was cracking jar after jar, breaking free all those babies' trapped souls. And with the help of liquid, the fire burned high to the ceiling. I caught sight of Don Vicenç's body on fire, and I hoped he would face a more horrible death. I didn't want his body to be burned at the same time as these poor souls. But I knew in my heart that his soul would never go to the same place as these poor innocent children. And with that idea in my mind, I felt somewhat satisfied.

I retreated from the room as the heat that was blasting out became insufferable. Before I left, I went first for my mother's letter. Stuffing it in my pocket, I walked out and started looking for Agnes to finish my business before the fire consumed everything. And I knew quite well where to find her. Cecilia told me of a door in Don Vicenç's private study that would lead me to a secret room. I headed towards it.

What business had Don Vicenç told Agnes to do? I knew that it could not be anything pleasant, as I had found out that Don Vicenç was a psychopath, and Agnes, after knowing what kind of person Don Vicenç was, still helped him through and through. And she was the one who told him about my mother, so she had to die.

As the castle was eerily quiet, I could trace the sound of movement once I got closer to Don Vicenç' study.

The door wasn't securely closed, so I carefully slipped in without making a sound. There was no one inside as I had suspected because Agnes must have been in the secret room. I went around the room to look over at a misplaced wall, and there, between the gap of the shelf, I could feel the wind blowing out, and along with it, a faint horrid smell, a smell of death.

I slipped through the secret passage quietly. Along the small corridor, the candles were burning. It was a sign that Agnes must have passed through here. Something dark on a sand-coloured stone caught my attention, a trail of blood leading from the doorway deeper inside the passageway. The blood was still quite fresh, trailing down through a curvy path that led down and down. I quickly followed, and the further I went down, the smell worsened. I could hear a faint moaning sound along with laughter and a murmur. I trod quietly, expecting that Don Vicenç's men or Itzal would be down here. With a pistol in my hand and my back against the wall, I braced to face them, but when I peeked over the wall at the end of the path, I only saw Agnes, crouching down on the floor in front of an open metal bar, a bunch of keys jiggling at her hips. She was murmuring something to the woman who was laying on the floor. However, once I cast my eyes around, whatever this place was, it wasn't just a secret room, instead, it was a huge dungeon with metal bars along both sides of the passageway.

With a pistol pointing at Agnes, I walked inside, not bothering to keep my footsteps quiet. And when Agnes heard, she just calmly looked my way, but after she spotted that it was me, and not her master, she jumped up to her feet.

'Jacobo, I——,' uttered Agnes.

'Shut up,' I cut her off before she was going to utter some bullshit excuse.

'Jacobo?' I heard another raspy voice, whispering my name. Turning towards the sound, I saw Martín, frail and dirty, in the cell to my right. His hand was wrapped around the metal bar, and his face was full of guilt when he looked at me. I could hear more whimpers and whispers from the other cells. Within the darkness of the cells surrounding me, I carefully looked inside, and there, I could see a silhouette of women inside each cell. Some were crouching down on the floor, and some were looking out at me through the metal bars. All of them were frail and dirty.

'Jacobo.' One of the women whispered my name. I tried to find the origin of the voice, and deeper inside the dungeon, I could see a hand extending out of the metal bars. 'It's Alba, help, help us,' the voice that rang out was weak and sickly. I hadn't seen the woman's face as her cell was deeper within this dungeon, but I remembered Don Vicenç pointing to one of the foetuses in the jar and said that it was Alba's. And I did remember Alba as one of the maids, who I first saw at the beginning of my time here, but then one day, she was just gone along with the others. And there were always new women who would come and replace the old ones. I didn't pay much attention to it, the same way I hadn't really been associating with anyone inside the castle. Now, I understood why I was forbidden to deal with the matter that had been going on inside this place.

Alba's fate must have ended like every other woman whose baby had been stolen from them. But she must be one of the few lucky ones who survived the brutal process of abortion. Did Martín kill Alba's baby, too? Before I could walk further inside the dungeon, I had to make sure that Agnes wasn't going to try any tricky business.

I turned back to Agnes. 'Throw those keys to me,' I told her

'I—'

'Shut up! And do as I say,' I said.

Agnes shuddered as she stepped back. She must have noticed the bloodstain on me. And the look on my face must have shown that I was in no mood of saying things twice. She slowly removed the bunch of keys on her hip and threw them at me. The jingling sound of the keys hitting the floor caused another murmur and a soft wail around me. But my eyes trailed after Agnes' every movement, for I could not let her play any tricks on me. 'Now, get inside that cell,' I said.

Agnes froze her ground, trembling. And when she didn't do as I said, I took another step closer. She screamed as if she thought I was going to shoot her, but as she realised that her body was still all intact, she hurriedly went inside the cell. I slammed the metal bar shut, making sure that it was securely locked. And that was when I looked away from Agnes to a woman who was lying at Agnes's feet.

Amelia stared lifelessly up at the dungeon ceiling.

A shiver ran down my spine from a realisation as I quickly trailed my eyes over to the woman who was lying next to my feet. Everything in me crumbled when I saw Cecilia's face. Her dress was soaked with blood in her middle. Her hair was loose and clinging to her freckled face.

I got on my knee and held her body.

A faint whimpering sound escaped from her. It made my heart swell with hope that she was still alive.

Her eyes fluttered open just a little. The corner of her mouth curled up into a small smile, and it revealed her bloody teeth. The hope I felt before withered. I knew that she didn't have much time left, for the wound on her stomach must have caused internal bleeding, and she must have lost a lot of blood as her skin was so pale. Her fingers twitched, but she could not move further than that.

Cecilia's mouth gaped open, but as she tried to draw in a breath, she struggled. She was trying to speak. I lowered myself nearer to her so that I could catch her words.

'You're here . . .' Cecilia's word was like a wheeze of air. 'I'm . . . sorry that I've betrayed you. Your blood couldn't lie and . . . because of my stupidity, I told him that you were his son. I'm sorry . . . Jacobo.' She gasped for more air, but it was getting harder to see how she was struggling.

'Cecilia, it's alright.' I kissed her forehead and tried to calm her from speaking. 'It doesn't matter now.'

'And my stupidity also caused my sister's life . . . He—he made me watch her die. . .' Tears trailed down her cheeks. 'But, I'm glad you're alive, Jacobo. I . . .' She struggled to form her last word as she was unable to grasp for more air. It was almost impossible to hear her words now.

'I . . . just only wish that you . . . loved me.'

Tears escaped from my eyes and dropped upon her freckled face.

'I . . . wish . . .' Cecilia's last breath wheezed out of her lips, and everything went still.

I cursed myself for letting this happen to Cecilia. I knew that my reckless actions had led her to betray me. She had decided to tell Don Vicenç this in order to take her revenge on me after I had betrayed her trust. And Don Vicenç must have decided to kill her because he knew Cecilia had kept my secret that she should have had told him when she first suspected it from the beginning.

And because of that woman sculpture, it must have brought out the worse in her and heightened every bit of malice and jealousy.

I hugged Cecilia's lifeless body.

'No! No! Please,' I mumbled to myself as if I could change anything.

Teardrops kept rolling down my face. I cried for Cecilia's life that I'd lost and for the fact that her death was my fault.

# Chapter Twenty-Six

I kissed Cecilia's cold lips as the last goodbye before I slowly got up to deal with Agnes, who was standing with her back against the wall.

When she saw that I was looking at her, she said, 'I didn't kill them.' Agnes's trembling voice rang in my ear. 'It was the master. I—I was just doing what master bid me to. I just have to bring the bodies here before Itzal gets rid of them. I—'

I had to summon all the good that was left in me in order not to shoot Agnes in the head. 'And what about these women here? What have you done to them?'

'Please,' Agnes' voice trembled.

'Why are you so afraid of me now?' I asked her, wondering where the woman who had played an authority over whoever was below her had gone.

'I just did whatever the master told me to do,' said Agnes. And out of fear, her voice trembled, but she kept talking. 'You must know about Don Vicenç's purpose in this world! He must have told you, for he is the chosen one, who will deliver all the believers to the land of eternity. I was just doing my part as a humble servant. All I needed to do was to find a beautiful woman for Don Vicenç as a tribute. But they also serve a purpose. They are meant to give him pleasure as well as serve him. We

282

fed them and gave them shelter. And soon enough, with a touch of Don Vicenç's grace, they all converted into believers. And when they are, they have this ultimate purpose, where they will provide a child for Don Vicenç, and the children would serve as a sacrifice to the god.'

I thought about what Agnes said and what Cecilia used to tell me. Everything that they said must be associated with some kind of dark cult. Don Vicenç must have really believed that he was someone special, some chosen one by this god of darkness. Martín asked me once whether I believed in God, but I had no idea the God that he was talking about was this god of darkness.

'You said you gave these women food and shelter, but why are they here? Tell me!' My hands trembled as I looked around the women who were trapped inside this horrible dungeon.

'These women aren't true believers! They tried to take the child as their own when they know that those children belong to the god,' said Agnes.

I wondered what lies Don Vicenç had been feeding her. And how she could be deeply influenced by him. Then, I thought about Don Vicenç and his influence. He was a man of charisma and authority. It must be easy for him to manipulate people with his words. He had always spotted each person's weakness, and he knew what each person wanted the most in their life. Then, he would give that person the thing they needed the most in order for them to look up to him. And when he had the upper hand, he would use their trust and loyalty as his weapon, to lure people and influence them into doing whatever he needed them to do. I was one of his pawns, too, I realised. But I never thought that Don Vicenç had gone this far into brainwashing many people into believing that he was god's chosen one. But in reality, he was just a cold-blooded psychopath who was obsessed with women and the prophecy that his own flesh and blood would come to kill him one day.

I could not help but say to Agnes, 'I am sorry Agnes, for you have been living a lie all your life. What did he promise you?' I asked, willing to know the trick that he had bought Agnes' loyalty with.

'He said that he would set me free. He said that my soul would be purified and eternally free in the land of eternity,' said Agnes.

I wondered how many people fell under his web of lies, the one he had made up and moulded into a glorious tale where he was this chivalrous knight who would deliver everyone to some gibberish eternal land that didn't really exist. I also could not stop myself from chuckling at Agnes' answers. So, Don Vicenç didn't have to do anything much to gain Agnes' loyalty. The woman was just a fool who happened to believe in Don Vicenç's madness and lies. And because of her delusion, she became one of the tools for fulfilling Don Vicenç's perversion, and she had played a part in killing off many innocent lives. But now that her master was dead, her part in this whole madness must end.

'Oh, Agnes, your master is not the chosen one from this god of darkness you are talking about. He was just a perverted man who was scared shitless of death. Did you know that he was given a prophecy by his wife, who he used to lock up and torture, that his child would be the one who would take his life? And with that, he was obsessed. He was just an egoistic psychopath, who enjoyed beating up women and killing innocent children just because he was scared that they would kill him first!'

'No! This can't be! You don't know everything. You don't understand!' Agnes protested.

'He is dead. I have fulfilled that prophecy. And you, with everything that you have done, you don't deserve to live anymore!' I said my last sentence to her before I lifted the pistol and fired the shot right through her chest. Agnes didn't have time to scream. She staggered back. 'It is you . . .' she whispered. A glimpse of bewilderment flashed on her face before it turned into horror, and finally, she fell to the ground.

I felt no regrets for the deed I had just done as I stared at her body alongside Amelia. It was the righteous thing to do, I knew it in my heart, to give her the justice she deserved, for she deserved to die a thousand times and maybe once more.

I looked at Cecilia's body. Seeing it laying cold on the ground made my heart ache and erupted my anger. I told myself to help the rest of the people here before I could take her body out and give her a proper burial.

Picking up the keys, I went straight to Alba's cell. There must have been around ten women in this dungeon, and I wasn't so sure if all of them were still alive because they just lay on the cold stone floor when I walked past their cell.

After I managed to help Alba out of her freezing cell, out of the quietness inside that dungeon, I could hear rapid footsteps coming closer. I lifted the pistol and braced for Don Vicenç's men to enter, but I was faced with Andrea. His chest rose and fell rapidly like he had been running for miles, and his hand held a metal club.

'You!' said Andrea, his words echoed through the stone wall. His eyes glared with hatred. And the crooked nose on his face reminded me that it was Don Vicenç's doing.

Alba must have seen the look on Andrea's face that he came here for blood. In her frail voice, she said, 'No, Andrea. Jacobo is saving us. It was Don Vicenç and Agnes. They put all of us here. They—they,' Alba didn't finish what she was going to say, as the memory of the terror she had been through seized her. She started to weep quietly and signalled me to let her sit. Slowly, I let her sit on the floor outside the cell.

Andrea's face was full of confusion and pain when he looked at Alba.

'Alba? What have they done to you? I—I thought you just left the castle without saying goodbye. All these times, they put you here? And where is Flor? Is—Is she here?' said Andrea as he took a step closer to Alba, but then he was aware of my presence next to her. 'You said Jacobo is saving you? How can you know that it's not his plan? To fool you, to fool all of us?'

'No, no, Andrea. It was all Don Vicenç's doing. When Don Vicenç was here, he mentioned to Agnes to make sure that you and Jacobo stay out of the castle and away from their business.'

Andrea looked between Alba and me, and his face turned pale when he looked carefully at what had become of Alba. He came to sit beside her.

'I heard a gunshot. What was that?' said Andrea.

Alba snorted before she said, 'Finally, Jacobo sent that woman to hell. He shot Agnes.'

Andrea's eyes went wide when he looked around and saw Cecilia's body on the ground. 'Isn't that a—'

286

'Don Vicenç killed her.' I said before Andrea pronounced Cecilia's name or whatever he had in mind. I didn't want to be reminded of her death. I knew that when all this was done, I would take Cecilia out with me and give her a good burial.

'I knew some crazy things must have happened in that castle,' Andrea blurted out. 'That was why they never allowed me inside. And when Flor left, Agnes told me she ran away. Flor was pregnant with Don Vicenç's baby! She told me. She would never run away! I knew something was wrong. So I left and hid nearby. Days later, Don Vicenç's men came. I heard they spoke my name, and that was when I knew that they must be looking for me. I thought Don Vicenç was just playing with Flor and whenever he got bored, he would break her heart, but this is worse than I thought! All these days, I hid, but never too far away from the castle, until I saw a fire, and when I came here, I heard a gunshot. It led me to a room with a hole in the wall. Then, I found this place,' Andrea said as if everything was too much for him to take in. 'What is this cursed place? What have they done to you, Alba?'

Alba kept her head down when she started to talk, 'It all began when Agnes found me on the street in Barcelona. She took me in, fed me and gave me work. She told me it was all because of Don Vicenç, the master of the castle's kindness. I thought how lucky I was for my fate to change overnight. You must know Don Vicenç, he was a man of—'

'Was?' Andrea blurted out, to which I turned to him. 'He was trying to kill me, but I got the chance to kill him first,' I said, leaving every other part out.

Andrea snorted and chuckled, 'I guess he was done with you

too after whatever profit he made from you,' he said before he turned his concentration back to Alba, 'I'm sorry Alba, please go on.'

Alba took a deep breath before she continued. 'Don Vicenç was a charming and charismatic man. He treated me as one of his class, and he was a very persuasive person. He told me of this idea that he wanted to change the world. He no longer wanted people to suffer from every kind of suffering. And it was true. He helped me and other women from hunger, cold and poverty. I didn't have to sell myself to survive the day. I began to fall for the idea he had explained to me. And in the end, he said that everything that he had done was because he had received a message from god. And the people he selected to help were special. I suppose we all fell for him in the same way.

'We—I let him bed me.' Alba looked as if she was ashamed. 'He told me that I was special, and yes, I was treated that way whenever he called me to see him at night. I fell head over heels with him, until I found out that I was pregnant. Don Vicenç told me that the baby could not be born within the world of impurity. He told me that the world needed to be cleansed before a child of his could be born. I did listen to him at first, but when I felt that baby inside me, I told him otherwise.

'I said that I wanted to keep the child and that our baby would be born in a world where he would lead, and they would all turn out right. Don Vicenç refused to listen to me. And the more I protested, the more he started to show his true self. At last, when he saw that I no longer shared his belief, he dragged me to this cursed place and locked me up.' Her body shivered as she kept talking.

'One—one day, Don Vicenç just came in and beat me in order to kill the child inside. I had to stay here until my dead baby
came out of me, but it never did. I was already four months
pregnant when Don Vicenç found out.' Alba sobbed. 'Then, he
took me to that horrible room and tied me up to wait for Martín
to get the dead child out of me. Everything was horrible. I was
one of the lucky ones who survived. And Flor, I am sorry Andrea. . .'

'Is she dead?' said Andrea.

'She—' Alba swallowed and turned away from Andrea. 'She
lost her baby the same way I lost mine. I don't know what she
knew, but she kept the secret that she was pregnant until the
baby must have been around five months. Don Vicenç brought
her here, but he didn't beat her like he did with me. He just
brought her here and left. Then, days later, Itzal. . . that monster
came in with Martín. He dumped Martín in the cell, then he
went inside Flor's cell—'

'Please, you don't need to tell me the rest,' said Andrea, his
face was pale and blank.

'Andrea, Flor is here,' whispered Alba, 'in the last cell on the
right. But I think her mind was never the same when those two
men brought her back here. I am so sorry, Andrea.'

Wide-eyed, Andrea got to his feet as fast as he could and ran
with the key to the cell where Flor was supposed to be.

'Alba, you have to get out of here,' I said, helping Alba up to
her feet. 'There is a fire in the attic, and soon, it will reach us. I
will help the rest of the people here. You must warn the others
who are still inside the castle. Take whatever valuables you need
and leave.'

Alba nodded with an alarmed expression. She hurried across the stone floor to the exit, but before she was about to disappear through the door, she turned and said, 'Thank you, Jacobo, stay safe.'

I looked away from the dungeon exit and caught sight of Martín, who was crouching on the stone floor. Hate and anger burned inside me, but I told myself to deal with him later.

I followed to where Andrea was. Looking inside the dim cell, the woman who sat at the corner of the cell was really Flor, but I would not have recognised her, for her dress, her face and her hair were all dirty. In her hand, she was carrying a bunch of hay as if it was a precious thing.

I heard Andrea called out her name, but she didn't respond, and when Andrea walked over to her, she just looked at him as if she didn't recognise her own brother.

'Flor,' said Andrea. 'It's me.'

Upon hearing Andrea's voice, Flor slowly got up and walked towards him. 'Oh, I knew you once,' she said. Her eyes were constantly staring at Andrea without blinking, and Andrea who must have been too shocked to utter anything, stood in front of Flor, as rigid as a rock. After a few seconds, Flor uttered softly, 'Are you going to hurt my baby?'

What had I done to deserve such a fate? Was damnation the only path fate had planned for me? Was it because I had taken the road of a sinful life? Everyone I had come to know ended up dead or worse than dead. Looking within the dark cell where Flor sat with hay in her arms, I felt terribly sorry for her. She hummed a melancholic tune for what was supposed to be her baby. Seeing her now, I noticed how frail and thin she had become. Her once beautiful hair was now dirty and sticking to her face. Flor must have been locked up here since the day Don Vicenç dragged her away. I could not imagine what she had been through while I was spending my life in sin and cherishing every minute of it. Don Vicenç must have ordered his men to kill Flor's baby and put it in the jar in that damned room. They must have forced her out of her will. And this was the consequence she had to suffer for the rest of her life, not dead, but dead on the inside.

'No, Flor, it's me, please,' Andrea pleaded as he tried to approach her once again. With Andrea's slow steps and the tone of his voice, Flor could sense that Andrea wasn't going to hurt her or her baby, so she slowly eased up and let Andrea approach her.

Tentatively, Andrea led Flor out of her cell. With each step Flor took, a pain of guilt and pity was gnawing in my heart. She was limping, her once white skin was stained with dirt. The rag she was wearing could not possibly protect her from the cold within these cells. I thought to myself, if I had followed Flor and Don Vicenç that day, could I have changed any of her fate?

When they passed through the metal door, Flor caught sight of me. The blankness in her eyes shifted to recognition. It was a deep pain that I saw, hidden behind those blue eyes.

'Oh, finally, Vicenç, you are here at last,' said Flor, but I could not respond to her words when she called me by that monster's name.

'They hurt me, Vicenç!' Flor raised her voice as she hadn't received any reaction from me. I hated it when she called me by that monster's name. I hated it that I shared Don Vicenç's blood and that his face reflected in mine.

I looked at Andrea, and I also saw the pain in his eyes, the same kind of pain that was hidden in mine. Even if it was caused by different circumstances, it was the same kind of pain.

Andrea tried to lead Flor away. He kept whispering in her ears that I wasn't the person she was calling. Flor looked confused as she kept looking between Andrea and me. And when she realised that I wasn't the person she was waiting for, she turned away and sobbed quietly.

'Go, Andrea, before the fire catches us,' I said.

'I will help and save the others too,' he answered.

'But—' I was going to comment about Flor but Andrea cut me off. 'Flor will be fine. She will wait for me. Now, hurry! We have to get them all out.'

After Andrea led Flor to sit on a wooden bench, he and I went through each cell, freeing each one of them. Andrea seemed to know all these women as he called out their names and told them to get out of this place as quickly as they could. However, we found some women lay breathless on the floor. We came for them too late, as they must have suffered the cold for too long.

'All these times, I thought they all left because of Don Vicenç. I had never thought that bastard Vicenç kept them all here. That monster . . .' Andrea placed his hands behind his head as he looked around the dungeon with an unbelievable expression.

I wondered what Andrea would have said if he had seen what Don Vicenç kept inside the attic.

We managed to free the women who were strong enough to get out by themselves, and they managed to take the ones that were too weak to walk by themselves out as well.

At last, Andrea helped Flor up to her feet. But she refused to leave. She kept saying, 'No, no, I could not leave, I am waiting for Vicenç. He will come for me and our baby.'

I was sorry to hear Andrea's words when he told Flor that Vicenç was waiting for her outside of the dungeon, and he would take her to him. Flor believed Andrea's words as she slowly walked away with him without resisting.

'Go, Andrea. I will take care of Martín,' I said.

Andrea looked at me one last time as he uttered, 'I hope you will be safe and well.'

I gave him a faint smile before he walked away.

# Chapter Twenty-Seven

Now, I was left with the last person I had to deal with, the old man, who thought that by repenting, he would be spared. With anger burning in my heart, I went straight to Martín's cell. He was crouching with his head in his hands next to the metal bar, so small and so hopeless.

I pulled the man up by the collar for him to face me as his nemesis. Looking closely at Martín's face, his once blue eyes were murky, like he was staring at me through a fog. It was a guilt-ridden face, and there were tears brimming in his eyes.

There were so many curses that I wanted to utter to him, but nothing could possibly come out of my mouth right now. I wanted to kill him right there. And it took everything in me not to do it. I released the collar of his clothes and walked back and forth in front of his cell.

Finally, when I was more restrained, I said quietly, 'Did you really help that monster kill the babies?'

'Oh, Jacobo . . . I know I have done wrong,' said Martín. His words triggered my anger. I abruptly stopped in front of him. My voice raised as I said, 'You have no idea!'

The old man staggered back a little, his eyes full of fear. 'I have always been a humble and loyal servant to Don Vicenç,' said Martín. 'I believed that he was my almighty, my saviour and liberator. That was why I have sinned for him, blindly. Oh, I was so blind, and I was a coward and a fool. I did an evil deed, and all along, I thought that I was doing the righteous thing. I did everything I did because I thought it was an act of gratitude.'

'It's too late for you to repent now,' I said. 'The thing you have done is far too great to be forgiven. You have helped that monster take away innocent lives.'

'It wasn't the right thing to do, I know now. I could have refused Don Vicenç but I was too deeply devoted to him. I had been telling lies to myself that I was—I was doing those babies a favour. If they weren't destined to live, at least I could preserve them the way they were. But, I—I never took their lives. They were all dead when Don Vicenç told me to take their bodies out of their mother's belly.'

'You are sick! You are fucking sick!' I shouted right in front of him. The old man took a step back.

His words reminded me of the scene in the small attic room. Tears brimmed in my eyes when I thought of those poor souls and Rosalia.

I looked at Martín. Did he even know that Don Vicenç killed her? If not, I did not want to be the one to tell him about the tragedy. Why had Martín been locked up here if he had always been Don Vicenç's faithful servant?

'So, why did you end up here, old man,' I asked.

'The day you left for Barcelona,' said Martín, his voice shivered. 'Don Vicenç dragged me here and locked me up. He told Agnes to only let me out of this dungeon once I had finished the deed with Flor, and only when I came to my senses. He told me to kill the babies and put their bodies in the jar like he usually told me. Then, he just left.

It seemed that he was in a hurry, but that day, I could not have forgotten my master's face and what he was holding in his hand. It was that sculpture of yours, the woman, the devil in disguise. And it made my master's eyes shine with greed, more greed than I had ever seen in him.'

Martín slowly took a step towards the metal bar. 'I am sorry, Jacobo, I dragged you into all of this. That day when I met you on the road, I should have just let you go. But I see it now that it was a plan of the devil all along . . .'

His voice shifted, and fear shone on his eyes, 'You—you said that you killed Don Vicenç?'

'Yes . . .' I approached the old man and looked directly into his murky blue eyes. 'I have fulfilled the prophecy. I killed him. Your master was wicked! He was a monster, and he deserved to die.'

Martín lifted his shaking hand and placed it on the metal bar, 'Oh, I hope it's not too late.'

'Too late for what?!' I snarled.

'The devil has won after all. It has gotten him, and it has gotten you. Oh, you . . . have gotten him.'

'What?' I said, confused.

Was the old man still being hysterical? I looked into his eyes and found no madness in them, just raw sadness and guilt. I did not believe in all this dark magic cult that everyone around Don Vicenç believed in. Then, I remembered the woman devil and what it could do. It was telling me that I was the one who set her free.

'You said that—that you have fulfilled the prophecy, but did

Don Vicenç tell you the whole prophecy?' said Martín.

'What is it, old man?'

'"Blood will be spilt, of his own flesh and his own blood. Life in exchange for death, and when the task is fulfilled, he, who is banished, shall return to the land of darkness." That— that's the whole prophecy, Jacobo.'

To the land of darkness . . . Martín's words rang in my head. What could it possibly mean?

It never occurred to me, this strangeness inside of me, of my ability.

Who was I?

What was I?

Why did I possess this power?

Was it a curse?

'Oh, Jacobo . . .' the old man's voice snapped me out of my thoughts. 'Do—do you remember when I asked you to leave the castle before it was too late? It was because I didn't want the prophecy to come true. I found out who you were the day before you left for Barcelona.

'I had this suspicion that you could be the missing son of Don Vicenç. You are so much like him, both physical and in character. And then when I think of Rosinda, you do share her eyes,' said Martín.

I contemplated Martín's words. It was too much for me to take in as the truth knocked me and left me speechless. I felt that fate had made a fool out of me. And it was sneering at me. Martín must have known my mother because he has been serving Don Vicenç's family since the time of his grandfather.

'It's just that feeling in my gut that emerges whenever I see you,' he continued. 'You look so much like Don Vicenç when he was young. Somehow it even felt like I was going back in time, and I was talking to Don Vicenç from the past.' Martín's voice was soft. He had a longing look in his eyes. I hate it when I think how my face resembles my dead father. I stepped back and started to pace back and forth, trying to calm myself.

'And when I think about it, another thing that added to my suspicion is that you could read and write,' he said. 'And you told me once that your mother taught you. You said that you are from the hanging town, somewhere far away, a town of peasants, but a peasant's son could never read nor write. It's very unusual.

'Of course, at first, I thought it was just my stupid theory. How could a stupid man like myself be able to figure such a thing out . . . But I overheard a conversation between the twins, the witches. One of them said that she could feel something in you, something out of the ordinary that would threaten Don Vicenç's safety. But the other one with freckles said that she believed otherwise. She believed that Don Vicenç was threatening your safety. Their conversation added more weight to my suspicions. So I went to your room, just to find anything, any evidence at all, to lay weight on my suspicion. I found a knife, some herbs and a letter hidden inside the bag in the cupboard.'

I halted in front of his cell, letting everything sink in. I didn't look at the old man but from my peripheral view, I could see him looking at me. Both of his hands were holding onto the metal bar.

'I could not read what was said on the paper, so I asked my wife, Martha, to help me read it and told her all about my suspicion,' said Martín. 'You see, Martha used to work in the castle when Don Vicenç's father, Don Alfons, was still alive. By that time, we were already married. We are made for each other, we are almost the same in our devotion to our masters, but one difference that made her better than me was that Martha wasn't blind as I was.

'After Martha finished the letter, her face went pale. I could tell by the look on her face that my suspicion was true, that you are really the son of Rosinda.

'And finally, Martha told me everything that happened before—why she suddenly wanted to leave the castle after she had sworn to spend her life in service to Don Alfons and his son. Martha confessed to me that it was her who helped your mother escape. And she was afraid that anyone could sense the secret she had been trying to hide.

'It started one evening when Martha was told to bring dinner to Rosinda's chamber. You must know that Rosinda wasn't allowed to leave the room per Don Vicenç's order. So every day her food has to be brought to her in her private room. But that day, Rosinda's personal maid was sick, and it was Martha who brought the food to Rosinda. She was there half an hour earlier than Rosinda's usual dinner time. And upon arriving at the door, Martha heard Rosinda talking to someone. No one was allowed to enter Rosinda's room, except Don Vicenç and her personal maid, but the voice that Martha heard wasn't the voice of Don Vicenç. She said that it wasn't the voice of anything she had heard of before, for it was like a sizzling sound so quiet that it did not make any sense. Nevertheless, she understood everything that the voice was saying. "You prayed for help, and

I have come," said the voice, "yes, soon you will be free, but another thing that you have asked of me, I could not help you, for it's not the time. But his fate is set—blood will be spilt, of his own flesh and his own blood. Life in exchange for death, and when the task is fulfilled, he, who is banished, shall return to the land of darkness. The prophecy has been foretold. And now you shall wait."

'Martha said that the room went quiet after. So she quickly entered just to see who was inside with Rosinda. But it was only a second when Martha finally unlocked the door and entered. She found no one inside. And the time between her unlocking the door and entering would not give enough time to let whoever was inside the room to hide or escape through the window.

'Martha found your mother sitting alone at the far end of the room in front of the mirror. Her eyes came to rest on Rosinda's reflection. She said that she could never forget the anguish on Rosinda's face. And Rosinda, still in a haze of fear and some kind of trance, got up off the chair and walked towards the bed. She didn't even notice that someone had entered the room. But when Martha called out her name, Rosinda turned to her with an utter shock. But Rosinda's expression was like a mirror, mirroring Martha's face. What she saw on Rosinda's face were bruises. Her once white neck was full of black and blue marks.'

I swallowed down the bitter truth and kept listening to the old man's words. I thought of my poor dear mother. And I thought of the death that Don Vicenç deserved.

'Martha had heard that Don Vicenç beat his own wife, but when she witnessed the outcome, she could not believe her own eyes—how could a man do this to his own wife?

'Martha went to your mother and told her how sorry she was for the man she had helped raise. And, of course, any servant so devoted to Don Vicenç would never utter such a thing. Rosinda took this as a sign that her hope wasn't lost. She took this chance to ask Martha to help her escape. Rosinda told Martha that if she agreed to help, Martha would be saving two lives and not just one, as she was pregnant.

'Even though the prophecy wasn't clear, Rosinda could not fathom seeing any of it come true. She could not ever watch her child be killed by his own monstrous father, or risk having her child kill his own father and lose himself completely to the darkness . . .

'But one thing that I see wrong is that your mother made one mistake. Before she escaped, she left Don Vicenç a letter, cursing him and telling him about the prophecy that one day he will die by the hand of his own flesh and blood. And I suppose that was the beginning of it all.

'I had no idea about all these stories until Martha confessed to me. She was very meek and shy, and from other's people point of view, she was very devoted to her master. No one would ever suspect that it was her who helped Rosinda.

'But after she found out that your mother was still alive, she begged me to help you and to prevent the prophecy from coming true. She told me that she also wanted to repent for her sin, as she was the reason for the death of Rosinda's personal maid. Don Vicenç whipped her because he thought that she failed to do her deed. The maid died the day after. And it haunted Martha's consciousness until today.

'But when Martha asked me to help you and keep your secret from Don Vicenç, I knew that by helping you, I would betray Don Vicenç. However, I also developed a fondness for you, Jacobo. Might it be because you reminded me of Don Vicenç when he was still innocent? So I was left in between the dilemma of a fool. Should I be the same devoted servant to my master, or should I listen to Martha and at least tell you to leave, so this whole mess of a prophecy would not be fulfilled.

'I—I did not know what to do . . . I told Martha that it was too dangerous because if Don Vicenç found out, he would definitely come back for us all. But that day, Martha stood up to me. She never thought that Rosinda and the baby were still alive. But once she knew, she told me she'd had enough of being a coward. She told me that if I wasn't going to help you and let this madness end, she would help you herself. I was left to choose between Don Vicenç and my family, and that was when I knew that the feelings I have for Don Vicenç were not of love. They weren't the same feelings I have for Martha and Rosalia. The line between the two was so thin I could barely see it.

'That left me no choice. I had chosen to protect Martha and Rosalia. I promised her that I would try my best. But I warned Martha that if something ever went wrong, she should take Rosalia and leave. Martha agreed. She told me that she would go find your mother at the hanging town. And I should meet her there.

'Then, the day after, when I went back to the castle, I saw you with Don Vicenç, dressing and acting like him. I did not know what Don Vicenç was plotting. But I could see the pieces of prophecy were starting to fall into place.

'Like your mother said, you are not overly white or black,

but you could be dragged into the darkness easily. I knew at that moment in time, you could never take anyone's life because you are a boy of a good heart. Your mother must have taught you well. But once I got to know you better, I could also feel that you have a seed of evil somewhere inside you. And I thought under Don Vicenç's influence, you would be corrupted, and that you would become the person your mother was most scared of.

'And when I met Don Vicenç that day, he told me that he was going to Barcelona soon, and he was going to take you with him. I knew that it might already be too late, but I tried to warn you anyway. And then, in the attic, I saw that sculpture of yours. It—she, she is a devil in disguise. She laughed and shunned me when she knew what I intended to do. She knew that I was trying to prevent your prophecy from falling into place. She told me that a person like me could never be helped. That devil! She possessed the power of destruction! She really saw through me and destroyed what was left of me.

'I was left hopeless and broken beyond repair after the conversation I had with her. She showed me who I could have been and the person I really was. Yes, now I realise how small and utterly hopeless a person I have become. All my life, I have been devoted to a man who, in return, used my devotion and loyalty to manipulate me. I suppose I wanted to be loved and praised by Don Vicenç so much that I blindly followed his orders. My master was a very smart man, wasn't he? He turned my loyalty, which should have been a strong point of mine, into weakness. Now I see why he had given me a house and allowed me to marry Martha. He even gave Rosalia to me . . . I thought Rosalia was a gift from him to me as a reward for being a humble servant.

But it was just his plan all along. Don Vicenç knew how useful I was to him and how deeply I was already involved in his evil deeds. He could not possibly risk my betrayal. So he used Rosalia and Martha as a tool to bargain with me.

'Deep down, under my subconscious, I was doubtful. I was scared that what Don Vicenç had given, he could take away. I was afraid that he would take Martha and Rosalia once I disobeyed him. I know what my master was capable of. I know what he did to those people who defied him. But with all these feelings in my gut, still, I turned a blind eye to it because I was too devoted to him. And because of my stupidity, this is the fate I have to live with.

'I am less than a person. I am a fool, and I am worthless . . . The devil had almost succeeded in encouraging me to take my own life, but the only thing that still kept me alive is the hope that Martha and Rosalia are safe somewhere with your mother.'

I stood speechless in front of Martín's cell. Inside of me was a storm of feelings.

Somewhere, deep down within me, I felt sorry for Martín. But I couldn't hold that feeling for a long time, for it was all clouded with a black smog of corruption and hate that was polluting me.

I also felt scared of the darkness that I had unleashed. I started to understand the power of darkness I could embed within my sculpture. The part of the evil that I let it slip out had managed to destroy Martín from the inside out.

'Jacobo,' said Martín. 'I fear for you. I don't want you to go down the path of sin. Right now, I felt remorseful for every life I could have saved. And with you, I think maybe it's not all too late even though part of the prophecy has already been fulfilled. But I do not believe you have completely lost yourself to the devil yet.

'Go back to your mother. Let her help you. And forget about all these things as if you had never met any of us. Do not take hate and malice into your heart. I think it's the only way for you to not fulfil the whole prophecy. Go, Jacobo, go to Rosinda and let the love of your mother guide you.'

I went for the pile of keys and opened the old man's cell. Upon noticing my action, he looked up at me, his face full of hope, of expectation that I had overlooked his sin.

'I am sorry, Martín,' I said under my breath when the old man slowly walked past the metal door. He caught my eyes and tried to approach me, but I took one step back, hating the idea of having him touch me. I said to him, 'Your remorse could not be compared to the deeds you have done. I could never forgive your actions. And isn't it ironic that a sinful man like you is trying to tell me to repent my for sins?'

'Please, Jacobo,' said the old man. 'I know that I cannot undo the past, but I don't want you to suffer the same fate as me.'

'Oh, you have not gotten to the suffering part yet,' I told him as I thought about Rosalia's body floating lifelessly inside the glass jar. Something deep within my consciousness triggered me not to tell Martín about Rosalia's fate.

'Are you going to kill me?' He said.

'No, I am not going to kill you. But I am going to tell you something,' I said, ignoring that small warning, a sense of right and wrong. 'You have been living under false hope all this time. Vicenç got his hands on Rosalia before you. He ordered Itzal to murder her and put her inside one of the glasses just like you did with the other babies. And I suppose if he got Rosalia, Martha must also have suffered a similar fate.'

Martín plummeted down to the floor, 'No! No . . . You are lying to me.'

'Why should I lie about such a horrible thing?' I said as I started to walk away. The old man's sobs echoed with my footsteps inside the quiet dungeon. 'Killing you would not satisfy me. You don't deserve it. You deserve to die slowly, taking this guilt with you to your grave. I set fire to that cursed room of yours. It will bring down the whole castle. So I am going to let you decide your own fate whether you want to continue living or not.'

I wasn't any kind of god who could pardon his sin. Whatever he did, whether he did it blindly, he deserved all his guilt and sorrow. Why did he ask me for absolution when he knew that what I could give was just the opposite?

I took Cecilia's lifeless body in my arm and headed towards the exit.

'Goodbye, Martín. I hope we never meet again.'

# Chapter Twenty-Eight

Outside the castle, the fire was burning; its orange flames swayed like an angry dancer that reminded me of the forked tongue devil woman skipping her devil dances when she manifested herself into my vision.

The fire reached the top of the castle and vividly burned its way down. The women who used to work there ran out with a sack of what I supposed were valuable things of Don Vicenç's. I spotted Alba among them. She was wearing a type of cloak that used to belong to Don Vicenç's guests.

I laid Cecilia's body down on the ground. It would not be hard to bury her as the rain had softened the ground beneath the earth.

I looked around me and saw no trace of Flor and Andrea. When Alba spotted me, she came over.

'I am sorry about her,' said Alba as her eyes cast to Cecilia's body. 'She must be someone you care about.'

'She was, but it doesn't matter anymore,' I told her. 'Where are Flor and Andrea,' I asked, intending to change the subject.

'I have not seen them come out yet.'

'I will go back and see if Andrea needs help. You and the others should leave before the fire attracted unwanted thieves or Don Vicenç's men. They can't be far away.'

'At least let me help you with your friend's body. You don't know how many of our lives you have saved here.'

'No, I will take care of it. At least she deserves that. Now, go far from here and start your new life. I hope you have taken enough valuable things.'

'Oh, each of us has more than enough,' she gave me a faint smile as she moved closer. Alba seemed reluctant before she took my hand. 'Jacobo, be careful, and thank you, truly,' she said.

I felt a little squeeze from her cold hand before it disappeared. Her soft and cold touch reminded me of Cecilia's hand, which made me look directly into her face. Slowly, I started to see those freckles across the bridge of her nose, spreading out onto her cheekbones. I blinked once or twice, and Alba's face was clear of those freckles once again.

'Stay safe, Alba,' I finally told her.

Alba nodded and went to join the other women who mouthed the word thank you to me. I acknowledged them with a nod before I slipped into the burning castle in search of Andrea and Flor.

Inside, the smoke was beginning to creep through the ground floor, sending a whip of smog straight through my nostrils and throat. I couldn't help but cough from that burning smell.

I hurried on to find a trace of Flor and Andrea as the sound of fire crackled above me, eating away raw what was in its way.

'Andrea!' I shouted. But there was no reply.

I went down every possible corridor and paused to hear any unusual sounds. Within one of the rooms, I could hear a woman's voice. I followed it, and I recognised this corridor as the same one I first entered in this castle when I was searching for writing materials. The voice that echoed through the quietness came out from the same room where I first saw Don Vicenç and Delilah. I went straight to the door and pushed it open.

I saw Flor sitting on Don Vicenç's bed, humming the same melancholy tune to the haystack in her arms. It took me a second before I spotted Andrea sitting in the far corner of the room, cradling his head in his hands and holding a pistol.

'Andrea?' I said.

He looked up, and his face was full of tears and misery.

'What are you doing here? You should leave,' said Andrea.

'Alba said she did not see you and Flor come out of the castle.'

'Flor never wanted to leave. I—I did not know that she really loved that mad man, that monster who erased all the goodness in my sister. I think I have already lost what was once my sister.' Andrea was talking through his tears, but his eyes shone with the same look that was on Martín's face; a man who had lost all hope and a will to live.

'Andrea. Let me help her,' I said as I tried to approach Flor.

When I reached for her arm, Flor screamed. She snarled at me like a feral animal, baring her teeth with wild eyes. I stood frozen to the ground and withdrew my hand.

Flor giggled and went back to her baby and kept on humming the same tune.

'She is not the Flor we used to know anymore,' Andrea said. 'I have lost my sister already. She is no longer Flor but a devil!'

Andrea stepped into the light, and I could see a fresh bite and nail marks on his face.

'Andrea,' I whispered his name. He abruptly pushed his hair

that usually covered half of his face away, and with a quick glance, I could see the unevenness of his face. His right cheek-bone was totally out of place, and the skin of his right eyes sagged, making him look half-human, half-monster.

Andrea did not care to hide his face any longer when he looked at me. 'Leave now, before I find it in my brain that you have played some part in Flor's destruction.' He pointed the pistol in my direction.

'What are you doing?' I said.

'I can't let the devil take her,' he said before he fired. The bullet flew past me and went straight to Flor. Everything happened way too fast for me to process. A second after seeing Flor's body slumped on the bed, Andrea, with his miserable face, cocked the pistol again and lifted it at his head, 'And I will not leave here without her.'

'NO! An—' I did not finish his name before he fired. The effect of the pistol destroyed both the devilish and beautiful side of his face.

The quietness that came after the shot and the scene of both Flor and Andrea lying dead haunted me. I had to quickly leave the room.

Upon grabbing the door handle, I noticed that my hand was shaking. I ignored it and walked out of the castle as quickly as I could.

It was raining again, a shower of rain as if the sky knew my misery and was weeping on my behalf. The scenery I saw from the front of the castle glowed orange from the blaze. Outside, beyond a stone and metal fence, everything was quiet now, apart from the crackling sound of the heat. The wind blew quietly, and the spurt of rain kept on falling.

I turned and looked back at the burning castle. It was as if I was looking inside myself; the fire was burning me alive on the inside.

I walked over to Cecilia's body and finally dug a hole under the weeping willow tree with the shovel that I'd found near the stable. Cecilia's body lay amid the wet dirt, inside a hole that was a little too small for her body. I felt pathetic for the thing I had done to her when she was alive and the thing I had done for her body when she was gone. But I felt so tired, so numb all over my body, all over my soul.

As I was throwing the dirt over Cecilia's body, I could not utter anything or even say my last goodbye. The only thing driving me was the need to see my mother's face. I knew that at that moment, I needed her light to guide me.

I looked at Cecilia's nameless grave one last time before I walked to the stable. It was almost empty, except for some horses that were neighing as if they knew that danger was lurking nearby.

I chose the large black horse that seemed to calm when he saw me and freed the rest.

Riding off towards my home, I looked back at the angry flames that the spurts of rain had been trying to tame. And there, at the foot of the castle, a movement caught my eye; I spotted Martín, staggering and wandering to nowhere—a lost soul.

So I thought, the old man was not so valiant in the end.

I rode off with a tired body and a bitter soul. I suppose that the expectation of seeing my mother's smile and hearing her voice was, after all, like those spurts of rain that tried to extinguish the angry flames, for now, in my heart, I felt the fire burn lower.

On the horizon, it was still dark, but the sun was waiting to be set free from this vast line of darkness at any moment.

I could feel the sharp wind on my skin, but the coldness could not cut through me, for the numbness had already crept through my bones.

When I reached the bottom of the mountain where the hanging town was situated, the light had already begun to shine, glowing dimly through the darkness. The black horse did not show any signs of fatigue as it gained speed across the small stone bridge of the hanging town.

When I finally passed through the small street that cut through to the wood, I heard no noises of life, the only sound echoing down the small pathway was the rapid rhythm of horse hooves. I kept on riding until I came to a familiar path within the wood. The winter season had left the tree's branches bare, only darkened trunks stood haphazardly, uncanny bony limbs trying to reach for me with their bony arms. The ground was coated with the fiery red colour of fallen leaves and dried leaves, piled up in a thick layer.

I jumped off the horse once I spotted the silhouette of my humble home, blending in with the stillness and the quietness of the wood.

'Mother!' I shouted as I pushed through the door, expecting to see her grinding herbs as she always did in the morning. But there was no one there, and there was no answer from my mother.

'Mother,' I called out for her again, and still, my voice dissolved away in the emptiness and quietness of this cold and foggy place. The bedroom was also empty, but there, where the bed lay, it was made as if waiting for her to come and rest her tired body after a long day at the market.

I looked out through the window. The fog had not dispersed and the light had not penetrated through. And out there, among the thick fog and the darkened trunks and empty branches of the trees, I spotted one tree that hadn't yet shed its leaves. The fiery red colour stood out among the foggy black and white scenery in front of me. It took me a second to realise what I had seen wasn't the last leaf of the autumn.

'NO!!!'

Everything in me fell apart as I ran to the spot, to see the last thing that Don Vicenç had been preparing for me. My mother's fiery red hair stood out among the darkened branches. Her body was suspended above the ground by the loop of rope around her slim neck.

I stumbled to my knees, under my mother's feet with no word, no feelings and not a single drop of tear.

I hated myself for not being there for her, and I hated myself even more for my own stupidity that had dragged my mother's life into the hand of fate.

Fate! Why was there such a thing as fate that could make fools of us all? Who was it that reprimanded us? Someone must be at the end of the string, weaving and pulling me into this tragedy. Was it this God, or was it the god of darkness? I would denounce them all.

If fate had decided to hand me this, then I was going to take my revenge.

The dampened fire in my heart burned once more. This time it churned and burned and twisted. An immense amount of hate and anger melted my corroded heart into hot black tar, slowly eating up everything that was left inside. Everything fumed up and exploded from within—like erupted lava, until there was nothing left of me but pure darkness.

'Arghh!!!' A voice of anger and desperation shuddered through the quiet of the wood.

Shrouded in mist, I was half-awake, half-delusional, trying to accept the truth of what had happened, for it all seemed like a dream. I wished to wake up in a different place or a different time. But there I was, sitting underneath my mother's feet. I do not know how long I was there until I realised that I had to end her prolonged suffering. I cut her down from the branch.

Seeing her pale and lifeless body in my arms, still, I wished her lips would curve into a smile from the happiness of seeing her only son, but as the time went on, I knew it was a wish that I had wished for in vain, for my mother's lips remained dim, just like the light in my soul.

A string of necklace with a small squirrel hanging from it caught my eye. I remembered it well, as it was one of the first pieces of sculpture I had made. It seemed like forever ago. It was one of the summers when my mother was cooking, and I was playing outside the hut when a tiny brown squirrel came down from the tree and tried to steal my chestnuts. That little brown creature wasn't afraid of me, and nor was I afraid of it. It took its time to eat and crack the chestnut open, allowing me to observe it in wonder. I took my time to remember all of its movements and its curiosity. That afternoon, I made a small duplication of that curious little creature from my little hands.

When I was done, I showed it to my mother, and she told me she had been observing me while I was observing the squirrel. 'I saw you, I saw the wonder in you, my dear boy,' she said to me that day. I never noticed that she had kept that particular piece with her this whole time.

I was left with only memories of her, that I swore would be eternally imprinted in my heart and mind.

It was such an unspeakable misery and an unfathomable pain.

How was I supposed to endure it?

How would I go on?

A soundless sob rose up from my empty soul. 'Oh, mother, please, I need you. I need you to tell me that it will all be all right. Please, don't leave me alone in this world. I cannot bear it.'

All regrets, shame and sadness squashed my heart and my whole being. Beside me, my mother's body still remained lifeless. It killed me each time I looked at her ashen face.

Mother, mother, mother . . .

My mother, mother, mother . . .

Her hand felt so inhumane, so lifeless. She was stiff. Was it because of the cold? But I knew better than that, I just could not accept the fact that her body was decaying as she had been dead for hours. Don Vicenç must have sent Itzal here to finish her off while he tried to finish me.

At last, I told myself the thing that I had to do. I buried her body near the hut where we used to live. Each and every time the dirt covered her body, my heart broke for the millionth time.

When the last pile of soil finally covered her, I still did not know how to say goodbye, as I would never be ready, but there was nothing I could do. I begged for everything in my power to give life back to my mother. There was no one who could answer my prayer; there was only darkness and the echo of my wishful wish.

My dreams and my life were lost now.

Besides my mother lifeless body, I crumbled.

I fell under . . .

. . . And under . . .

. . . Until I became submerged on the other side.

# PART FOUR

Long gone the sails
'Til we meet again
Once in this life
Twice in the next
Knock upon my door
Save me with your spell.

# Chapter Twenty-Nine

'Y ou came back at last. We all have been waiting.'

Something that was similar to a voice murmured, for I did not know what to call what I was hearing. It was like a sizzle that cut through the air, sending a vibration throughout the complete darkness, but it managed to form a word, a sentence that conducted meaning.

As I turned left and right, the sizzling noise grew all around. It was coming from every direction, a hissing that seemed to echo from externally and internally. I became irritated.

'Where am I?' I said, but my voice was not my voice, but the same sizzling sound that echoed through the darkness, just like the same echo I'd heard a second ago.

Suddenly, a figure appeared right in front of me. It possessed no shape or form but was some kind of shadow, however, as I looked closer, it was composed of an eerie touchable smoke. I extended my hand, and through it, my hand went smoothly, like I was touching thin air, though I could feel the heat emitted from this figure. Then, it expanded in a swift motion, and once I pulled my hand away, it recoiled.

A swift noise of sizzles hissed again, 'You have fulfilled your prophecy. You have proved yourself worthy, you have fully embraced the darkness as you should. You will unleash all of us with your wrath. We will feed on their sin, and we will thrive. And with that, you and I, and all of us, we will live through eternity.'

# Chapter Thirty

I awoke under the midnight sky next to my mother's un-
marked grave. I didn't feel like myself. Something in me
had completely changed. It was as if I was manifested
with calamitous evilness at the tip of my fingers.

My dreams and my life were lost now. But there was only
one thing that kept me alive. If I was determined to release my
wrath and take my revenge, so be it; it shall be my new purpose
in life.

I stood up, and when I cast my eyes around, I was no longer
in complete darkness but surrounded by a glowing pair of eyes.
The creatures' wings fluttered, and I knew what those reflec-
tions were—an owl, a creature of the darkness, of death and
of evil.

A heaving breath of the large black stallion came closer and
closer to me until I could feel the muscles of its strong legs. I
embraced the sign of what I needed to do.

On horseback, I rode on. My destination was Barcelona, and
one by one, I would search for Don Vicenç's little treacherous
mice, his followers and servants.

Death was what they all deserved.

First, I would start with Delilah.

It was not much effort to find out where Delilah lived. My foot-steps trailed without a sound and left no footprints behind. Darkness enveloped my presence. I was a shadow of destruc-tion, a devil in disguise.

The burning torches on the wall and the candles in the cor-ner went out one by one as I approached.

It was eerily quiet inside Don Bernado and Delilah's house. Shadows clouded every corner of their place, and the air was damp and cold like a forgotten tomb. I thought to myself, even after sunrise, this would remain unchanged, for the life of the master of the household would end tonight.

It wasn't hard to locate Delilah's bedroom, for the scent of Don Vicenç's lustful perfume was still branded on her.

I stood at the edge of Delilah's bed, watching her sleeping form that looked carefree as if nothing in this world, except her own self-interest, could affect her. I thought to myself, was this the woman I had fallen for? Looking at her now, I saw a person who lived between mirrors, unable to look past her own self-obsessed ego.

And that man sleeping next to her, Don Bernado, he was just a stupid man who fell into the wrong hands of the wrong people. But there was nothing that could be changed now. There would be no forgiveness or exceptions. If he was a follower of Don Vicenç, then his fate was set.

I knew I was going to have some fun with these people with the evil I was going to bestow upon them, an evil that would corrupt them from the inside.

Delilah stirred in her bed. Her chest heaved as her breathing became more rapid. I watched as the nightmare consumed her once peaceful sleep. She startled awake, but the darkness concealed my existence.

'Bernado,' said Delilah as she shook her husband awake, 'wake up. I—I had a horrible dream, so horrible.'

Don Bernado stirred under the force of his wife's hands. Irritated by his wife, who woke him up from his blissful dream. Drowsily, he said, 'Go back to sleep, darling. It's just a dream.'

'It was so real,' cried Delilah as she sat up in bed. Her long dark hair fell down her white nightgown. 'I saw a baby in my arms, but it was deformed, and it had these pitch-black eyes. It looked so devilish, Bernado. Oh, I wanted to throw it away, but it grabbed hold of me with its claw. I screamed, but it wouldn't let go. And in my arms, it—it turned into this pale, wrinkled creature. There was no trace of the baby in it, only horror! And it talked to me. Oh, it told me horrible things. And its voice!'

'Darling, darling,' Don Bernado turned over. He placed his hand on Delilah's arm. 'As I said, it was just a dream. Go back to sleep. When you wake up tomorrow, you will have forgotten all about it.'

'It said that—' Delilah's eyes widened as she sniffed in the air around her. 'What is that smell? Can you smell it? It is like something sweet but burnt.'

'Please, darling, I can't smell anything. You are just being paranoid.' Don Bernado turned away from his wife and tried to go back to sleep.

Delilah looked around. Her eyes went past my shadowed

presence.

She breathed in again. 'It is like burnt sugar. Bernado! It is the same smell as that baby in my dream. Bernado! Wake up!'

'Dear Lord, woman! Do not shout. I have to get a good night's sleep tonight,' Don Bernado said, annoyed, but his back was still turned to her. 'Tomorrow I need to justify to the authority what happened to Count Alfonso. And if I don't get enough sleep, I won't be able to concentrate.'

Delilah got out of bed and walked to the window. She pulled open the tapestries. The moonlight shone inside some parts of the room, but the darkness and I was one, it still concealed my presence.

'Are you being serious? Did you have to let the light in?' Don Bernado pulled the blanket over his head.

'I am scared, alright? And you did nothing to ease it,' Delilah said as she walked back to the bed. 'And I don't understand why you are afraid of the authorities. You did not kill Count Alfonso. That fat man jumped out the window by himself.'

'To tell you the truth,' Don Bernado mumbled under the blanket. 'I did not see what happened. Don Vicenç and Count Alfonso were in the room, and I was waiting in the other room because Don Vicenç told me he had some private business to discuss with Count Alfonso. I heard them having an argument.'

'So what? Are you suggesting that Don Vicenç pushed him out the window? Don't be ridiculous. You would have heard something even if you were just sitting in the next room.'

'You are right, but after a loud argument, everything went quiet, and not long after, Don Vicenç came to fetch me, saying that the meeting was over, and it was time to leave. I did not see or hear Count Alfonso afterwards.'

'Don Vicenç could not have pushed him out of the window,' said Delilah. 'Anyway, are you going to tell the authority that you did not see? That could get Don Vicenç in trouble. Don't you think we owe him that small favour? You could testify that you saw Count Alfonso before you left.'

When Delilah saw that Don Bernado's form was still and gave her no answer, she pulled the blanket off him. 'Are you still listening to me?' she said.

Don Bernado gave an apparent sigh in annoyance before he sat up in bed. 'I'm not sure about that man. Can't you see that these past years, Don Vicenç's motives have begun to change little by little? It is like he is consumed by greed and something worse. To be honest, I'm beginning to doubt everything about the belief. And don't you see that, one by one, each of the members has met a terrible end instead of flourishing like we have been promised? Count Alfonso is dead, and Countess Helena went mad. It could be anyone next. It could be us!'

'I can't believe what you just said,' Delilah said in a mocking tone.

I thought to myself, Don Bernado was not a total fool after all.

'This could get back to us, too!' Don Bernado hissed. 'If in any way Don Alfonso's death was a suicide, the authorities would investigate his motives, and it would not end there. All of the nobles in Aragon will know the news of Count Alfonso's death. And don't you see? They will investigate everything, and not only will they find out about our cult, but they will also know that we are backing the Habsburg. The king is dying, and he wanted his cousin to succeed to the throne, but his cousin, the Duke of Anjou, is a Bourbon. Once the authority digs deep into Count Alfonso's business, they will find out everything. And then, we will become both traitors of the church and of the country. I am afraid, Delilah.'

'So what? You are going to blame everything on Vicenç? Are you going to say that he killed Count Alfonso?'

'I am just saying that I will tell them the truth that I did not see what happened in that room, and I did not hear and see Count Alfonso after Don Vicenç left. And if they want to investigate Don Vicenç, let them. In the meantime, we should leave Barcelona.'

'Oh, you are such a coward,' she snorted.

'Why do you want to protect Don Vicenç so much? I'm doing this because of us! Do you want to end up in a noose?'

'We won't! Don Vicenç will know what to do. He would never let the authorities interfere with his purpose and plan! All you can think of is to escape? And let him be a scapegoat?'

Don Bernado went quiet as he stared down blankly at his hands, 'So it is true then . . .' he whispered.

'What is?' Delilah said as she looked at him as if her husband had gone mad.

'Don't look at me like I am stupid. Tell me, are you unfaithful to me? Are you having an affair with Don Vicenç? I want to hear it from your mouth,' Don Bernado said as he looked at Delilah. 'Please, do not lie to me, at least you owe me that much after everything I have done and sacrificed for you.'

'What? No? Of course not. What are you talking about? I can't believe you are asking me that right now. Don't you think—'

'Do not change the subject. And, please, Delilah, no more lies. Everyone has been telling me about it. At his castle and his apartment, the nights when I woke up and did not see you in bed and those nights and days when you disappeared when you said you were with your friends. Were you with him?'

'Of course not.'

Don Bernado snorted, 'You said that I am a coward, but I think the real coward is you. You can't even tell the truth to my face.'

'How dare you say that to me. Fine, if you want to know the truth. Yes, I have been cheating on you, and you know what? It was not only with Don Vicenç but also with Lord Cristobal. And you know why? It is because you are an incompetent person! Everything that you have in life is because of your father. You by yourself, you can't achieve anything. For God's sake, you can't even father a child, and you can't even keep a wife in your bed!'

I grinned as I watched how the evil I had unleashed manifested in Delilah's heart and mind, bringing out the worst in her. And slowly, I let the evil creep up into Don Bernado's inner self as it made his heart and mind recoil with anguish.

I could feel how Delilah's words burned into Don Bernado's skin and cut into the deepest part of his soul. Nothing could ever undo the wound that had been punctured in his heart. He knew that he was incompetent, but nobody had ever said that to him, so day by day, he kept building up courage and telling himself that if Delilah, the most beautiful woman, chose him as her husband, he must be a person of some quality. But, alas, her words and actions were nothing but lies.

327

Whatever confidence and self-esteem were left in him evaporated into thin air. He could not hear what his wife was saying now. Everything else went quiet, except for the word incompetent . . . incompetent . . . incompetent . . . that kept ringing in his ears.

It brought him back to when he was young, when he was hiding under a table on the day of his older brother's funeral. He hid away as if he could hide away from the truth and all the responsibility that would come after. The door of the dining room opened, and young Bernado could see his father's shoes, and young Bernado remembered his father's words, 'It should have been Bernado and not my Carlos. How could Bernado inherit the title from me? He is such an incompetent person. And where is he when he is supposed to be a man?!'

Don Bernado quietly got out the bed and went for his coat. He pulled a pocket knife from a hidden pocket. And without any word, he went straight to Delilah. With a knife in his hand, he slashed her beautiful face.

Delilah screamed in horror as the knife slit across her left forehead through her nose and split her lower lip.

'Let's see if Vicenç still prefers you this way, and you should tell my family how incompetent I am,' said Don Bernado before he struck the knife in his own neck. And that moment in the dark, he looked in my direction. I stepped out of the darkness and tilted my head in a mocking way. His eyes met mine, but it was too late. His time in life was running out. His face was full of confusion, then once he realised that he could not talk nor breathe, it turned to horror. He saw me smiling, but he gagged on his own blood, unable to form any words or make any sense.

He struggled for a second before he fell to the floor.

His time was up.

Delilah still screamed in horror, but I bet it was for herself, for her lost beauty and not for her husband's death.

Delilah deserved to spend the rest of her time suffering, to live with a face that matched her heart, scarred and distorted. I watched her as she sobbed and as her blood dripped down, tainting her pure white nightgown.

Who was going to be next?

# Chapter Thirty-One

One by one, all of Don Vicenç's followers went down a slope towards damnation, the path that would take them towards endless suffering that would last centuries, and then, only then, they would begin to wonder how they had ended up in the black pit of purgatory, suffering endless agony. And little by little, each and every minute in between the centuries of their lives, I would feed on their unforgivable sins. They couldn't escape from me wherever they were.

And when the sanity of Don Vicenç's last devotee had been ripped away, I went back to Barcelona.

Of all the fun I had, I had to keep the best ones to last; Itzal. . . that cold-blooded man, He was the one who took the life of my mother. With his treacherous deed, he would never be allowed to live. Life in exchange for life, and Itzal's life was mine.

I knew Itzal had been tracking me, but as I was constantly on the move, he had to work harder to find me. But I always knew that he was near. Itzal was good at what he does. He moved quickly and quietly like a shadow moving through the water. He was also cautious and careful but lethal, like a leopard on the hunt. I gave him some warning by leaving behind a trail of my work, of what I was capable of. I knew the more he witnessed the death under my hand, the more he would be anxious to take my life, as it would add flame to his ego and lunacy that he would have outsmarted the person he believed to be better than him. And that would make him the best of all.

In the narrow streets of Barcelona, it was eerily quiet. Not a single person came down the streets tonight as if they could sense the smell of danger in the air. Windows were drawn shut, and not a glimpse of candlelight escaped through the cracks.

Along the street, my footsteps never gave away my presence. And here I was, standing in front of the large wooden door of the cathedral of the Saint Mary of the Sea.

I took a step inside, and a rush of wind fluttered the candle flames before they blew out.

It wasn't long after when I heard the door of the cathedral creak open, so quiet as if a mouse had slipped inside, and I knew that it was him.

In the middle of the basilica, I stood waiting. His eyes still looked the same as that day by the stream. They gave away nothing, but at the same time, they gave away everything. The coldness in his eyes showed that he had no feelings, no regrets, the look of a psychopath. And that was the reason why he ended up with Don Vicenç. The likeness of their souls was the same they attracted each other. And now, his soul attracted mine.

Itzal stopped a meter away from me. 'You are a hard man to find,' he said. 'For you, I have stepped inside a place I vowed I would never enter again. You have no idea how I have spent all my life under the rule of God and how he has failed me.

'Oh, and I have to say that I'm surprised you have come this far from that boy I saw at the stream. I don't know how you managed to kill my master and all of his friends.

'Don Vicenç gave me so much entertainment. All those animals he made me skin. And all those women's screams. Oh, Martín's old lady and that small kid. Their screams were like music to my ears. Now that Don Vicenç is dead, I have to find some fun elsewhere. But I would also say that chasing you and imagining what I am going to do to you brings me pleasure.

'You know, I missed all the fun in my life when I was in the monastery with those idiots who called me brother. And you have no idea how that abbot was so obsessed about having the top of my head shaved,' Itzal chuckled like an awkward child who just learned how to laugh. 'But before I left, I helped him take off the scalp at the top of his head, so he didn't have to be bothered shaving that hair anymore.'

'You talk a lot, don't you,' I said, unbothered by this mad man's words.

Itzal chuckled and smiled. 'Fine, soon, you won't have to listen to my babbling.'

'Or soon, no one will ever have to listen to you babbling,' I replied.

Itzal didn't laugh this time. He swiftly unfolded a long blade from his hand, the one that I didn't realise he was even holding. It was the length of my forearm and slightly curved at the pointy end—a deadly weapon.

He charged towards me with the swiftness and precision of a true killer, aiming below my left rib, a least deadly spot. So he didn't plan to give me a quick death.

But what he didn't know was that he was no match for me.

Itzal kept on charging, but I was quicker. My movement was even quicker than his own shadow. A second before he came at me with his knife, I had already moved away to the other side. I kept on evading his knife like he was playing a childish game with me. And I knew that it would boil up his anger and frustration. He thought that he was the best and the quickest, but he thought wrong.

Once he knew what he was up against, he tried to distract me with his words while trying to get past my guard. 'You are full of surprises, aren't you?' he said. 'I suppose you have your mother's blood after all. You don't fear death, and neither did she. Torturing her didn't give me that much pleasure. She didn't scream, you see. But I got to her eventually. I told her about how Don Vicenç was finishing you off. That was the only thing that made her tick. Oh, but hanging her was fun after all. The way she squirmed for air.'

This bastard knew too little of me. His miserable life would soon come to an end.

In a swift second, I knocked the blade out of his hand. It flew upward, and before it started to fall, I caught it mid-air. Itzal's eyes went wide, following every move I made. It happened so quickly that the only thing he could react to at that moment was the movement of his eyes that followed me. And before he could command his own body to move, I was already behind him. With a quick and lethal movement, I slit deep into both tendons behind Itzal's knees, making sure that they were severely torn.

Itzal fell on his hand, but he kept on chuckling. It was an unbearable sound I no longer wanted to hear. I went over him before kicking him to the ground. He was lying face-up, looking at my face. I hated his cold eyes and his perfect teeth. And before he was about to say something, I stabbed his vocal cords. The chuckling sound was replaced by a gurgling that I considered much more pleasant.

Itzal's blue eyes were looking at me now. I thought about plucking them out, but then he would miss what I was going to do next. So, I spared those eyes for him to witness everything.

I slit the skin on his arms open, just for him to feel the pain, but not enough for him to pass out. Each time the sharp blade sliced into him, I thought of the life that he had taken.

The movement of his lips caught my attention. The bastard was crazy, after all. Even though he could not talk, he was still trying to do anything just to intimidate me. I didn't bother trying to understand what he was trying to say. Without hesitation, I dragged him by the hair up the tower steps until I reached the first level. The stone floor was now painted red from the blood flowing out from his wounds.

Itzal's cold eyes shone with fear now.

I smirked at him. I thought he was going to be brave enough to show no fear until the end.

I took out a rope from my coat and tied a tight noose around his neck and the other end to the stone at the top of the facade.

The last look I saw on his face was the look of a defeated man, and it shone with terror. I ignored the pleading in his eyes. He tried to form a word but failed. From the facade of the cathedral, I threw Itzal's body down. The sound of his snapping neck rang through the quietness of the night. His lifeless body dangled from the church door, right in front of the sculpture of Jesus Christ that seemed to be condemning his past deeds.

# Chapter Thirty-Two

The king died that year, and what followed were years of unleashed of evil, corrupting everything in my path. Barcelona fell under siege. There was no peace for another thirty years or years that followed.

Wars raged on every corner while hate and malice kept burning through human's hearts. And I fed and thrived on those sins.

Ashes of what was left were carried by the wind into the greyish sky. The dust of the crumbled memories twirled around ashes of bone, and hand in hand, they disappeared, leaving us with only unfinished tales.

And here I was, still unleashing destruction and thriving from the corruption of the human soul.

How long had it been now?

Dew froze the tips of fading green glass. Colours that once remained slowly wilted, fading away one by one.

Time slowly changed everything for better and for worse. I had witnessed the famine when the water rose in the land, drowning every surface and all the life underneath. Then, the drought caught up in the once soft soil, cracking the surface of the earth, transforming it into a hidden maze.

I looked upon a vast land when the air vibrated from the heatwave upon the surface of the stone like a string of bow drawn when shooting.

It came, then it went . . .

# Chapter Thirty-Three

One random evening on the last day of the year, I looked out to the horizon and the reddish light that beamed over the sky. I had witnessed this kind of sunset a thousand times, especially during the war, but the sunset on that particular day triggered something within me . . . The memory of my mother.

I had taken my revenge on a person who had wronged me and more of them just to justify the bitterness and anger that burned within me. More than half a century had passed. But even then, even when the flame had not been put out, I just felt lonely and tired.

The hanging town wasn't far away from where I stood. So I went on down the road and across the mountain, back to the place where it all began.

Across that stone bridge through the small street in the hanging town, everything remained unchanged through time. The sandstone of the building had withstood endless counts of wind and rain. It made me think of humans, for they constantly change, both mentally and physically; their lives are dictated by time, and the course of their fate is dictated by me. It was like a string that was wrapped around my finger, waiting for me to operate.

At the end of the small town, I came across an old man who was sitting beside a large tree. He looked up as the sound of the horse's hooves approached. What was left of his hair reflected the colour of white from the light. Age had reached him.

As I rode closer, the old man looked up and was stunned for a moment, and I thought it was because of the large black beast that made him stir from his seat. But then, a hoarse shaky voice told me, 'You remind me so much of someone . . . a long time ago.'

I looked at him without any reply, though I know who he was, a freckled boy I used to play swords with.

I rode past him, heading towards the wood. But the hoarse voice caught my attention, 'Why are you heading there, young man? That wood is cursed!'

And I thought to myself, wasn't everything?

Within the wood, everything looked so gloomy and lonely. All the light was obscured by the shadow of the day. Along the path, the colours that I knew had melted into darkness. It took me a while before I could see the silhouette of the hut. It wasn't the same hut that I used to know anymore. Naked vines had swallowed up the whole place. This wood must be cursed just like the old man believed as I could not hear any sound of birds or fluttering leaves from curious creatures when the intruders had entered their territory. Everything was completely still and quiet.

My footsteps left no marks upon the soft soil as I walked over to my mother's nameless grave. It was impossible to tell that underneath that pile of leaves and soil lay someone who was once very dear to me.

A cool breeze blew against my face, and it reminded me that everything was over. I left my mother's grave and walked over to the hut. The crumbling door gave way when I pushed it.

Almost everything had stayed the same, just like I last remembered, except for the dust that clouded every surface of the place. Along the shelves on the wall and inside a cupboard, my mother's jars and my sculptures still laid there, untouched. The whole place was full of memories, of what once was, of a boy whose dream became an echo that was carried away by the wind. But now, the place felt so empty, just like the hollow in my chest. I was just a substance, some kind of creature without a soul.

Death defined me now, as wherever I went and whatever I touched melted into destruction.

I wanted everything to end. I wanted everything to stop.

The only thing that I could cling to now was the old obsession I used to have.

And at the last ray of light, I started to form my last sculpture, a piece where I could embed myself.

Gliding along with my finger, I let what was left of me flow underneath the layer of the clay that was formed into the shape of an owl; its face looked so peaceful and serene, but what was hidden beneath it all was death and destruction.

I took a deep breath and stared beyond the endless darkness of the night. And I thought to myself, maybe it was time for me to rest after all.

# Acknowledgements

This novel would never have been published if not for my husband, Santi, who encouraged me to put my work out there. So, I would like to say a big thank you to my number one supporter. Thank you so much for your encouragement and for always being there for me whenever I have self-doubt. Your support means the world to me.

I would also like to thank my sisters, who were my first readers and told me they would want to watch my story in a movie version. It really meant a lot.

Thank you to everyone in my family. The most fun parts of my life are always the ones when I share them with you guys.

Thank you to my father, my guidance and the wisdom of my life. Thank you for teaching me what happiness means. And to my mother, your loving memory will always be in my heart.

Thank you, my fellow writer friends. You guys are my inspiration.

Finally, thank you to my editors Lucy Rose York and Lucy Christmas. I have learnt a lot from your help and your suggestions.

# About the Author

Mai Lertkachonsuk Herrero was born in Thailand. She is a constant traveller. Her most favourite activity is reading in the comfort of her home or by the beach. She also loves to sing and is a member of Barcelona English Choir. She lives in Barcelona with her husband. The Echo of a Lost Dream is her debut novel.

mailherrero.com
Instagram: Mai L. Herrero (@mai.sl)

Lightning Source UK Ltd.
Milton Keynes UK
UKHW010954251021
392600UK00019B/429/J